# Endgame

## WILLA GRAY

Copyright © 2026 by Willa Gray

All rights reserved.

No part of this book may be reproduced in any form or by any electronic or mechanical means, including information storage and retrieval systems, without written permission from the author, except for the use of brief quotations in a book review.

This is a work of fiction. Unless otherwise indicated, all the names, characters, places, events and incidents in this book are either the product of the author's imagination or used in a fictitious manner. Any resemblance to actual persons, living or dead, or actual events is purely coincidental.

No AI use or training: Without in any way limiting Willa Gray's exclusive rights under copyright, any use of this publication to "train" generative artificial intelligence (AI) technologies to generate text is expressly prohibited. No AI was used to write Endgame.

First Edition February 2026

Paperback ISBN: 979-8-9937175-0-0

Cover illustration and design: Dan Blaushild (DanBlaushild.com)

Epilogue illustration: Dan Blaushild (DanBlaushild.com)

Line and copy editing: Julia Ganis (JuliaEdits.com)

Proofreading: Britt Taylor (PaperbackEditor.com)

Published in the United States by Postscript Press LLC

*For anyone who needs the reminder:*
*Love you're scared to lose is love worth fighting for.*

# BEFORE YOU READ

While ultimately Endgame is intended to be a swoony love story (with some light & funny moments), it covers some heavy and sad themes. To avoid spoilers, I've listed these at the back of the book. You can also find them at www.willagraybooks.com/books or with the QR code below.

# PROLOGUE
## ellie

I always imagined car crashes would feel like they were happening in slow motion.

I can picture it in my mind—the sudden impact followed by a sedate roll of the car, bodies seemingly suspended in midair as the car pitches. Hair floating around your head like you're underwater. The sound muted and far away, as if it isn't quite in full focus.

Undoubtedly, I've been influenced by Hollywood in this imagery, but it somehow seems appropriate. Such a big, tragic moment should feel slow and quiet. You know, like the whole life-flashing-before-your-eyes thing. Time to process what's happening, what you might lose.

Well, Hollywood *lies*. I know, shocking.

Car crashes aren't slow or quiet. They're fast, loud, and painfully chaotic. I didn't have time to process anything. Didn't even have time to panic. I think I remember a flash of bright light beforehand, but I can't be sure. Replaying the moments before the crash feels like trying to recall a dream that keeps slipping out of my grasp. The harder I try, the farther away it gets.

The crash itself, though, feels like a vivid movie scene I can't get out of my head. So big and traumatizing it eclipses anything else that happened before. I want to scrub it from my memory.

The sound is forever branded in my brain, the loud screech and ear-splitting clash of metal. The unexpected force of going sideways in the car—something that feels entirely unnatural and wrong—made me think of being on a roller coaster with a blindfold.

I wish I could forget it all, every single moment. The reprieve of just having a black hole in my memory taunts me. What a relief it would be not to feel the crushing weight of this...this nightmare.

I don't want to remember the blinding pain or the blackness that followed.

I don't want to remember the sirens or the screams.

I desperately don't want to remember the night my mom died or the drunk-driving assholes who killed her.

Sometimes I wake up and forget for a moment. Just a tiny instance of escape from my reality. *Ignorance is bliss.* That's the saying, right? I get it. Not knowing feels infinitely better than the alternative.

Because the very second I remember what happened feels like the first time I woke up in the hospital and the memories came rushing back. There is no ignorance with memories. No matter how much I want to, there is no way to remove them from my head. I've checked.

One day this anger and grief won't be suffocating.

One day I won't be afraid of getting in a car.

One day I will think of my mom and smile, not cry.

*But not today.*

# CHAPTER ONE
## *ellie*

My dead mother just called me.

Okay, obviously *she* didn't call me, but I cannot overstate the absolute mindfuck of seeing *Mom* on my caller ID five years to the day after her death.

Dad, one. Ellie, zero.

Not that he was trying to be funny—he would never pull a joke like that on me. Poor guy didn't realize the trauma he'd inflict with a simple phone call announcing he'd found Mom's phone while going through some of her things. From said phone. I can't believe he's still paying to keep it active.

He's at home, excited to be scrolling her saved pictures and messages. And I'm fourteen hundred miles away, drinking alone in a bar at two thirty in the afternoon. You could say we process differently.

"Another?" The bartender interrupts my staring contest with the empty shot glass.

Glancing up, I feel the burn take over my cheeks as I realize I don't know how to answer him. I think if I ask the bartender the question that's on the tip of my tongue, he's going to cut me off.

I'm definitely not drunk and I don't think I can handle the embarrassment of him and the single other bar patron thinking I am. Because I've only taken two shots.

I think.

How did I lose track after so few? Why don't they use a new glass for each one? I came here to get a specific level of intoxicated, and two shots is too few, but four would be *way* too many. This is a finely tuned process, you see.

I'm debating which error would be preferable when the bartender raises an eyebrow and the side of his mouth ticks up. "Everything okay?"

*Crap.* He probably thinks I'm already drunk. Maybe the blush will make him think I'm just really shy? He's pretty cute—mid-thirties or so with dirty-blond hair that curls around his ears. He's quite tall and broad; I'd have guessed he was a football player if it weren't for the fact that he's working at this bar right now. He's got a decently well-groomed beard and bright blue eyes that are currently twinkling at me in amusement.

Hopefully he just thinks I have a crush. I clear my throat. "Yeah, sorry, just...trying to decide." I point my finger at the shot glass and feel like slapping a palm against my forehead. Obviously he knows I am referring to the drink he *just* asked me about.

I am unintentionally selling this shy-girl thing.

His smile stretches across his face and he glances at the only other person at the bar before looking back at me. "You visiting from out of town?"

My eyes flick over to the other guy a few seats down from me. He has his baseball cap pulled low and is nursing a light beer. I think he's around the same age as the bartender, but it's hard to tell with his head turned toward the TV in the far corner. As far as I know, he hasn't looked at me since I came in fifteen minutes ago. Must be sports.

When I passed this place on my walk to a different bar, there was just something about the unassuming nature that drew me in. It felt like the perfect place to quietly accomplish my mission. It's a narrow, long room with a bar top spanning almost the entire right side. Liquor bottles are stacked on the wall behind it with exposed brick peeking through. The two TVs at opposite ends of the bar are loud enough to hear but not so much that they're the focus. High-top tables line the opposite side of the room, the wall there covered in a random collage of framed memorabilia. It's somehow both eclectic and simple, like it can't quite decide if it's a sports bar or an old-school pub.

Hat Guy's glass makes a thud on the bar as he sets it down, drawing my attention back.

I look over at the bartender and wonder why he glanced at him before asking me a question.

"Uh, no actually. I just moved here." The reminder makes my stomach clench. Okay, I just need to figure out my shot consumption and then I can get out of here and commence Project Forget Today and That Mindfuck Phone Call.

"Hate it that much already?"

I whip my head to the right in surprise. Hat Guy *was* listening, apparently. Oh frick, Hat Guy is *hot*. He's got a Clark Kent vibe going, sans glasses, and…I need to stop staring before they mutually agree I have to leave for being weird. *Crap, what did he ask?*

"Sorry?" I feel my brow furrow a bit.

"I don't think I've ever seen someone come in here and slam two shots in the middle of the afternoon. Trying to stay warm? Newbies always struggle with the cold. No offense." He has the decency to wince a little on the last words.

"Two!" *Shoot.* "I mean, um, excuse me?" I look over at the bartender, who is right where I left him, wearing an amused expression. He definitely thinks I'm crazy. Oh well, I'll be out of here soon. "I've decided I'd like another. Please." I tilt my head toward my empty glass and give him a polite smile.

He keeps the amused look in place and nods, glancing at Superman over there again before turning to grab the tequila.

I twist on my stool to face the most handsome stranger I've ever met. Is this some gift from the universe? A little distraction to help me through this shit day? If so, I'll take it.

"Sorry about that," I apologize, fully aware of the impression I'm leaving with these two. "Nothing wrong with Minneapolis, no. Not all that different from where I'm from in the weather department, actually." I feel my face fall at the thought of home. Grief is such a bitch.

Clark's mouth is slightly downturned and, dammit, even that's super hot. *Thanks for the eye-candy diversion, universe.*

Focusing on using my normal, adult conversation skills, I try to dispel his frown of what I assume is confusion.

"Just a pretty bad day." I shrug. "Kind of a long, weird story, but figured I'd try to forget it a little." I shake my empty shot glass for emphasis and then set it back down.

Superman gives a slow nod at that, but his slight frown remains. I think back to what he said and feel myself talking before I can make a decision to stop.

"Did you know that a 'beer blanket' is actually a total misconception? You just think you're warm because the blood vessels close to your skin expand when you drink, but your body temperature is actually getting lower. So it will feel like it's working for a little, but then you'll just be colder than you would have been without any alcohol," I explain, probably totally unnecessarily. Hot people make me nervous.

"Noted," he says, a hint of a smile pulling at his mouth.

"I swear I wasn't a nerdy buzzkill in college."

That hint of a smile turns into a full grin and I have to force myself to look away before I embarrass myself any more.

I turn back to the bartender as he refills my shot glass. I suppose refills make more sense than a new glass for every shot, but damn. Could've been signing the check by now if I had known how many shots I had taken. I grab the glass that's now full and pause before raising it up. "What's your name?" I ask.

"Nate," the bartender says, amusement slipping into his tone.

"Thanks, Nate," I say as I lift my drink and then bring it to my lips to shoot back. *Blegh*. I close my eyes and relish the burn running down my throat. Soon I'll have that Fuzzy Haze that puts a slight blur to my dark thoughts and makes the day bearable.

January eleventh is always hard. I know that's not going to change. But sometimes there are moments... Moments where I forget for just a second that my mom is gone. And the tidal wave of fresh grief that follows when I remember is always crushing.

So pair that with today's date *and* a delusional moment of thinking I might hear my mom's voice one more time? Absolutely debilitating.

Feeling my chest tighten and a lump form in my throat, I shove a mental block in place as fast as I can. Almost there, just have to close my tab and hightail it out of here.

I open my eyes to a very concerned-looking Nate. He's tracking something on my face, and to my extreme embarrassment I feel a tear rolling down my cheek. *Goddammit.* I wipe it away and force a smile.

"Can I close out, please?" I say as cheerily as I can manage, trying to hide the shakiness in my voice.

Nate nods and heads to the far end of the bar, passing Clark Kent on the way. Again he makes eye contact with him and I almost ask if they're friends before I realize I don't really want to initiate any more conversation today. As Nate prints and brings over the check, I grab my jacket from the back of my chair and slide off to stand and slip it on. I sign and then go to grab my keys, accidentally knocking them off the bar instead.

"You're not driving, right?" Nate asks with far more genuine concern than I would expect from a random bartender.

I bend to pick up the keys and give him a quick, reassuring smile. "Nope, wouldn't do that. Just walking home." I angle my head in the general direction of my apartment and hope the bitterness in my voice wasn't noticeable.

I'm about to turn and leave when Nate glances at Clark *again*. I've decided *one* question won't hurt and open my mouth to ask how they know each other when Clark surprises me for the second time.

"Want me to walk you home?"

There's no suggestive look or anything really that gives me creeper vibes. But you can never be too safe and I'm fresh off a true crime documentary binge.

"Oh, thanks. But I'm okay. It's pretty close and, you know, not trying to get Ted Bundy'd or anything like that." I let out a low laugh and replay that in my head. *Ted Bundy'd?* Now he thinks I think he's a serial killer. And a hot one at that. I feel a blush heat my cheeks for the millionth time and tighten my purse on my shoulder.

Nate and Clark Kent—I wonder what his real name is—share a long look and I catch Nate raising his eyebrows. I think I'd normally feel embarrassed over the idea of them silently communicating about me, but the Fuzzy Haze has started to seep into my body and I just need to focus on getting home.

"All right, well, bye, and thanks again." I smile tightly, glancing between the two of them, and then turn to head out.

I try not to think about what they will say about me once I'm gone. Time to succumb to the Haze and forget this fucking day.

# CHAPTER TWO

## *matt*

I think I just got compared to a serial killer.

In my own bar.

By a *really* pretty girl.

"Dude," Nate laughs, "cute as hell and didn't even know she was talking to Matt Anderson. You should see your face. What a goner."

I swallow and try to wipe whatever expression he's referring to off my face. "Like you weren't trying to flirt when you asked if she was *visiting from out of town*," I scoff at him.

"Hey that was for you, man," he huffs and points at me, but I catch his face getting a little red before he turns and grabs her empty shot glass.

Thirty years as friends means shit like that doesn't go unnoticed. In either direction.

Nate finishes putting the shot glass in the bin and turns back to me. "Too bad she seemed to be having a rough time. Wonder what happened today," he muses with a frown, grabbing a rag to wipe the bar top.

"Yeah," I mumble and glance at the door where she walked

out a few minutes ago. Why *was* she sad? I don't even know her, and the grief that took over her face during our minimal conversation set me on edge. Nate's wrong though; no way it was just something that happened today. That look did not scream bad hair day or flat tire. Or "it's too cold." I cringe at the reminder of my stupid comment. Her rambling response was pretty cute though.

Maybe she's lonely? She did say she was new to town. Shit, I didn't even get her name. Those honey-brown eyes and freckles are going to haunt my dreams. She seemed young, though, maybe even too young for me.

The reminder of my age is not what I want to be thinking about. It doesn't carry quite the grief I felt on Pretty Girl's face, but thinking of my inevitable decision regarding retiring puts a heavy weight on my shoulders I could live without. Hockey is a brutal sport and I feel every single one of my thirty-six years these days. But it's also my whole life, so how am I supposed to decide when to give that up?

That's not even an exaggeration. I've been playing since I was five years old and was getting scouted early in high school. By the time I was fourteen I had my own agent, and by seventeen I knew I was likely to be an early round pick for the draft. Over thirty years I've played and loved this sport. It's pretty much all I know. Thinking about being done sends a sharp pain through my chest—both at the idea of not playing professionally for the team I've been on my whole career, and at the unknown of what to do next.

One could argue that now's the time to retire. I'm still putting up big numbers and living up to the hype that's surrounded my career since the beginning. Going out while still on top certainly has some appeal. But what if I have more to give? What if I can continue to lead this team and, selfishly, set some more records? I could definitely go for another Cup too.

There's also the chance I wait too long and get to witness the decline of my career in real time. God, I think that might kill me—to lose my edge and watch my reputation shift. It wouldn't be seen as a voluntary retirement then, no. It would be seen as my only option. The old guy finally showing his age. *Get off the ice before you drag the team down.*

Yeesh, that shit gives me nightmares. Literally.

I love hockey so much I don't know who I am without it. It's been my focus for as long as I can remember. So how do I live the rest—and hopefully the majority—of my life without this pillar that defines who I am? Fuck, I don't want to think about this. *Half the season left*, I remind myself. No pressure to make a decision until after it's over, anyway.

Shaking my head and trying to think of literally anything else, I turn to the TV to catch the last of the soccer game that's been on for the past hour. I don't think Pretty Girl looked at the TV once. Not a fan of sports, maybe? That would further confirm she wouldn't have recognized the captain of the Bears.

We don't often get people coming here to seek me out, but some regulars certainly know I'm here a fair amount. Some even know that I co-own the bar with Nate—information I'm sure gets shared. Thankfully, locals are generally respectful of my privacy and don't make a thing out of my presence. Being a small, bare-bones place means we don't attract tourists either, so luckily we aren't seeing a ton of new people. And when we do it's usually pretty obvious if they recognize me: the shifty eyes, the sly selfies, the double takes and whispering.

I don't think Pretty Girl even noticed I was here until I interrupted her conversation with Nate. Refreshing and yet oddly frustrating.

I wonder how much she paid attention to the bar itself? It's not exactly a *nice* bar, but it's got character and that old-school charm you can only really acquire over time.

Not that I should care what a stranger thinks about it. Even one as cute as her.

My eyes catch on the dust on the TV and the liquor shelves next to it. Maybe in the offseason I can do a little work to spruce the place up, focus on projects Nate can't get to while running the day-to-day. I scan the room and take in the cracked paneling on the frame gallery wall and the permanently sticky wood floors under me. Okay, more like a *lot* of work. Maybe this should be my retirement plan...

I can figure it out later, I remind myself again.

"Did you happen to catch her name when you closed her tab?" I try to sound casual, turning back to the TV.

"Stalker much?"

I turn to a grinning Nate and wonder if he's going to fuck with me. He laughs at whatever he sees on my face. He relents. "Eleanor Ford."

*Eleanor.*

My legs burn and sweat drips down my face as we rerun a play for the fourth time. One of my favorite parts of hockey is watching a maneuver we've practiced over and over get executed flawlessly in a game. Just imagining the buzzer going off as I slide out on one knee sends a little hum through my veins. That shit never gets old.

I push back up to both skates as the whistle blows and give Alex a friendly shoulder bump before heading over to the bench for some water. He's been putting in the work and it shows. Since he got traded to the Bears last week, he's been playing first line with me and has really impressed everyone with his handful of goals and assists. Hockey takes a lot of natural talent and learned skills, but the drive to be better and master the game can't really be taught or bought. It's just something you have to want badly enough.

It doesn't happen often, but I see a lot of myself in Alex. If he can keep his head down and not get distracted by the hoopla around being a pro athlete, I think he could really make a name for himself.

"Killer no-look, man. That release was perfect," I tell him as he leans against the boards to grab his water.

"I just hope we can do that tomorrow. Would really like to fucking bury Boston," he says. "Maybe even lay out that fucker McCormic."

I smile at the fervor in his voice—something hilariously on-brand for the younger players. Maybe a few more years in the league will temper that a bit.

"We're ready for 'em," I promise him with a slap on the back as I get up and head toward the locker room. I won't admit to him that Bryan McCormic getting friendly with the boards sounds fun to watch. No need to encourage him.

I remember when the passion for winning felt more like an angry emotion than a happy one, when I felt like I had something to prove and the other team was the enemy. I still have that passion for wins, sure, but these days it's more about perfecting our playing, working to read the other team like a fucking book, and improving our record one game at a time. Getting to the Cup is a heck of a marathon, and treating every game like a methodical battle has long since been my viewpoint. Getting angry doesn't work for me and only serves to detract from my game. It's also why you won't find me in the penalty box too much. Focusing on my game instead of defending baseless aggression has served me well.

Not everyone has that approach though.

"So how many power plays are you gonna give them tomorrow?" I ask Niko with a smirk as I sit roughly and start to unlace my skates.

Niko's been on this team almost as long as me. And, despite the tenure, he always seems to get baited into penalties when playing our rivals. It's something I both love and (fondly) hate about him—he'll defend not just himself, but the whole damn team till his dying day. Even when it's pointless. However, that loyalty is one of the main reasons he's one of my closest friends on and off the ice.

"Whatever, man. Those fuckers always have it coming," he grunts as he starts ripping his tape.

I guess not *all* of us lose the fervor with age.

"Fair enough," I laugh. I get to work on ripping my own tape, thinking about how I'm going to mitigate my teammates' rage tomorrow against Boston. Some rage is good, but too much interferes with our ability to play well. Cliché as it sounds, balance is key.

"You want to grab a few beers tonight? I was thinking of hitting that new bar near yours over in North Loop. My buddy says it's not too crazy," Niko promises, correctly assuming I'd be concerned about that.

Another thing I love about him: he never fails to invite me out even though he knows I'm probably going to say no. Hockey isn't the most popular sport in the US and *most* of us don't draw too much attention. But having a household name is a blessing and a curse, and being recognizable falls into both categories. Major perks and huge downsides. One of which is being hounded at a sports bar by fans and…admirers.

*Hard pass.*

I'm about to say no when an image pops into my head. One of light brown eyes and a sprinkling of freckles over her nose. It's a Friday night... She could conceivably be out. She said she was walking home from my bar that day a few weeks ago, which is right around the corner from where Niko's headed later.

I feel like such a loser. I'm debating doing something I never do—and something that might lead to me getting mobbed—just for the slim chance I might run into her. Slim is even pushing it. There are a million places she could be on a Friday night.

Eleanor is a pretty tempting fucking image though.

I shake my head at my own antics and give Niko the answer he's expecting. "Thanks, bro, but I gotta pass. Maybe next time. Let me know how the bar is," I tell him, collecting my pads and skates.

He gives me a nod. "Usual lunch before the game tomorrow?"

I give him a quick "Yessir" before shoving my shit in my bag and heading to the showers, trying to convince myself there is no way Eleanor would be at that bar tonight.

*Right?*

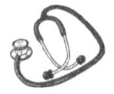

# CHAPTER THREE
*ellie*

Holy fudgenuts it's cold.

I hate to admit it, but Clark Kent was a little bit right. My Bostonian blood is failing me. According to my weather app, the "feels like" temperature is negative fifteen with the wind chill. *Negative fifteen.*

Would it be morally wrong to call out of work today? Maybe. Also, I'm already fully bundled up for the very daunting thirteen-minute walk to the hospital. Turning back would be illogical. And yet...

I longingly look at my door down the block, imagining my warm bed. I'd like to curl up and rub my legs like a cricket until the cold fades. I turn around and spot the skyway up the road. Boston could take note of the indoor walkways Minneapolis has around the city to help pedestrians when it's freezing. I forge ahead and try not to think about my bed. Being an adult is hard.

I'm on the last of my three, twelve-hour shifts for the week, and holy moly, I can feel it. People think having four days off per week sounds cushy. *Pssshh.* I welcome every single one of them to try working my shift in an emergency room and then talk to me.

The absolute chaos and nonstop nature of the ER is both exhausting and thrilling. Back when I decided to pursue being an emergency room nurse, I hadn't thought about the schedule too much, but it's proved to be one of my favorite things. With virtually no lulls, the shifts fly by, and by the time I get home I'm so tired I could fall asleep brushing my teeth. And then on my days off I can focus on catching up on reading, trash TV, grocery shopping and sleep, and, occasionally, going out.

I glance over at the bar parallel to where I'm walking now. It's been almost four weeks since I embarrassed myself in there with Nate the bartender and hot Hat Guy.

I take a moment to study it as I pass by. It's—I glance at my watch—two thirty-four. That's right around the time I was in there shooting tequila. I wonder if Superman is in there now.

I get little butterflies thinking of his handsome face and have a momentary pang of regret for not taking him up on his offer to walk me home. I have Dev here and I've made friends with some of the other nurses too, but a little bit of loneliness is inevitable with such a big move. And the idea of a partner is…daunting, I guess, but also appealing. I don't necessarily miss my ex, Josh, but I do miss having someone to talk to about my day, try new hole-in-the-wall restaurants with, and just plain old hang out with. Solitude has its limits.

And, god, I miss *sex*.

It's been over six months and I'm starting to worry I'll forget what to do. Is that possible? Oh god, what if I'm bad at it? Josh never complained, but he would never do anything like that anyway.

I just need to rip the Band-Aid off, I suppose. Maybe I'll go out this weekend and find a proper suitor. That phrasing classes it up a bit, right?

Tearing my gaze away from the bar that's now almost behind me, I realize it doesn't even have a name visible from the outside. I wonder what it's called. I don't remember seeing any branding inside and the door just has a neon *Open* sign out front. Ooh, maybe it's one of those secret places only locals know about! Cool points for Ellie.

I make a mental note to find out the name at some point and focus on getting to work without freezing. I know this would go a lot faster—and be a lot warmer—if I drove. But I don't like driving. Scratch that. I *hate* driving. Driving in the snow? My personal hell. My old therapist told me it should get better with time, but I haven't seemed to shake the aversion over the past five years.

So I picked an apartment within walking distance to the hospital. And thankfully the walkways mean the feels-like-negative-fifteen-degrees weather doesn't give me frostbite. I glance at my car parked down the street behind me.

And at least I *can* drive. If I have to. I guess time did help with that part.

Mentally fortifying myself for the last few minutes of the cold, I put my head down and power walk up the sidewalk. Just twelve hours of work today and then rip-the-Band-Aid sex is next on the list. After a shower. And sleep. And finding some much-needed boldness for such a task.

Piece of cake.

*Why is this so hard?*

My internal whining is not productive, but it is making me

feel slightly better. It's Thursday night, and Dev—another nurse and one of the reasons I moved here—and I are at a newish bar close to where I live that she promised would have "lots of cute guys." I should've asked for more qualifiers.

Aside from being moderately attractive, all of the guys I've talked to have been too grabby or too drunk or way too eager. Not once have I even considered picking one for practice sex. I knew this wouldn't be easy, but I did not think it would be this hard to even find an *option* to get back on the proverbial horse with. I haven't even had the chance to be nervous about my elevator pitch I rehearsed.

Maybe my standards are too high? I really don't think they are.

Although...

It's possible Clark Kent from a few weeks ago has set an unfairly high bar in terms of looks. Sometimes I think I made him up. Like my brain needed something else to focus on that day and delivered what I would consider a perfect specimen to obsess over for a little while.

*Why can't he be here tonight?*

It comes out as another whine in my head and I almost physically pout just thinking it. I know it's still early, but I'm feeling so hopeless I might call it a night. Too bad my fancy matching lingerie is going to waste. At least I got to show off my new chunky thrifted boots. I kick them out from my stool to admire them. Guess I should tell Dev I'm ready to go.

I'm startled from my personal boot-admiring session when the bartender drops two fresh mojitos in front of us.

"From the guys over there," he says with a quick point to two guys at the other end of the bar. They look mid- to late-twenties, and fine, they're cute, but there is just something missing. I don't feel excited looking at either of them. Neither is particularly…superhero-y.

*Dammit, Ellie.*

Normally there's at least a little rush of pleasure at the attention when you get hit on, but I now feel so committed to *not* practicing with anyone here that I don't really feel anything. Well, maybe some frustration at now having to deal with these drinks and those men. I mean, what is the protocol? Do we say thanks and drink them and hope they don't want some kind of reciprocation? Or do we refuse drinks that have already been set in front of us and look rude?

I feel so out of practice. I know, poor me, getting free drinks. But it feels like a lose-lose when you don't want the extra drink, the extra attention, or the potential extra responsibility of handling someone's fragile masculinity.

I look over at Dev so we can game plan, but she's smiling at one of the guys that sent us the drinks.

*Well, then.* Guess I'll be sticking this one out. I follow her lead and hold my drink up in thanks before taking a quick sip and putting it back down. Avoiding eye contact like it's my job, I grab my phone to check the time. Barely ten. We've only been here an hour.

"You trying to go home?" Dev asks me.

I put my phone down and give her an angelic, guilty smile. "That obvious?" I laugh.

"Only to me." She winks.

"I can just walk home though. You don't have to bail," I tell her, feeling bad for cutting her night short too.

"No way, I'm leaving if you do. My bed sounds amazing right now," she says. "Wanna finish these and then head out?" She lightly shakes the new mojito.

"You're the best."

"I know," she says while she bats her eyelashes dramatically. "So now that you've been here for a bit, you still liking the neighborhood? You missing Boston? I'm gonna feel bad if I sold you on Minny and you hate it."

I laugh at Dev's nickname for the city. "She's pretty different from Boston, but it's been good. Neighborhood's close to work and takeout options are awesome. Those were my only two requirements. So check and check." I joke with her, even though that *is* mostly what I cared about when choosing a place. "And I miss some specific things, yeah, but it's okay. Minny treats me well."

"Okay, phew. I obviously love it here, but I'm biased of course." Dev's parents immigrated to Minnesota from India when she was three, so it's home to her. She only left here for nursing school in Boston, where we met just before we graduated. Once we became friends we both wished we'd gotten closer sooner. "All right, let's get outta here. Just give me a sec."

I watch her slam the rest of her drink, get up from her seat, and walk over to the guys who bought them. She pulls out her phone and, presumably, either gets the hotter guy's number or gives hers to him.

*Devna Mathur is a boss.* A petite, dark-haired, cute-as-a-button boss. Don't tell her I said that.

I quickly take a few more sips of my drink and signal to the bartender that I want to close our tab. Dev makes her way back over and starts putting her jacket on while I'm signing. I watch her pull up an app to call a ride on her phone.

"You sure you don't want to share with me? It's fucking freezing and I doubt they'd mind dropping you on the way," Dev offers.

"Nah, I'll be fine. It's only a couple blocks." I grin at her and jerk my chin at the bar. "You gonna call him?"

"Eh, not sure. My vibrator *has* been a little boring lately," Dev says as she looks up from her phone at me with a mischievous smile.

I laugh at her candor and feel a swell of warmth that I have a friend like her here. Dev is bold and fun and extremely kind. She often surprises me with her honesty, but I've found she's still never anything but nice.

"You could just get a new toy," I tell her as I pull on my beanie.

"I feel like I own them all," she huffs.

"I bet Drink Guy would like to see them." I waggle my eyebrows at her.

"I bet he would." She flips her hair out of her scarf and sashays to the door.

*Gosh, I love her.*

# CHAPTER FOUR

## *matt*

BEING AT A PACKED BAR ON A THURSDAY NIGHT IS NOT MY definition of fun. It's specifically why I turned Niko down last week. But after Nate mentioned he'd seen Eleanor walk by a handful of times since she was here a month ago, I decided one night at the bar was worth a little bit of delusional hope.

With my hat pulled low and Nate keeping an eye on non-regulars, I try not to stress about getting harassed. It rarely happens, given the low profile of the bar, and thanks to Nate I'm not exactly *worried*. But the general noise and chaos has me on edge. You'd think regular exposure to screaming arenas would make me immune to the racket, but there's just something about this up-close commotion and volume that has me feeling a tad claustrophobic.

"Those two girls want to buy you a drink."

I look up at Nate and try to fight my reflexive grimace. "Guess that's my cue to go," I tell him, tipping back the last of the beer in my glass.

"You don't even want to look? They're pretty hot," he says with a smirk.

"Well then maybe *you* should—"

I stop talking as I see Nate's gaze snag on something outside the bar. I follow his line of sight to something passing the front door. *Someone.*

Eleanor. Holy shit.

Despite the time that's passed, her pretty face has been burned into my mind exactly as I predicted. The regret of not getting her number or even her name—in a normal way—has been weighing surprisingly heavily on my mind. I was sure I would never see her again and it's been strangely more upsetting than I would expect from some fleeting encounter. Hence the out-of-character night out.

I don't pursue random girls. And that's not some cheesy intro into *girls pursue me.* I mean, I guess they do, but that's not why I don't go after them. I just don't trust myself to know a stranger's intentions. I've been a professional hockey player for eighteen years, and from the very first day, they warn you about the minefield of dating as a pro player.

Only date friends of friends. Or friends of friends of friends. That's your best bet, they'd say.

I was pretty casual the first few years, but then I experienced firsthand what they were talking about. So I took their advice. No more random hookups, no strangers in a bar. No matter how pretty.

Playing it safe made sense and still does, but as I watch the little pom-pom on her hat disappear from view, I rush to grab my jacket and jog to the door. I'm not letting her slip away again.

Nate's chuckle is cut off as the door swings shut behind me and the noise of the bar fades to muted chatter. I turn right and catch sight of Eleanor walking down the street. How long has she been walking? It's cold as balls out here.

"Hey," I call out. Like a total fucking creep.

Fuck, what if she doesn't remember me and now I'm some dude a few steps behind her on a dark street? Not exactly the start I want.

She turns around and—*shit.* The seared image I had in my brain takes a back-row seat to the sight in front of me.

Honey eyes and rosy, freckled cheeks. Dark brown hair falling to her shoulders under her blue hat. Glossy pink lips curving into a smile that gives way to perfect teeth.

I swallow and try to remember how to talk.

"Clark," she says as her smile takes over her whole face.

*Wow. Okay.* Except then there is an almost comical little record scratch sound effect in my head. *Clark?* Shit, does she think I'm someone else? We did only meet once... Perhaps it was more memorable for me.

I tilt my head and try not to show too much confusion on my face. "Clark?"

"You know, Clark Kent?" She looks down and I see that pink blush turn a little more red.

My own smile catches me off guard. She thinks of me as Superman? That's got to be good, right? Way better than a serial killer, at least.

I reach my hand out and watch as her eyes flick down to it and then back to my face. "I'm Matt."

She softly places her hand in mine and I feel my heart give a little jolt at the contact. "Ellie," she says.

Ellie, not Eleanor. I catalog the switch in my mind and nod my head in the direction she was going, reluctantly releasing her hand. "You walking home?"

"Yeah, just coming from Lola's. I'm another block down this way," she says.

Lola's... Why does that sound so familiar?

*No way.* "Is Lola's that bar that just opened a couple blocks away?" I ask her.

"Yeah, my friend convinced me to check it— What?" Ellie pauses at whatever she sees on my face.

"Ah, nothing, just my buddy also tried to convince me to go there last week. Maybe I'll say yes next time."

I'm momentarily distracted when I see Ellie's teeth start to chatter. *Shit*, I've been making her stand here in the cold.

"Now that I'm not a stranger, can I walk you the rest of the way home?"

"Hmm. That depends, Matt. I usually know more than just a first name when I allow such intimate behavior. Can you tell me a little more about yourself?"

I stiffen at the thought, but remind myself she doesn't know who I am and there is plenty else I can tell her that doesn't involve hockey. Well maybe not *plenty*, but enough.

"It's a big ask, but I think I can do that." I smile at her. "Let's see..." I pause to think for a minute, trying to come up with some random facts. "Just off the top? I don't have any pets, but I have a lot of plants. I co-own that bar with my friend Nate. I'm not sure if you remember him, he was bartending." I hike my thumb over my shoulder. "I think the best ice cream flavor is vanilla and I'm willing to die on that hill. Hmm...I hate the beach. My favorite book genre is science fiction. And my mom's name is Shirley, like the drink."

I study her face as I talk and watch her smile slip at the end. She seems to straighten her posture a little and nods before announcing, "That'll do," as she tucks her hands in her jacket pockets and continues down the street.

I sidle up beside her and take her in properly. She's probably a little over half a foot shorter than my six-foot-one frame, but her heeled boots have her standing only a few inches below me. She's got a long tan coat and a blue beanie with a familiar logo on the front. Any player would recognize one of the top-ranked schools for hockey.

"You from Boston?" I ask, angling my head toward her beanie.

Ellie reaches up to touch the logo there. "Oh, yeah, I am. I guess I should return the favor, huh? Can't have you walking with a stranger either." She looks over and the side of her mouth curves up.

*That is a distracting mouth.*

She faces forward again and I listen carefully as she shares tidbits of information I plan to hoard like a reality TV show spectacle.

"All right, I don't have any pets either, but I'm thinking of getting a fish. Although I've really struggled to keep even plants alive, so maybe that's inhumane to consider. A little ironic because I'm an ER nurse over at General. Should be good at keeping things alive and all that..." She trails off with a huff. "Hmm what's next? Oh yes, I actually agree with you on the ice cream front, so no dying for you. Team vanilla, baby."

She says the word "baby" with enthusiasm, emphasizing and dragging out the *y* sound slightly, making it sound more like *bay-beee*. Her energy is infectious enough to make me forget about the cold.

"I love two very specific beaches, but otherwise don't feel strongly about those. And my favorite book genre is historical romance. If you make fun of my reading preferences, Matt, we can't be friends. You've been warned."

She gives me a faux glare and I laugh, internally delighting in her easy use of my name. "I would never, promise," I say with my hand over my heart. "Besides, my mom loves those books too, and I may have read one or two back when I lived at home."

"They're pretty good, right?"

"Oh yeah, very entertaining, but I couldn't get past the idea of knowing my mom read...ya know. Teenage Matt was scandalized." I give a little shudder at the memory.

"Gave you the ick, huh?" she jokes and pauses, pointing to the red door up a small set of stairs we've stopped at. "This is me," she lets me know. She shifts a little on her feet and I'm not sure if it's the cold or something else. I'm definitely not risking another semi-coincidental run-in as my only way of seeing her again.

"Do you think I shared enough personal information to get your number?" I try to keep the uncharacteristic nerves out of my voice, but I'm not sure how successful I am.

Ellie beams at me and my breath catches in my chest. *Christ*.

"I'll do ya one better." She tips her head toward the door. "Do you wanna come in?"

*Um, hell yes I do.*

But shit, I think I could actually *like* her. And I don't want her to think I'm looking for a one-time thing. Although maybe she just wants to talk more out of the cold? Or maybe *she* just wants a one-time thing.

I look from the door to her face and notice her smile start to fade. *Fuck*. Guess I can figure it out as we go.

"I promise you're safe with me." She elbows me lightly in the side.

I know she means it as a joke, but there's something so adorably endearing about her offering that up. She has no way of knowing why that would mean a lot to me. And I don't know if I've ever felt *unsafe*, but I've certainly had my fair share of feeling uncomfortable or even targeted when I'm with new people who might be around me for specific reasons.

I have a hunch Ellie has never made anyone uncomfortable in her life.

"I guess I'll have to trust you." I gesture for her to lead the way.

# CHAPTER FIVE
## *ellie*

My hand shakes as I unlock the front door with the shared building code. I push it open and glance back to make sure Matt's close enough behind me to keep it open. Holy crap on a cracker he's hot. How am I going to pull this off?

I lead him up the two short flights of stairs to my apartment, careful not to catch the toe of my heavy boots. The tripping hazard they present when I'm *not* nervous is already high.

And right now my heart is *racing*.

I remind it we're just trying to get laid, not getting hunted for sport. I played that conversation as cool as I could, but now I have to figure out how to actually make this happen. Oh god, this is going to be a top-five embarrassing moment. I can feel it.

*Okay, deep breaths.* Matt is hot and tall and giving major gentleman vibes. He mentioned his mom, so he's probably a good person. I think that's a thing. He also offered to walk me home and didn't jump on the chance to come inside with me. So he's polite and not just some fuckboy.

Oh crap.

*He's not just some fuckboy.*

He's totally going to turn me down. Ugh, he's probably going to think *I'm* the fuckboy.

I have to stop using that word.

At least he'll probably do it really nicely. I still have to give it a go, right? He was practically handed to me on a silver platter. Feels like a sign from the universe. Have to shoot my shot and all that.

I muster the confidence of my alter ego fuckboy and take the last few steps to the door of my apartment. Trying to think about what Matt's seeing for the first time, I study the entrance as I pull my keys out. The black paint is slightly chipped in some places, but overall the wood door has classic charm with its little brass knocker.

This place has become my home away from home over the past few months and I'm proud to call it mine. It's small, only one bedroom, but the exposed brick and parquet floor give it so much character. And it's just me here anyway.

Well, usually.

I think of the slight (okay, massive) mess I left in my room while I picked out my "time to get laid" outfit, and falter slightly. I guess I wasn't thinking this night through fully. All right, this is probably just a one-time thing anyway, and anyone who can't handle my disorganized self probably wouldn't work out in the long run if it came to that.

Squaring my shoulders, I turn the key in the lock and push the door open with my arm, angling myself to let him through.

Matt smiles at me and then walks in, pausing in the entryway as he waits for me to shut and lock the door. He's still smiling when I slip my shoes off and hang up my jacket.

"What?" I ask him, my own grin growing on my face.

"Nothing. This is cute. Is it just you here?"

I narrow my eyes at him.

He laughs and shakes his head. "Oh man, is that like a classic Ted Bundy line?"

I preen at the notion he remembered what I said all those weeks ago. "Just a little," I tell him.

"I just meant because it seems small." Matt winces. "Not that that's a bad thing," he rushes to explain. "I'm gonna shut up. Can I put my jacket there?" he asks, pointing to the wall rack where I hung mine.

I give him a nod and head into the kitchen—two steps away—and open the fridge. My apartment *is* small, the living room, foyer, and kitchen all kind of one room. Other than a small stacked laundry closet, it's just the bathroom and a bedroom that barely fits my queen bed. A real estate agent might call it quaint. Or cozy.

"Would you like water or...sparkling water? Shoot," I huff as I look at the contents here. "I thought I had more, sorry."

"That's okay, I'm done drinking for the night, so water is great," he responds.

I fill two glasses and set them on the bar, then rest on the counter across from the two barstools I have there.

Matt sits on one facing me and reaches up to pull his hat off before flipping it backward and putting it back on. He leans forward on his elbows and rests his chin on his hands, looking so striking up close like this I feel like I have to stave off a physical reaction. The word *swoon* floats through my mind.

I take advantage of my first unhindered view of Matt and commit this sight to memory.

His dark hair is trimmed short on the sides and looks longer up top where it peeks out the front of his cap. I can see some grays coming through at his temples that only add to his good looks. There's a small scar through his right eyebrow that catches my attention, making me wonder how he got it. Maybe a bar fight or some accident? I fight the involuntary urge to press a hand to my own.

Below that, his dark green eyes are focused on me as I continue to survey his handsome face. And other than where another small mark scars his chin, uniform stubble covers a defined jaw and a bit below. He's got a mostly straight nose with a little crook in the bridge, and disgustingly perfect, pouty lips that are stretching wide as I fail to hide my casual perusal of his features.

I stop staring and grab one of the water glasses from the counter, holding it up in cheers. He grabs the other and clinks my glass with his. That broad smile is slowly covered as he brings the water up to his mouth.

Superman is in my apartment. Drinking out of my favorite thrifted cups. Unknowingly cheersing my decision to shoot my shot.

*Bombs away.*

"So I have a proposition for you," I blurt.

Matt sputters a bit and coughs, setting his glass down on the counter with a loud clink. *Whoops.* Could've timed that better.

"A proposition?" he asks with raised eyebrows.

I can feel the blush on my cheeks, but I know this is my chance, so here goes.

"Yes. So"—I clear my throat—"before I moved here a few months ago I lived in Boston with my boyfriend, Josh. Well, ex-boyfriend now, but current boyfriend then. I'm single now, we aren't still together. You get it. Anyway, we actually broke up a couple of months before I moved so it's been a while since we were, like, *together* together."

I don't think Matt's eyebrows can go any higher at this point.

"And I don't know about you, but that's kind of a long time, ya know? And the more I think about it, the more worried I am that when I eventually get together with someone new, I'll forget what to do or be bad at it. And what if I ruin my next relationship before it starts because the first time we have… you know…I forget what to do and suck? I mean, it's a lot of pressure, and I was with my old boyfriend for a longish time, so it's not like I have a lot of experience with what different people do. I just kind of know what we used to do…"

I trail off and take a breath. I study my hands holding the water glass. *Very smooth, Ellie. Word vomit is sexy.*

"I know I sound crazy and I swear I'm not. I just feel like it would be best if I could kind of rip the Band-Aid, so to speak, and try…getting together…with someone."

I look up at Matt and notice I have his full attention. His eyes are trained on my face and, thank friggin' heavens, he's not laughing at me or looking at me like I am, in fact, crazy. Time to wrap up this pitch.

"What do they say? It's like riding a bike? Or something like that. So…um, yeah, I guess my proposition is asking you if you'd be willing to do that. With me. And go into it with all the information I just shared so you aren't disappointed if I'm not…well…*good*."

*Riiiip.*

Okay. I did it. Well, I did the first part. Still an accomplishment. I give myself a mental high five and take a breath.

Matt picks up his water and drinks the rest in three big swallows. I watch his throat bob and feel the first inkling of excitement over the possibility of doing this with him. He's so attractive it's borderline offensive, and probably…seven years older than me? Ten? So he's got to be experienced. This would be perfect. If he says yes.

Matt sets his glass down and studies my face. He opens his mouth to say something, but then closes it.

"I know this is weird," I hurry to add. "I'm not exactly a super-forward person, so that should speak to how nervous-slash-desperate I am." I take a few sips of my water and find myself wishing it was one of those mojitos. One, because *yum*. And two, liquid courage. I had three drinks at the bar earlier tonight and the buzz has long since worn off.

*This is so embarrassing.* I set the glass down and spin it a little, watching my hands.

"So, to be clear. You want to have sex. With me. As... *practice*?"

My head jerks up at his question. Crap, did I insult him? I give him an apologetic smile. "Sounds pretty bad, huh?"

*He's going to say no.* Okay, that's okay. Plenty of other fish in the sea and all that. Probably not pretty, sparkly fish like him, but maybe there are shiny enough ones around somewhere. Just not at the bar I went to tonight.

"I can honestly say I've never been propositioned like that."

I huff out a laugh. "I would hope not."

"When did you move from Boston?"

"October," I say slowly. It feels like I can see him doing the mental calculation for when I last had sex.

"And you want to do this...tonight?"

*Wait, is he considering this?* "Well, yes? If you're...you know... up for it," I ramble, cringing at the unintended innuendo.

Matt smiles again, blessedly ignoring my bad choice of words. "What would you have done if we hadn't run into each other tonight?"

I hesitate. "Gone to bed?" I suggest.

"And who is going to rip the Band-Aid if I don't?"

I cannot believe this conversation is happening. "Well, you see, tonight was the first night I was, uh, actively looking, if you will."

*Please kill me.*

The side of his mouth curves. "Looking for what, Ellie?"

"A proper suitor for the occasion," I tell him with a straight face.

Matt barks out a laugh. "That's very cute. Okay, am I the first proper suitor you've propositioned?"

I nod.

"What is it that makes me a proper suitor?" His grin turns wicked and that's when I realize he is trying to make me work for this.

*Game on.*

"Convenience," I say sweetly and bat my eyelashes.

Matt lets out another laugh and shakes his head. "Fine, I'll stop fishing for compliments." He pauses. "So if I'm practice, who's endgame?"

# CHAPTER SIX

## *matt*

Ellie's face loses some of the humor, but her smile remains.

"I'm not sure yet," she says with a shrug.

"No criteria in mind?" I ask her. I want to know what she's looking for and if I'm really only going to be a passing ship here.

She grabs her water glass and takes a sip before setting it back down. She hums as she glances around her apartment for a few moments. She's not smiling anymore—she looks thoughtful. I sit up straighter in my seat.

"I guess I want a real partner," she says a little shyly, like she's not sure it's a good answer.

I sober at what she said, my shoulders falling forward. That's somehow both a simple and complex answer at the same time. "Like someone who prioritizes you?" I ask. That type of thing is not really a big ask for most people. Professional athletes though? It can be. And it sums up why most of my previous relationships didn't work out.

"Kind of? I would prioritize them too, though. Obviously

there is a lot that goes into it, but I want someone who builds a life *with* me. Not around me or for me. If that makes sense."

"What kind of plans was this ex making without you?" I hedge. Now I'm curious as shit. I try to be patient as I watch Ellie think, tilting her head from side to side.

"It's kind of a long story." She sighs. "Anyway, this isn't really the proper thing to talk about on a first da—"

Was she going to say first *date*? I feel a new smile grow on my face as I watch a blush creep onto hers. "On a what, exactly?" I don't think I could school my cheesy grin if I tried. Her use of the word *proper* again is killing me. I work hard to keep a laugh from slipping out. So fucking cute.

Her mouth pops open before she abruptly shuts it. She covers her face with her hands and tilts it up to the ceiling. "This night is so embarrassing," she mutters.

I can't stop my laugh this time. Ellie propositioned me for sex and yet calling this impromptu meeting a "first date" is what's embarrassing her.

The blush still peeking out from where her hands are on her face reminds me of the way she asked earlier. I cannot believe someone this fun to be around is stressed about having sex. About being *bad* at sex. She's stunning and cute and obviously smart and funny. She could do absolutely nothing and I'm one hundred percent sure it wouldn't be *bad*.

Man, the thought of her propositioning someone else for practice sex is making some baser caveman instincts surface. Everyone else can fuck right off. *This one's mine.*

"Ellie?"

She removes her hands and gives me a skeptical look.

"I wouldn't have asked about your ex if I didn't want to know. So, proper or not"—I can't help my smile as I use her word choice—"I would've been happy to talk about it. But maybe we can save that for our second date."

I watch her now predictable blush deepen, satisfied that I already have a tiny part of her figured out. I have a feeling it's only going to get worse with this next part.

"How about you convince me why I wouldn't hate your two favorite beaches tonight and then we rip the Band-Aid on a night when I haven't just come from a workout followed by a crowded bar. That way I can shower first and—"

Ellie's expression changes from embarrassment to something else I can't quite figure out.

"Why are you looking at me like that?" I ask with mild caution, not wanting to guess at what she's thinking.

"What if you took a shower here?" Ellie asks. "With me. Tonight."

Now my mouth pops open. *Oh fuck.* I did not see that coming. Why did I mention the shower? How am I supposed to say no to her?

Do I want to see a wet, naked Ellie? Fuck yes. But I also don't want to be just a one-night stand.

Worse, a *practice* one-night stand.

Maybe if I can make this the best shower sex she's ever had, she'll consider a regular "practice" schedule?

The more chances I have to convince her I'm worth more than rip-the-Band-Aid sex, the better.

*All right, Matt. Don't fuck this up. Guess you'll just have to woo her.*

In the shower.

Thank fuck for hockey-trained leg strength and stamina...

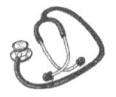

# CHAPTER SEVEN
## *ellie*

"Okay, you first. Take your clothes off."

"What about we both go at the same time?"

"Nope. My house, my rules. Strip."

Matt puts his hands up and mutters a quick "Fine" as he starts to undress. He reaches behind himself and pulls his black long-sleeved shirt over his head.

I think there's an audible *pop* sound as my lips part and my jaw drops.

"Are you kidding me?" I say as my eyes run over his chest and abs for the...third time.

Matt pauses unbuttoning his pants and quickly looks up at me and then down at himself. "What? What's wrong?" He's still looking down and around his body like there's something *wrong* with it. What a freaking joke.

"Okay, nope. I'm calling this off. What do you do for a living at that bar, hurl kegs?" I throw my hands up. I know I'm being dramatic, but he looks like an actual Superman and I look like...a normal human. Could be described as soft, if you will. Likes ice cream. Does not like working out. You get the picture. I like my body just fine, but I'm not normally next to a literal perfect specimen.

"Hey, Ellie?"

"Hmm?" I take my time moving my gaze from his abs to his face.

His eyes are twinkling at me and my nerves skyrocket. He's *celebrity* handsome. Like, "too attractive to be a normal person" handsome. This was a bad idea. My heart is pounding almost painfully in my chest. I guess ripping bandages is supposed to be painful. But it's also supposed to be fast, dammit.

Matt continues to look at me with what I would describe as warm amusement. "Do I have your permission to be bossy tonight?"

*Excuse me.*

"My..." I think my brain short-circuits. "You want my permission to be...bossy?" I'm sure my face is the color of a tomato based on the heat I feel rushing through my body. "Like...with sex stuff?" Oh god, he's going to realize I'm about as vanilla as they come. Maybe his preference for vanilla extends to sex? *I hope so.*

He gives me a nod and waits for me. I look over at the shower to avoid eye contact. The fluorescents in here basically feel like spotlights and I have a feeling my lack of athleticism is about to be put to the test. I look back over at him and scan his body again. I think one of his legs has more muscle than both of mine combined. Maybe he'll do most of the work? Hopefully I can find some way to contribute. Ugh, that was a weird thing to think. I'm *so* regretting opting for shower sex.

"I'm just...a little nervous," I admit, my voice low.

His face goes soft at my admission and he moves over close

to me to perch his probably perfect ass on the edge of the counter.

"I'm assuming you're not talking about what I just asked," he says gently, nudging my leg with his knee.

I shake my head in answer.

He dips his head. "Well, aside from the obvious, which is that we don't have to do this tonight, is there anything that would make you less nervous?"

I look down at my feet. *Um, the lights off? Shots?* Shower sex is like the Olympic version of normal sex. Possibly the worst way to practice. Why did it sound like such a good idea at the time?

I glance back up at Matt's face.

*Right.* That's why.

I catch the side of his mouth twitch as he waits for my answer. His bottom lip is a little fuller than the top and his stubble looks a few days old. I bet it will feel good pretty much everywhere.

*Screw it.*

I step forward into him and press my mouth to his, jumping him before I can think better of it.

He grunts in surprise and steadies me with both of his hands on my waist. Angling his head, he dips his tongue into my mouth and tightens his grip on me. He doesn't break our kiss as he stands, instead taking advantage of the added height difference to lean down farther and tangle his tongue with mine.

Holy smokes, Matt knows how to kiss. I push onto my toes to try to taste more of him, putting my hands around his neck.

The slight stretch causes my cropped sweater to rise and Matt's hands move underneath. His thumbs trace my skin up and down as he continues to kiss me, gently pushing me against the wall. His fingers stop their rhythmic movement as he inches his hands up around my ribcage until he reaches the underwire of my bra.

Chills break out over my skin and I feel my nipples tighten as one of his thumbs nudges underneath my bra, skimming the underside of my breast. A slight moan slips out of me at the thought of those hands moving farther up.

Matt pulls back abruptly, dislodging my hands from their position as he breathes much heavier than before. Without breaking eye contact he leans over through the shower curtain and turns the water on. His blown pupils nearly cover up the green of his eyes.

"So do I have your permission?" he breathes out, leaning into me with his hands resting on the wall behind me.

Permission...? *Ohhh*, right. I'm about to embarrass myself. Again.

"Do I need, like, a safe word or something?" I scrunch my nose a bit and hope the flush from that kiss will hide any new redness making its way to my face.

Matt makes a huffing sound and drops his forehead to the wall next to me.

Burning humiliation floods my body. "Was that a stupid thing to ask?" I say quietly, unsure what his reaction means.

Matt jerks his head up and looks directly at me. "God no, Ellie. I didn't mean to imply that just now. You caught me off guard, and the idea...threw me for a loop. It's not something I'm familiar with in practice. I just... 'Permission' was the wrong word. I don't know what you like and that was my shitty attempt at asking if you'd be okay with me being in charge tonight. I thought it might help with the nerves. But in case it isn't painfully obvious"—he glances down at his significantly tented pants—"I'll have you any way you'll let me." He pauses and pushes a piece of disheveled hair behind my ear. "And to be clear, lack of enthusiasm would be enough. No objection, verbal or otherwise, would be required. But obviously listened to right away. We're here to have a good time, yeah? To practice?"

I feel myself relax and give him a nod.

He glances back and forth between my eyes. "Can I kiss you again?"

Another nod.

He leans forward and brushes his lips against mine before slowly tracing the seam of my lips with his tongue. I sigh and part my mouth, letting him in and reaching my hands back up to feel that tempting stubble. The gentle scratch against my palm sends shivers down my body. Less frantic than before, Matt takes his time exploring my mouth and trapping my body against the wall with his.

The pressure of his length against my stomach makes me whimper. Matt presses a little harder and I *want it*.

As the bathroom fills with steam, I can't tell if my labored breathing is from the thick air or kissing Matt like my life depends on it. He tugs at my sweater hem and pulls his mouth from mine to talk. "Can I take this off?" he pants.

I nod eagerly and quickly put my arms up above my head. He chuckles and steps back, gripping the bottom of my sweater before pulling it up over my head and arms.

"Christ, Ellie," he groans quietly, eyes roaming my chest.

I glance down and remember I'm in my see-through black lace bra. Ah, yes. My *I'm going out to get laid by a stranger for the first time in like four years* bra. Guess it's serving its purpose after all. And my tits look really good.

I focus back on Matt and notice his cheeks are tinged pink. "Want to get in the shower?" I ask him.

He looks up at my face and gives a quick jerk of a nod.

I unhook my bra behind my back and let the straps fall down my arms, grabbing it and tossing it to the floor. Matt's Adam's apple bobs as his eyes drop back to my chest. I quickly unbutton my jeans and yank them and my black lace thong down my legs before I can chicken out. I am going to have hot shower sex, dammit!

Righting myself, I find Matt still staring at me. I clear my throat and refrain from smiling as his gaze jumps to my face. I raise an eyebrow at him.

He swallows again and then unzips his pants and mimics my moves, pushing them to the floor before grabbing my hand. No striptease for me, I guess. He pulls me toward the shower and steps in, tugging me after him.

As soon as we're inside, he turns us around and pushes me through the hot water up against the shower wall. Before I have time to yelp over the bite of the cold tile, he slams his mouth to mine, delving his tongue inside to *devour* me.

I pull away to gasp for breath and Matt trails his mouth down my neck to the hollow of my throat. He starts moving down farther as my chest heaves, but pauses and pulls away, studying something near the top of my chest. His eyes flick to mine for a second before he bends and plants a chaste kiss to the jagged scar over my collarbone.

I don't have time to process the intimate gesture before he gently bites and tugs on my nipple, sending a jolt of pleasure down my core. He licks over the bite and sucks the now taut peak into his mouth.

"Oh fuck," I moan.

He releases it with a pop and uses his pointer finger to trace a tight circle around my nipple on the other side. "Perfect fucking tits," he says almost absentmindedly as he continues to torture me with that finger.

"Matt."

He pauses his ministrations and jerks his head up.

"Quit teasing me," I breathe out at him.

A full smile stretches across his face. *Wow.* He leans in and pecks my lips before dropping to his knees. I look down at him and then quickly back up, covering my eyes with my palms.

Large hands resting on my upper thighs, Matt laughs. "What's wrong?"

I shake my head in disbelief at the situation and slight embarrassment at my reaction. I uncover my eyes and gesture vaguely to him on his knees. "This is...very hot."

"Good." He nips my inner thigh before tugging my calf, lifting it up and over his shoulder. I steady myself with my hands against the wall by my sides.

As soon as Matt leans in and licks slowly up my center, I wish I had something on the wall to grab on to. *Holy fuck.* He groans and I think I could come from that sound alone.

He continues a steady, pleasurable assault with his tongue. I move one hand to his hair, trying to hold myself up as my legs begin to shake. Matt latches onto my clit and sucks, making stars speckle my vision as my knees begin to buckle. I tug his hair, wanting more and less at the same time.

I think I might fall in this shower and I think it might be worth it.

Matt releases my clit and goes back to a leisurely glide of his tongue up and down, lapping at a combination of water from the shower and me. He removes my leg from his shoulder and carefully sets it down, not once stopping the movement of his skilled tongue.

He finally pauses and pulls back, staring directly at my

pussy. He bites his lip and looks up at me. God, it's like the best porn I've ever seen.

"Do you want to switch to the bed?"

I rock my head back and forth slowly from where it rests against the tiles to tell him no. I'm committed to hot shower sex, shaky legs be damned. Matt nods and stands up, his hands going to my waist.

"Stay put," he orders.

I frown in protest and hear a chuckle as Matt turns. I close my eyes and listen as the shower curtain is pulled open and to the side. Curiosity has me snapping them back open.

He leans out and grabs something before turning back to me. "Can you wrap your legs around me?" Eyes never leaving mine, Matt puts a condom packet between his teeth and picks me up by my waist.

I wrap my legs like he asked and rest my hands on his shoulders as he presses my back into the shower wall. He leans his head in toward mine, angling slightly so the condom packet is right in front of my parted mouth. The packet is pushed in between my lips so I instinctively bite down to keep it from going farther. Matt releases it and leans over to my right ear.

"Good girl," he says before gently tugging my earlobe with his teeth. Chills break out all over my skin. He leans back and focuses on my face with barely concealed amusement. "Don't drop it, okay?"

I nod and feel my heart thudding at the anticipation of what's going to happen next.

Matt's dark hair has turned inky-black in the water, the color emphasizing his Superman likeness. I watch that hair disappear from view as he leans forward and licks a path from the hollow of my neck to the base of my ear. He starts to suck on my sensitive skin as his grip on my thighs moves to my ass. Those large hands knead my flesh as he leisurely makes his way to the other side of my neck. I feel heat pooling down low as more than just water drips down my center.

"You. Taste. So. Good. *Everywhere*," he groans, sucking and biting my neck, no doubt leaving marks.

I angle my head to the side, trying to give him further access and moaning at the barrage of sensation.

Matt breaks his connection to my skin and shocks me as he leans over to my mouth and rips the condom packet open with his teeth. Keeping one hand under me, he uses the other to remove the condom from the packet my teeth are still holding.

I spit the empty, now wet wrapper out onto the shower floor and watch Matt freeze. Shoot, that was probably not a sexy move.

Matt drops his head to the wall beside me and shakes with quiet laughter.

I can't help but laugh along with him, my body physically moving from the vibration of his. "I was sick of it in my mouth!" I explain with another laugh, water dripping down my face.

Matt leans back and gives me a full, heart-stopping smile. Ugh, even his teeth are attractive. Pearly white with slightly longer canines and a chipped incisor, the imperfections making them that much more appealing.

Keeping me pressed against the shower wall with his body, Matt uses both hands to roll the condom on and then angles my hips to notch himself at my entrance.

He nips my mouth before licking into it, sucking my tongue and totally invading my senses. I squirm against him and try to sink myself down his hard length.

"Good?" he asks, his breath tangling with mine and teeth bumping into my own.

I nod my head frantically and feel him push in slowly. *Oh god.* I didn't get a proper look at his dick before, but it feels way bigger than I remember a dick feeling.

Matt gently pulls at my bottom lip with his teeth, tugging harder until I feel him bottom out. He releases my lip and I drop my head back against the tiles. *Oh fuck.* The stretched and full feeling... *Holyshitthisfeelsgood.* This is definitely better than I remembered.

"Fuuuckkk." Matt's forehead falls to my shoulder. "I'm going to embarrass myself," he lets out in a huff.

I test out a squeeze of my muscles and Matt curses again.

"Ellie," he groans. "Give me a minute."

"Mmk. Sorry," I force out.

Matt lifts his head off my shoulder and nudges my nose with his. "C'mere," he says against my mouth. He captures my lips with his, seeking entrance with his tongue.

I open for him and slowly...lose...my...mind. I could kiss Matt—

"What's your last name?" I ask, pulling back.

He lets out a startled laugh and says, "Anderson," before claiming my mouth again and beginning a slow thrust in and out.

I could do this with Matt Anderson all day. All. Freaking. Day.

I flex my inner muscles again and get a jolt of pleasure. Matt grunts into my mouth and picks up his pace, my back being pushed roughly into the wall with each thrust. I feel pleasure coiling tighter and tighter, like I'm on the brink of shattering.

Matt draws away from my mouth and presses his teeth into the spot where my neck curves into my shoulder.

"Oh, fuck," I let out.

The unexpected bite sends me over the edge, my vision blacking out as I drop my head roughly against the wall. Waves of pleasure roll through me as my surroundings fade away. All I feel are Matt's teeth and the ongoing ripples of ecstasy flowing through my body.

As the waves slow, I feel Matt thrust twice more before stilling and groaning into my neck where his teeth are still indenting my skin. A few moments later he releases me from his bite and rests his head on my shoulder. We breathe heavily in sync for a couple minutes while we both come down from the high.

Matt eases himself out and sets my feet on the floor as I realize for the first time that the water isn't hot anymore. Matt seems to realize at the same time and disposes of the condom, tying it off and setting it in the small trash can right outside the shower curtain. He pauses there for a moment, staring at the spot where he dropped it. He finally turns back and looks around the shower. Grabbing my body wash from the ledge, he puts some in his hand and looks at me. "I'll be fast."

He quickly yet methodically washes my body, moving down on his knees to get my legs and in between them. When he reaches my upper legs, he pauses, taking note of the slight quivering of my muscles.

He presses a quick kiss to my inner thigh before finishing his task.

"Maybe a less vertical position next time," I tell him.

Matt pauses and looks up at me from his kneeling position, a wicked grin on that handsome face. "Next time?"

My cheeks burn and I grab the body wash from where he

left it in the corner. "Stand up so I can return the favor and not freeze to death," I quip, ignoring the massive smile on his face and squirting some soap onto my hands.

"Yes, ma'am," Matt says mock-seriously as he stands up.

I wash him with the efficiency of a girl who does not want to take a cold shower, only getting distracted by his semihard cock once or twice. Maybe thrice. Wow. That is a nice dick. I didn't really get a good look before, but now I can't help but stare. Remembering the stretched sensation from before is giving me flutters low in my belly. I want to experience that again. As soon as possible.

*Fudge, this water is getting cold.* Maybe the universe is telling me to calm down. Fair enough.

I turn the shower off and reach outside the curtain to grab two towels from the rack. I pass one to Matt and wrap the other around myself. As I step out of the shower in my towel I panic when I realize I don't know what happens next. Will he just want to get dressed and leave? What's the etiquette here?

This went about a million times better than I ever could have imagined and now I'm finding I'm not sure if I want this to be a one-time thing. Do I offer to watch a movie? He might have work tomorrow though and it's already pretty late…

I don't even realize I'm biting my lip and staring at his clothes on the floor until Matt tugs my lip free with his thumb and finger.

"What's wrong?" Matt has the towel wrapped low around his waist.

I force my eyes away from his happy trail up to his face. *Be brave.* "Do you want to watch a movie? I have…" I cringe. "No food in the fridge, actually, but we could order something to eat while we watch? What time is it? Maybe it's too late—"

Matt kisses me twice, quickly, before straightening and giving me that smile I now have memorized.

"I'd love to watch a movie. It's probably about eleven thirty so I would guess most places are closed, but I'll be okay because I just ate." He gives me a wink and hastily rubs his towel over his body before setting it on the counter.

Did he just...?

He bends to pick up his pants from the floor and pulls them on without his briefs. After shaking out his shirt and sliding it over his head, he grabs the towel and rubs it over his hair. He drops another kiss on my mouth. "Did you have something in mind you wanted to watch?"

I shake my head dumbly, still clinging to my towel and overthinking next steps.

"You can pick," I mumble absentmindedly. *Couch or bed, couch or bed, couch or bed.* Surely it doesn't matter, but I can't seem to make a decision for my life right now.

Matt smiles indulgently at me. "Okay. I'll go look for something on the TV while you get changed?"

I sigh in relief and nod, then head to my room to grab some sweats. "Make yourself at home," I call over my shoulder before I shut my door. I try to quiet the nerves, but the thought of spending more time with Matt sends excited butterflies to my stomach.

Kind, patient, so freaking *hot*. This is the definition of getting lucky.

# CHAPTER EIGHT

## *matt*

A NIGGLING THOUGHT IS KEEPING ME FROM FALLING BACK ASLEEP right now, but I can't seem to pick it out of my sleep-fogged mind. There's just something urging me to wake up...

*Game day.*

Ah, right. I try to keep track of the days of the week, but after playing this long my internalized schedule mostly consists of game days and non-game days. And today is a game day, which means my standard routine is breakfast, team meeting and morning skate, lunch with Niko, home for a break, and then back to the arena to get ready. Unfortunately my admittedly unfounded superstitions also mean there are a lot more little things too, but that's the gist.

I normally follow my routine like clockwork, waking up to my alarm alert and ready to start my day of scheduled events. But for some reason I'm feeling groggy and unable to just get up. I flex my arm to fight the feeling and squeeze...something? Someone?

*Ellie.*

Oh shit, am I still at her apartment? I force my eyes open and yep, I'm on her couch, arm wrapped around her like even my subconscious couldn't risk letting her go. I'm on my back with Ellie's head on my chest, her soft brown hair splayed all over. Her arm is draped over my stomach and her leg is bent and straddling my thigh. She's sandwiched between me and the back of the couch.

Up close like this I can see the individual freckles on her nose and the little dip from the bow in her top lip. Her mouth is slightly parted and she's breathing evenly. Still fully asleep.

For the first time in my life, I consider being late to the team meeting instead of the first one there. It's not a necessity for the captain to be there early, but I like to set a good example for the guys—especially the newer, younger ones who might need ego checks after "making it big."

Now that I think about it though, I might already be late. My alarm hasn't gone off yet, but it's pretty bright in here. *Shit*.

I very carefully use my free arm to grab my phone I pocketed before we watched the movie. A movie we obviously fell asleep during. I maneuver it out slowly and press the button on the side to check the time.

Dead.

No wonder my alarm didn't go off. I turn my head toward the kitchen and squint at the microwave. Nine thirty-seven. Well, fuck. I'm normally up at eight on game days. And the team meeting starts in twenty-three minutes. At least the practice arena is only about fifteen minutes away, but I still have no time to do anything but get up and go.

*God dammit.* I scrub my free hand over my face and debate how to do this. I know nurses work a lot of hours and I really don't want to mess up her sleep schedule. But I also *refuse* to be the guy who leaves without saying anything, so I'm just going to have to apologize when I wake her up.

I kiss the top of her head and take a quick inhale. She

smells like...vanilla? And maybe something floral. It's hard to distinguish, but it's fucking sweet and it's reminding me of last night. And now is *really* not the time to think about that.

"Ellie," I say lightly into her hair.

She makes some unintelligible noise and flexes her small hand on my stomach. Her brow furrows and I want to kiss that little divot between her eyebrows. *Fuck*, I already have it bad. I want to stay on this couch all day.

Ellie awake is...so many things. Stunning, unexpected, funny and sweet. Ellie *asleep* is tempting in a whole other way. She's soft and peaceful, her warmth against me quieting some restless energy I usually can't shake. The stillness right now is just...nice.

I sigh and kiss her head again. "Sorry, Ellie, I'm going to be late to my team meeting so I have to get going," I force out.

She starts to rouse and slowly sits up, her palm on my stomach supporting her. That adorable sleepy gaze is going to ruin me. She yawns and I have to fight the urge to drag her back down onto me and go back to bed.

"You have to get to the bar for that?" she asks, eyes squinted from the harsh light, that divot getting deeper as her brows lower more.

Oh fuck. *Fuck*. How did I forget I haven't talked to her about my *other* job yet? My way more important, way more public job. I don't even have time to give her a full explanation.

Okay, it's probably fine. Hopefully the cool factor outweighs the forgot-to-tell-you factor.

"The meeting is actually over at the rink—the one in Saint Paul?" I hesitate, unsure how to do this. "I, uh, play hockey and it's a game day so we have a meeting this morning at the practice rink before a quick skate. I would skip it if I could," I finish as genuinely as I can. I *would* skip it if I could. But I don't think that matters right now.

Sleepy Ellie is gone. In her place is a very alert and increasingly distant version of her.

"What?" She removes her hand from my stomach and scoots back a bit toward the end of the couch with my legs.

I sit up and swing them over the side, still keeping my torso facing her as much as I can. "I'm sorry I have to leave. And I'm sorry I fell asleep last night. I mean, I'm *not* sorry, I liked sleeping with you…" I cringe at the shit show this explanation is turning into and take a breath. "I just meant I know we didn't talk about it beforehand and I didn't mean to overstay my welcome. I actually slept really well next to you and I'm sorry I have to go so abruptly. I would prefer to stay."

Ellie seems to be assessing me in some new light and I'm not sure I like the concerned expression taking over her face.

"You play hockey? Like, professionally?" Her voice sounds strained.

I'm not going to lie—when people find out I play for the Bears they generally don't seem so…put out. I was expecting surprise and, honestly, maybe intrigue. But Ellie does seem to continually catch me off guard. And right now, I think I am reading acute distress in her voice. Is it because I didn't tell her yesterday or something else?

I open my mouth to respond and then close it, instead opting to just give her a nod. Ellie goes a little pale at my confirmation and slowly gets up from the couch. I watch her walk to the kitchen where she gets a glass of water.

"Do you need anything before you go?" she asks with a flat tone.

*Shit.* I am being dismissed.

I get up and head toward the door to grab my jacket and

slip my shoes on. How do I fix this? "No, I'm okay. I'm really sorry about this, Ellie. Can I call you later today?"

Ellie grabs a dishcloth and starts wiping an already clean counter. She looks up at me and holds my gaze. Something in her eyes sends a pit into my stomach, but I can't name it.

"Sure," she says.

I swallow and nod and then let myself out the door. I'd love to figure out how to unfuck this right now, but I think I'm already later than I've ever been. A fact that's not bothering me as much as it should. Not nearly as much as the fact that I might have messed things up with Ellie before we've even really started.

It's not until I get to my car that I realize I never even got her number.

# CHAPTER NINE
## *ellie*

*SIX MONTHS AGO*

There's something about the late summer sun that's so... melancholy. I'm not really sure why I feel that way. I don't think it's about summer ending. I like summer, sure, but I *love* fall. Maybe it's memories of going back to school? Or maybe it's the coming back from a summer vacation that I associate with the close of August.

My eyes are shut and the low sun is flickering through the trees, an alternating red and black flashing behind my eyelids as we take the train up the coast toward Ogunquit Beach. We'll still have to take a car from the train stop into town, but suffering through ten minutes is a hell of a lot better than two *hours*. My stomach clenches at the thought. Josh and I are joining our friends John, Chandler, Zoey, and Graham at a rental house like we always have, but it's feeling different than it has in the past. This might be the last one for a while. Maybe ever.

I got my job offer at General last week and I'd be crazy not to take it. I *want* to take it. But it means our favorite vacation spot is no longer an hour and a half train ride away. Not to mention how much farther we'll be from our friends. I feel a pang of worry at the prospect of not having a group of friends around in Minneapolis, but I remind myself that Josh and Dev will be with me and I will make new friends. Hopefully.

We haven't talked about it much, but I assume Josh will move with me sometime next month unless he has issues with his job transfer. I guess I could go first and he could follow if it comes to that. I've never lived fully on my own, so even the idea of doing it for a month or two is a little intimidating, but I'm sure it'll be okay.

After we get off at the train station, we make our way to the small line of taxis waiting for passengers. We slide into the first one and give the driver the name of the restaurant we're meeting at, knowing we don't have enough time to drop our bags off at the rental house first.

I can feel Josh watching me out of the corner of my eye. I buckle my seat belt, pulling it tight, and close my eyes. *Ten minutes.* One minute, ten times. I decide to count backward from sixty, ticking down one finger every time I get to zero.

I have one finger still up and am at twenty-seven when I feel the car stop and hear the driver repeat the name of the restaurant we gave him. Cautiously opening my eyes, I sigh in relief when I see the familiar building outside the window. I quickly unbuckle and get out of the car. Josh pays the driver and walks over to me, grabbing the bag from my hand.

"You good?"

I give a jerky nod and forge ahead into the restaurant. Thank god Zoey promised I can drive her car while we're here. And double thanks that our house is walking distance to the beach.

As we get inside, we're met with crowded-restaurant ambiance and struggle to give the hostess the name on the reservation. She finally hears us and lets us know our group has already been seated. As she leads us to our table I take in the old floors and cozy seating. The restaurant looks like it was just a house once, with lots of separate rooms instead of one big space. The lighting is low and the flickering candles add to the warm atmosphere. There's a reason we make a point to eat here every time we visit. I feel myself relax and get a little giddy at seeing my friends in one of my favorite restaurants. I do my best to hang on to that feeling so I don't get swallowed by the looming finality this trip represents.

I see Zoey first and nearly squeal. She's been gone most of the summer visiting her family in California and this is the first time I'm seeing her since early June. She's a high school teacher, and while I wouldn't want her job, her free summers always make me jealous. *Lucky bitch.* I met Zoey my freshman year of college and we roomed together every year of school after that. She's sporting a true San Diego tan and her dark hair is down in waves. Graham, her boyfriend, smartly moves out of the way as she nearly loses a shoe trying to get out of the round booth.

"Ellieeeeeeeee!" she sings as she hugs me so tight I can barely breathe. I do my best to give her the same treatment, but she's got about three inches on me and a smidge of muscle. Maybe more.

I should really join her for that stupid yoga sculpt class she keeps begging me to go to. *Ugh.*

"Hi. You look hot," I tell her, with not an ounce of jealousy. I scan her tan legs again and sigh.

"Oh hush, you know it's the tan. It's like makeup for your body." She laughs and scoots back into the booth, making room for me and Josh. I slide in and say hi to everyone else as Josh gives John their signature man-hug before settling next to me. His longtime friend thankfully made an excellent choice of partner, and now he and Chandler fit right in with the four of us. Chandler gives me a big smile and I promise her a hug when we all get out of the booth.

"I want to talk to all of you, but I'm starving so can we order first?" I ask with a guilty smile.

Josh laughs and hands me a menu, which I immediately begin to scan. I'm looking at the drink list when the waitress comes over to take our orders. I order a fancy cocktail and the salmon and try my hardest to ignore my grumbling stomach. I should've eaten before we left.

"So what's up with everyone?" Josh asks, dropping a hand on my bouncing knee.

I stick my tongue out at him and stop my shifting, turning to focus on the group. I see Chandler look at John, and watch John face everyone.

"We actually have some news," he says, a nervous smile on his face. He leans down and is reaching for something under the table. He comes back up and is holding...a sonogram?

"Oh my god!" I screech. "You're pregnant?!" I push Josh out of the booth and scramble over to the other side to give Chandler a squeeze.

"Congrats, man," Josh says behind me, giving John another hug and then leaning around me to give Chandler one too.

I move out of the way to let the rest of the hugs commence and settle back in my seat. *A baby! Eeeek!* I love babies. This is so exciting.

"Ellie, I need you to get pregnant so we can have babies together. I know Zoey is a lost cause," Chandler says.

I laugh at the last part, elbowing Zoey.

"Hey, I do all my parenting at my job. I have nothing left for these hypothetical babies," Zoey reminds us. She's always known she doesn't want kids and I respect the hell out of it. Kids are no small decision.

"We know," I tell her affectionately and pat her leg.

"So...how about it, Ellie?" Chandler asks with a waggle of her eyebrows.

I laugh at her antics and knock my shoulder into Josh next to me. "I think the plan is to wait a couple years," I tell her.

"Oh nice. Didn't know you changed your mind, man. You gonna get it reversed?" John chimes in, and my gaze shifts from Chandler to him, but he's looking at Josh.

I try to process what he just said while simultaneously watching his expression go from casual to...*panicked*.

It's like my brain is moving in slow motion. I can see the alarm on his face, plain as day, but I can't seem to connect the dots. *Reversed... Reversed...*

The loud chatter of the restaurant seems to fade to the background and a slight ringing in my ears takes over as my mind finally puts it together. I feel my face get hot and then it's like something is squeezing my ribs. I try to quell the rising emotion so I don't make a scene. A quick glance at the table and I know it's too late. Everyone, even Zoey, is looking like they'd rather be anywhere else.

If there was any chance of me playing this as if I knew what was going on, I blew it with my dumbstruck reaction thirty seconds ago. I'm suddenly glad I haven't eaten yet.

"I'm just gonna go to the bathroom real quick." I force a tight smile and angle a thumb toward the back of the restaurant. Josh isn't dumb enough to keep me at the table and moves out of the way to let me out. I feel him following close behind me and can't decide what to do.

I push open the bathroom door. He can wait.

I flick the lock and lean my forehead against the cool wood.

Okay. *Okay. What the fuck.*

Finding out my boyfriend of three years got a vasectomy in front of a group of friends was not on my bingo card. You know what else wasn't on my bingo card? My boyfriend getting a vasectomy.

My mind is spinning with so many questions and so much hurt I can't even form a coherent thought. When? Why? What does this mean about *our relationship*? I think back to when we started dating and how Josh asked about what birth control I was on. We've talked about kids, for fuck's sake.

"Ellie?" I hear Josh's muffled voice from outside the bathroom door as the handle gives a jiggle.

"This is the—" My voice cracks and I want to die. I swallow and clear my throat, trying to keep any tears from emerging. I really don't want to do this here. "This is the girls' bathroom," I remind him, hoarse, shaky voice be damned.

I hear a rough sigh and the handle stops moving.

Where do I go from here?

### PRESENT DAY

I tell myself it's not even close to what happened last summer, but those hardwired feelings of betrayal surface like a reopened wound—painful and all too familiar.

Matt lied. And I know it was by omission, but I've *been there, done that* and my radar is throwing up a little red flag.

A fucking hockey player, of all things.

I pace my kitchen like a sad, zoo-caged animal and debate trying the "screaming into a pillow" thing with this kitchen towel to see how that makes me feel. I don't think I could actually scream though. Also that's probably gross. I've been aggressively wiping the counter with it for the past ten minutes.

*Goddammit.*

He was so nice. And sweet and patient and...ugh, hot. No wonder he has massive quads and a literal six-pack. Obviously finding the perfect guy to practice with would come with a catch.

I don't know where to go from here. I laugh humorlessly at the cruel reminder of having that exact thought all those months ago. There's just really nothing like finding out your boyfriend of three years withheld life-changing information from you for your entire relationship. It leaves a bit of a mark.

And I know Matt and I weren't in a relationship of any kind, but I liked him. A lot more than I thought possible after one night together. But I don't really want to get involved with a pro athlete of any kind, let alone hockey. I just can't imagine we'd be...compatible.

Memories of last night might beg to differ though.

I'm just so...so *bummed*. With Matt. With myself. Of course he's a freaking hockey player. *I slept with a hockey player.* My stomach drops at the reminder. *How could I do this?*

I wish I had never gone to that bar. Does he even own it?

A prickle of unease crawls up my spine as I think about what else he could've lied about. People lie to get laid all the time. Then I remember *I* propositioned *him* and want to slap my forehead with my palm. He also didn't seem like a liar. I shake my head, desperate to clear this mess in my mind. I could find out if he was truthful about one thing...

Resolved to get at least one answer, I throw on some less sleep-ridden sweats and grab my jacket, beanie, and keys. I'm so singularly focused on my mission I don't even remember the walk, but by the time I go to open the bar door, my hands are practically frozen solid. I do my best to curl them around the handle and pull it open.

"Sorry, we're close—" Nate's shout from the back is cut off when he glances up and makes eye contact with me. "Oh, hey. Uh, Eleanor, right?" Nate asks with surprise, glancing between me and the door.

Good memory. "Ellie." I correct him on autopilot.

He nods and stands up straight from where he was crouched near some bin on the floor.

"Does he..." I clear my throat and try again. "Does he own this bar?" It comes out shakier than I wanted, but at least I asked what I came here to find out.

Nate's expression shifts from apprehension to confusion. "Matt? Yeah, he co-owns it with me."

*Oh.* Well, all right. I feel myself deflate, the initial shock and sting settling into something tamer. And without those things to focus on I find myself...embarrassed. *What am I doing here?*

"Okay, thanks." I nod quickly and turn to leave.

"Hey, Ellie?" Nate's voice stops me and I face back toward him. He's looking at me with some unreadable expression. "Is everything okay?"

What am I supposed to say to that? *Oh, yeah, everything is great. I just slept with your friend and am feeling unreasonably bothered that he withheld information I had no right to.* I fight a physical cringe. I aim for a casual shrug instead. "Yeah, sorry about barging in here," I tell him, my blush likely giving away my newfound shame.

I push the door open and walk out, desperate not to make more of a scene than I already have.

# CHAPTER TEN
## matt

Morning skate went...less than ideal. First, I was late to the team meeting. Not a good look. Second, I practiced like shit. Not *all* that concerning unless it translates to a bad game tonight, but still embarrassing to miss that many passes. I guess you could say I was distracted.

I can still picture Ellie's face when I left this morning, void of the emotion she previously had let me see so easily. I try to remind myself it was just one night and this isn't a big deal, but the thought rings false almost immediately. I scrub my face with my hands and lean back against my headrest, waiting for the heat to kick in enough for the steering wheel to not feel like the ice I just played on.

My phone buzzes on the passenger seat and I jolt upright, stupidly wondering if it could be her calling. *You didn't get her number, you dumbass.* I see Nate's name and sigh, grabbing it and answering. "Hey, what's up?"

"Oh, nothing. Just wondering how it went with Ellie." Nate's tone holds amusement, but I'm too busy thinking about the situation with her to read into it.

"Pretty great actually, until this morning," I tell him. "She found out I— Wait. How'd you know she goes by Ellie?"

"Ah, yeah. Well, that was actually why I was calling. She may have stopped by the bar earlier."

I barely contain a groan. "Way to bury the fucking lead, you jackass. What happened? What did she say?"

"She, uh, seemed upset? She asked if you owned the bar. Honestly, I was pretty confused. I tried to ask if everything was okay, but she left in a hurry after I answered her." *Fuck.* "So what happened?"

"Shit. How long ago was that?"

"Probably an hour or so? I would've called sooner, but I knew you were busy. Everything okay? Sorry, I really thought you were going to tell me she turned out to be crazy or something."

"Nah, I actually like her a lot." I swallow, feeling even worse than I did before. "I just messed up. Can I call you later?"

"Yeah, man, of course."

I hang up and toss the phone to the passenger seat, putting the car in drive. A singular thought is consuming my mind: *make this right.*

DESPITE THE POST-SKATE SHOWER AND THIRTEEN-DEGREE temperature outside, I'm sweating as I stand in front of Ellie's door inside her building. I may have been a little frantic after that call with Nate and *may* have jumped the gun in driving over here. She might not even be home. But I'm here now…

I adjust my black ballcap and take a quick breath before

knocking on her door. I look around while I wait, noticing for the first time there's another apartment door on her floor and stairs leading up to another level. I wonder how many neighbors Ellie has and if she likes them. Maybe it was one of them who let me in the outer door a minute ago as they left? Nice, but not very secure.

At the sound of the door handle moving, I turn back and reflexively hold my breath. Ellie swings it open, revealing that pretty freckled face I'm quickly becoming obsessed with. No signature smile and blush in place this time though. I withhold a frown and brace myself for this conversation not going as well as last night.

Ellie's wearing a green sweatshirt and matching sweatpants with her hair messily held up by a big clip. Her lips look glossy—and edible, fuck me—but I remind myself I'm here for a reason. "Hey," I breathe out. "Can I come in?"

She seems to be cataloging something about my appearance, a touch of concern clouding her face. I do my best to slow my breathing and quell any of the worked-up energy I might be giving off. I watch her squint at something on my neck and fight the urge to reach there.

"Are you okay? Why are you"—she pauses to gesture to my chest—"panting?"

Guess I didn't hide that very well. "I, uh, came here straight from morning skate and had to park a couple blocks away." I hike my thumb over my shoulder toward the south. "Then I kinda jogged," I add, feeling an uncharacteristic heat come to my face.

Ellie scans my outfit, landing on my sneakers. I follow her gaze and look down at them, noticing for the first time that they are only half tied. I wouldn't blame someone for calling me disheveled. I hear Ellie sigh softly and I glance up in time to see her turning away from me and heading toward her couch. She sits and tucks her hands under her legs, staring at her fuzzy-sock-covered feet moving against the shag rug.

She left the door open, but I'm not really getting "come on in" vibes. She finally looks up at me and raises her eyebrows in question.

I blink and clear my throat. "I can stay?"

Her expression shifts to something softer and she dips her head in answer. My shoulders sag with relief. Okay, now to convince her to give me a chance. I straighten my spine and walk through the door, shutting it quietly behind me. I make my way over to the leather chair that's angled toward her couch and take a seat. Elbows propped on my knees, hands loosely clasped in front of me. Time to shine.

"I wish I had told you about my job earlier, but I can't change that now so I want to try and tell you about why I didn't."

"It's okay, Matt. You don't owe me anything, it was one night," Ellie says before I can continue. "I didn't specifically ask you about your job either. I did assume it was owning that bar because of what you said, but I guess that wasn't really a lie."

I wince at that, thinking both of my call with Nate and how I *did* get selective with what I told her last night. Ellie also sounds...resigned. Which is not good. I hesitate, looking at the rest of the couch we were lying on just hours ago. Last night was the most fun I've had with a girl in a long time. I haven't felt that much immediate chemistry with someone maybe ever. And I still feel hopeful that this could go somewhere more serious. If this plays out okay. I just have to hope she understands and ultimately feels the same way I do. I focus back on Ellie.

"Well, in the name of honesty, I was, in a way, trying not to get into my hockey career. But I wasn't trying to manipulate you or anything else malicious like that, I swear. I just really liked that to you I was simply Clark Kent, random guy at the bar you liked enough to adorably proposition. And not Matt Anderson, professional hockey player, some trophy to be bagged. It's not very often people don't already know who I am when they meet me." I cringe and look at Ellie's fuzzy socks. "I know how that sounds, but it's just my life."

After a beat I make eye contact, determined to explain.

"I got famous at like fifteen. My whole life, everyone I'm with has known my name, and the people who try to get to know me don't always have good intentions. In fact, I would venture to say most don't," I mutter, fighting a sneer. "I own that this is the cost of living a dream. And I'm grateful for it. I know how lucky I am to be doing this for a living. But it can often be exhausting living this way. And meeting someone in this city who didn't know me was like... It's like a weight I didn't know I was carrying every day was lifted. I forget how heavy the burden is to be in the spotlight until I'm at home, with my family. Or now, with you, and it's...not there. I'm not trying to throw a pity party here. I know I have a good life. I just hope you can understand why I didn't tell you."

I've been watching Ellie, trying to assess how my explanation is landing, but her expression remains carefully neutral. I know she said I don't owe her anything, but I'd like to get to a point where she can have expectations of me.

"I do," she says. "Understand, I mean. I'm not upset, Matt. It just took me by surprise and brought up some old issues." She waves her hand in a dismissive gesture.

Despite her words and the casual tone, something about her demeanor is putting me on edge. In an effort not to be obtuse, I try to think through this from her perspective the best I can.

She could still be upset about me lying, of course. Feelings don't just vanish. Or it could be something else. She did mention "old issues." I try to think of what I know about her past from our minimal time together so far. As I'm replaying our conversation from last night, something occurs to me.

"Was your ex a hockey player?"

"What?" Ellie's brows draw down low. "God, no. I would never—"

I raise my own, taken aback by her reaction. Ellie grimaces. She said *never*...

"That came out wrong, sorry. I just...no. Josh wasn't a hockey player or pro athlete." Ellie sighs and sits back on the couch, tilting her head onto the cushion and looking up at the ceiling. "Despite how this is all coming out, I don't really have a lot of resentment for my ex. I just don't like being kept in the dark, and this morning kind of reminded me what that felt like."

A shorter piece of Ellie's hair is loose from her clip, softly curling behind her ear, along her neck. My fingers twitch thinking about playing with it. I curl them into fists.

I'm feeling a little at a loss here, like I might be fighting a losing battle. She didn't backtrack on her response to my hockey question, which means Ellie likely has something against hockey players. Or professional athletes, I'm not sure which. Guess all I can do is focus on what *is* in my control.

"Ellie?"

She snaps her head up to look at me, eyes steady on mine.

"I'm sorry I lied." She opens her mouth to say something, but I continue before she can repeat what she said before. "I know you said I don't owe you anything and it was only one night, but I *am* sorry I decided to withhold that information. I promise I won't do it again. I'm an open book for you, okay?"

Even though the offer is genuine, I am hoping it might influence her own response to this next question.

"Are you up for telling me about what happened with your ex?" I hedge. "Feels like the proper thing to talk about on a second date." I smile to let her know I'm referencing our conversation last night and to lighten the mood a touch. The side of her mouth ticks up and I feel like fist-pumping the air.

She scrunches her nose and softly kicks her foot against the rug, deciding to focus on that instead of me. It's almost a full minute before she responds.

"Have you ever had the 'do you want kids' talk with previous girlfriends?"

The question catches me so off guard I feel frozen to my seat. Ellie looks up at me, patiently waiting for a response. Have I had that conversation? Yes. Has it gone well? Not really. I'm not sure where she's going with this, so I guess honesty is the best policy, given what we've been discussing. "With the serious ones, yeah," I tell her.

"And you were honest, right? About what you wanted?"

I take a beat before I answer, thinking through all those conversations. "Yes."

Ellie nods, like she expected that answer. "Josh was not."

"Ah." *Josh*. She mentioned the name last night and it didn't really bother me. Today though? *Fuck Josh*. I could hazard a guess at which side of the coin Ellie is on, but I'm almost nervous to get to that part of this conversation given how it's gone previously for me. I settle on something safer. "How'd you find out he was lying?"

Ellie's mouth twists to the side before she talks. "His friend accidentally outed that he got a vasectomy. Thankfully he got it before we were together, but I didn't find out until last August. And by then we'd been together for three years and had several discussions on birth control, kids, our future, all that stuff. None of which was truthful apparently." She looks at her hands, which are now in her lap playing with a hair tie on her wrist.

"Did you find out why?"

"Why he lied?" She picks her head up and I nod in answer. Ellie shrugs. "I mean, he said he just figured I'd change my mind, or maybe eventually he would feel differently and get it reversed. And maybe he would. But it's hard to trust someone again who can keep up a lie for so long. That takes a lot of... intention. And it's not like he lied to get in my pants or something. We didn't even have those conversations until a little further into our relationship."

Ellie gets up from the couch as soon as she finishes talking and wanders to the kitchen directly in my view. She opens a cabinet and stretches on her toes to grab something.

"Water okay again?" It comes out slightly muffled from where she has her head behind the cabinet door.

"Sure, thanks."

She produces two glasses and brings them to the sink, filling them from the filter she has there. I'm guessing her sudden trip to the kitchen is her way of closing that part of the conversation. Her next question confirms it.

"So an open book, huh?"

I wait for Ellie to look at me before I respond. When she does, I incline my head. "For you."

She finishes filling the glasses and puts one in each hand. She walks them back over toward me and sets one on the coffee table with a low thud. I watch her curl back up on the sofa and take a sip of her water.

"What would you like to know?"

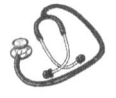

# CHAPTER ELEVEN
## *ellie*

As I sit facing Matt, I'm hit with the sudden realization that my description of "celebrity handsome" was freakishly accurate. Because Matt Anderson isn't just a professional hockey player. He's a *famous* hockey player. Like, *household name* hockey player. And he fucked me against my shitty shower wall in my tiny one-bedroom apartment last night.

I try to bury the unfounded, retrospective shame, but my earlier Google search was quite...illuminating. The hat he's wearing? That brand endorses him for millions of dollars a year. *Millions.* Matt is *rich* rich.

And worse? He's known as the most charitable hockey player to date, literally. Which means I have maybe one of the nicest hockey players to exist apologizing to me for trying to be normal for one night. And it totally makes sense, everything he said. He even has *me* feeling bad for *him*. Mr. Richy Rich.

And *yet*.

I'm not sure if it's enough. I'm not mad anymore, if I ever even had the right to be. I just don't think I can handle the hockey thing. Or the fame.

"You're kind of famous." The non-question slips out, my filter apparently not working at the moment.

Matt's cheeks tinge pink and his shoulders lift slightly before falling. A shrug. He's *uncomfortable*. "Hockey players don't really get famous." He pauses and then, "Comparatively."

Charitable and humble. I'm screwed. *Stay focused, Ellie.*

"Do you deal with public attention? Like paparazzi and articles and stuff?" I didn't see any tabloid-type stories about him during my search, but I also got the impression Matt doesn't elicit anything really scandalous. So it's possible they just don't get written about him much.

Matt's eyes are bouncing around my face, probably trying to make sense of this line of questioning. Maybe he thought the offer of being an open book would lead to things more like "how often do you hook up with strangers" or "why hockey." But I don't really want to think about the former, and the latter I already know the answer to, thanks to the internet: his parents got him a mini plastic stick and goal for their basement and he became obsessed when he was four.

"I try to keep my life as private as possible," he starts slowly. "So I don't have any social media or anything like that. I mostly just do what I'm contractually obligated to in the media department." Matt clears his throat. "We don't really have paparazzi here in Minnesota, so if you're asking about pictures then it's mostly just from fans. Though usually those are pictures *with* them—they tend to be respectful of my privacy and not take candids too much, that I'm aware of at least."

"And the articles?"

Matt's brows draw down and his mouth sets into an almost-frown. I can see the questions behind his eyes. *Why does she care so much about this part of my life?* "Some articles are inevitable, I guess. Most tend to be hockey-related though. I'm sure there's the occasional invasive story about some aspect of my personal life. I tend to only read things my family send me, so I wouldn't see those if they exist."

I think of how that would feel, having articles and stories about yourself get sent to you. I fight off a cringe. I've never thought about being in a position where privacy wasn't guaranteed. There's something to be said for mundane anonymity. Would I lose that if I kept hanging out with Matt?

"How did that all play into your past relationships?" I ask him.

Something flickers in Matt's eyes, like maybe he's started to connect the dots on where these questions have been coming from. "How did the public aspect of my life affect them?"

"Right, the lack of privacy," I confirm.

Matt seems to perk up as he answers this time. "Well, all of my serious relationships have started through mutual friends, so they all kind of knew what they were getting into. Honestly, they probably would've preferred to be in the spotlight more than we were, but that's not really what I'm into. There were other reasons, but that difference contributed to why we weren't compatible ultimately."

I'm now picturing his previous girlfriends as ultrahot Instagram influencers. The sharp pang of jealousy catches me off guard and I look to the water I've been holding in my lap. It's probably a good thing he doesn't have an account for me to stalk. I don't remember seeing pictures of him with any women in my search, but that doesn't mean they don't exist. "But they did get attention? Like they were photographed and stuff when you were dating?"

Matt doesn't answer for a long time. I pick my head up to

look at him and find him already watching my face carefully. He looks...despondent. I think he's surmised this might be an issue for me.

He gives me a nod and continues to watch my face. I look back to my cup. A few moments tick by in silence. I hear movements and glance up to see Matt rounding the coffee table to come to the couch where I'm sitting. He lines himself up beside me and drops softly, maneuvering that broad frame with more grace than you'd expect.

Matt surprises me when he plucks my water from my hands and sets it on the table, quickly reaching back toward me and taking one of my hands in his. He threads our fingers and rests them on his thigh. "Ellie."

I look from our joined hands to his face. It's really so striking up close, those green eyes sending flutters through my belly.

"I really like you."

Those flutters turn into a full swoop.

"You hardly know me," I remind him.

Matt shrugs and smiles at me. I feel his thumb gently moving along mine. "Well, I *really* like everything I know," he says.

I fight my smile and feel my face heat. Matt reaches up with his other hand and swipes a thumb over my cheek. "I'd also really like to take you on a date."

I know Matt can see my expression fall, but I can't seem to help it. A date. Dating. Potential pictures and attention. *Articles*. I don't think I can handle any of it. Don't think I want to. "I don't know if I'm up for all of that," I confess quietly.

Matt's eyes look back and forth between mine as his thumb stills its movement. "You're not just talking about the date," he guesses correctly.

I shake my head and feel the dejection of the situation settle in my stomach like a solid weight.

Matt looks down at our clasped hands. He seems to be mulling something over as his expression changes from understanding to thoughtful to...resigned? Maybe it's disappointment. He starts moving his thumb again, almost absentmindedly. Nearly a full minute goes by before he speaks again.

"What if we kept it all—us, I mean—a secret?" Matt finally looks back up at me after he says that and I can read the disappointment clearly now.

*He doesn't want this to be a secret.* But he's offering it anyway. And it's a relatively selfless offer for someone in his shoes. Matt's the one who will have to work to keep anything a secret. Not me, really. I don't have fans. No one cares what I'm doing every day.

But if we date publicly *they might.*

I look at Matt's eyes. His lips and nose. Those little scars that now make sense. I almost decide to give in and just agree to a date. I really like him too. Maybe even more so because of how he handled today. But I don't think I can handle the attention. So maybe keeping it on the "DL" would be the best of both worlds. And honestly? Hanging out in secret sounds kind of hot.

"So like confidential fuck buddies?" I ask him.

Matt smiles and shakes his head, a low laugh slipping out in the process. "I never know what's going to come out of here," he tells me, reaching up to swipe a thumb over my lower lip.

"Is that a good thing?"

He nods and looks at my mouth. All of a sudden Matt drops my hand and grabs my waist with both of his. In one quick move I'm lifted and turned, then deposited on his lap facing him. He keeps his hands firmly on my waist as I reorient myself and find that I'm straddling him with my knees resting outside his hips.

Matt squeezes me. "Sorry, wanted to see your face better." He says it gently, a soft contrast to the abrupt change in position I just experienced. He keeps eye contact with me as he rests back against the couch. I watch his eyes shift from my eyes down to my lips. Then back up. "Can I kiss you?"

I dip my chin and see Matt visibly sag in relief. He sits up and slides a hand around my neck, pulling me gently to meet his mouth in a soft kiss. I sigh at that contact and relax into him, tentatively offering a deeper kiss with a tilt of my head. Matt angles me further with his hand tangled in my hair and starts to kiss me in earnest.

I think I'd be happy just being Matt's *kiss* buddy. His skilled tongue traces mine like there's no rush at all. Nowhere else to be but right here, with me.

I break away and rest my forehead on his, slowing my breathing. "So you're gonna be my—"

"Confidential fuck buddy?" he says with a smile I feel against my own. He pulls my head back with a gentle tug of my hair so we're face-to-face. I watch his smile fade as he licks his bottom lip, his gaze jumping from my eyes to my mouth and back. "If you'll let me, Ellie."

I think there would be a public riot if anyone knew I wasn't one hundred percent sure about this. Who wouldn't want to have regular sex with someone this hot? Someone this… charming. And apparently also rich and kind of famous. *Ugh*.

He did say secret though. And I don't think he would offer that if he didn't mean it. I'm still trying to talk myself into it when an alarm goes off. Matt closes his eyes and then uses the hand not in my hair to maneuver a phone out of his back pocket. He looks at it for a moment before silencing it and setting it down on the couch next to us.

"Time for you to go?" I ask him.

He takes his time nodding, reluctant to give me confirmation. It's probably for the best. I need to figure out if this is what I want without his tempting presence right in front of me. It's hard to say no to ice cream when it's shoved in your face. Impossible when Matt Anderson himself is offering it to you. And now I have an image of a naked Matt feeding me ice cream...

"So, can I call my confidential fuck buddy later?" Matt asks me with a sly grin, breaking me out of my dirty thoughts.

I blush at the fading image in my head and feign a glare. "Are you ever going to forget I said that?"

"No, ma'am."

I watch as Matt grabs his phone again and types on it for a minute. He holds it up to show me a new contact: *Confidential Fuck Buddy*. The number is blank.

I roll my eyes. "Give me that."

Matt's eyes twinkle as he hands it over. I quickly type my phone number in and save it, handing it back to him.

"What's my contact name going to be in your phone?"

I get up from his lap and grab my phone from the kitchen counter. "Can you call me real quick?"

He complies and I see an unknown number pop up on my phone. I reject the call and open the contact, typing out my chosen name for him. Matt gets up from the couch and wanders to me, peering at the screen from over my shoulder.

"How's that?" I angle the phone so he can see better. I crane my neck to look up at him behind me. Matt glances at it and nods, taking the phone from my hand and setting it on the counter next to us. He gently pushes my hips back until they bump into the granite and presses a soft kiss to my lips.

"You can expect a call from Clark Kent, okay?"

He waits until I nod to release my hips and step away, turning to head to the door. I don't realize I'm holding my breath until I hear it click shut behind him.

I wish Matt was still just an attractive, superhero-y stranger I met at the bar, but I'm pretty sure he just left to go get ready for his nationally televised hockey game. And not even the promise of seeing those quads in action on TV is enough to get me to watch one of those.

# CHAPTER TWELVE

## *matt*

I MAY HAVE GONE OVERBOARD. BUT ONCE ELLIE AGREED TO hanging out, I was determined to make sure she knew this was a good idea. And tacos are always a good idea.

I'm standing outside her apartment building door, freezing my ass off, with two takeout bags full of my favorite tacos and one grocery bag. Just for us. I also have my backpack on, but I didn't put any food in there other than some protein bars for the morning. Wishful thinking and all that. I transfer one bag to the other side so I have a hand free to pull my phone out, bouncing on my feet to fight the cold. When I pull up Ellie's contact to text her that I'm here, I see the reason I over-ordered and smile.

Today 12:37PM

MATT

Do you like tacos?

CONFIDENTIAL FUCK BUDDY

is Minnesota cold in the winter?

> **MATT**
> Noted. See you tonight, C.F.B.

**CONFIDENTIAL FUCK BUDDY**
please stop

> **MATT**
> Never :)

I shake my head and chuckle again at her earlier responses before quickly shooting her a new one to let her know I'm out front. I probably should've just asked her what she liked instead of ordering one of almost everything, but my common sense seems to take a backseat with Ellie. And everything from my favorite taco joint is really good. Proven by the fact the hole-in-the-wall restaurant is literally always packed. They also only serve lunch, but I may have called in a favor today. One of the few perks of being me that I take advantage of—*food*.

Ellie opens the door and warmth assaults me from the heated foyer and her bright smile. Her hair is down and looks a little damp, her gray T-shirt dotted with wet marks just beneath her shoulders. She's wearing black leggings and thick white socks with smiley faces on them. There's a matching smiley face in the middle of her oversized shirt. I study her bare face and feel a tug of happiness at her casual, comfortable appearance. She didn't dress up for our date—for me, Matt Anderson. And I fucking love it.

Ellie pushes up on her toes and surprises me with a quick kiss on my cheek. She shivers and lets out a dramatic *brrrr* noise. I refrain from touching the tingling spot she kissed on my face.

"Hurry up, it's freaking freezing," she says in a chattering voice. She grabs one of the bags and turns to head up the stairs, which she takes two at a time.

I laugh and step inside, shutting the door behind me and following her up to her apartment. By the time I get up there, the door is ajar and Ellie is at the counter, ripping open the bag she carried. She pulls out the carton and holds it up to me, a pout on her confused face.

"This isn't tacos," she says.

I toe my shoes off and hold up the two bags I have before I set them on the counter in front of me. She claps and starts rummaging through them while I go shut the door and hang my jacket up, dropping my backpack underneath.

"Can I put this in the freezer?" I ask Ellie as I grab the ice cream from the counter where she left it.

I hear a muffled "Mhm" from where her head is almost literally inside one of the bags.

I chuckle and walk over to the freezer, opening it and looking for a spot to set it.

"Someone joining us for dinner? I'm not really dressed for guests," she says.

I turn around and see Ellie perched on her knees on a barstool, all ten takeout containers stacked in two piles in front of her. She peers around them at me with a raised eyebrow and gestures to her outfit. I'm nearly struck speechless by her casual reference to the fact that I'm not a guest to her, despite it all being a joke. I swallow it down and answer her while I start opening the containers.

"I wasn't sure what you liked. And everything from here is really good," I explain and then name each of the different types of tacos.

She listens and then hops off her stool, rounding the counter to a cabinet where she pulls out two plates. She hands one to me and then proceeds to grab one of everything except the lengua. I file that away for next time and follow suit, filling my plate and then trailing Ellie over to the couch where she's sitting. There's already two glasses of water placed on the coffee table she must have filled before I got here.

"I forgot to order drinks in my last grocery delivery, sorry," she says in between bites of food, nodding her head at the waters. "Yummm, this is good. Thanks for bringing food. I was starving."

"Water's always good," I tell her, leaning over and dropping a quick kiss to her mouth as she chews.

She makes a noise in protest but I pull back before she can actually say something. I smile at her and take a bite of one of my tacos, holding back a groan. *So good.*

"How was work this week?" I ask her. It's Wednesday and, despite my intentions otherwise, this was the soonest we could make plans after Friday. I had a game in Denver this weekend and it turns out Ellie works an unusual schedule. I'm still surprised—and impressed—by her long shifts.

Ellie sets her half-finished second taco down and grabs her water. After a few sips, she puts it back on the coffee table and then angles herself toward me on the couch, her crossed legs facing me now.

"It was actually great. Obviously I went to school already and did my training in Boston, but this hospital is really good about continuing education. So yesterday I got to sit in on a training for this new burn treatment and it's a freaking *spray*. It's so cool," she gushes. "I won't go into too much detail, but it will save time and it works better to help keep wounds clean. Science blows my mind."

Ellie lets out a little bomb noise as her hand makes an

exploding gesture. I smile back at her infectious enthusiasm and marvel at her passion for her job. My job is fun and easy to love—but Ellie's job is important and hard, and her loving it feels so much cooler. Bigger.

"Did you always know you wanted to be a nurse?"

She tilts her head back and forth while she finishes chewing. "Hmm, I guess yes? But it's not for the noble reason you might think. I was like seven or eight and me and my mom were out at the store. This woman was next to us and I loved her outfit so much." She giggles. "Spoiler alert—it was scrubs. I asked my mom what she did for work and she said 'a nurse, maybe.' So I committed then and there. Thankfully the actual job appealed to me once I learned more and got into *Grey's Anatomy*, but that's how it started."

Imagining a little Ellie infatuated with scrubs is pretty fucking cute. "And do you still love scrubs?"

"Heck yes, I do. I love not thinking about what I have to wear, and I still think they're pretty cute to be honest." Ellie smiles at me and takes a drink of water. "How's your week been?"

She picks up her taco and starts eating again, chewing and focusing on me. I mimic her previous movements and set mine down on my plate. I wipe my mouth with the napkin next to my water and angle myself toward her, resting my arm on the back of the couch.

"My week's been fine, got back from Denver last night. I don't love travel nights, but we didn't have to practice until three today, so there's that at least."

"What's so bad about travel?" Ellie asks around a mouthful of food.

"In general, nothing really. Although we have been

performing worse on the road," I grumble. "But anyway, my main annoyance with travel games is that we usually leave right after. So we are flying at like ten, eleven, or twelve-ish at night and don't get home until the early hours of the morning. It makes sense, but they suck. And the next day can be rough depending on our practice and game schedule," I explain with a shrug.

"You don't get the next day off?" Ellie's nose scrunches when she asks, and I want to kiss the little wrinkle it creates.

I clear my throat and focus on her question. "Sometimes we do. But we have a game tomorrow, so we had a short practice today even though we flew back last night," I tell her.

"That blows," she says.

I laugh at that and nod, picking my taco back up. I look at her empty plate and feel a bit of pride swell in my chest. She obviously liked the food I brought and it's one of my favorite restaurants. And she ate *five* tacos. Only one less than me. I take the last bite of mine and stand, grabbing her plate and bringing it to the kitchen.

"Ice cream now or later?" I ask her as I put the plates in the sink.

Ellie hums. I look up and see she's grabbed the remote and is scrolling movie options. "Now is good."

I grab the ice cream from the freezer and then scan the kitchen for where the utensils might be. I guess the drawer correctly on the first try and just barely stop myself from giving a fist pump. No need to highlight my ever-present competitive nature when I'm trying to impress. Not that Ellie is watching me locate spoons.

I think tonight is my unofficial chance to win Ellie over. I know we talked about it last week, but she seemed hesitant to commit to even a casual arrangement. I'm not sure if she's fully onboard even now. So the ice cream? Me sucking up, one hundred percent.

I was a little nervous to talk about hockey at all, given how she seems to feel about my job, but I wanted to be honest when she asked about my week. And it makes up my entire life, truthfully, so it would be hard to avoid.

I'm also hoping the dinner portion of our night makes this less of a hangout and more of a date. At least on some subconscious level. *Fingers crossed.*

Ellie looks over to me as I walk back to the couch and holds a hand out, curling her fingers toward herself a few times as she silently asks for the ice cream. "This is dangerous, you know," she warns me. "You're setting an awfully high standard for yourself. I don't think you know yet how much I care about food. And tacos and ice cream? Hard to beat."

I hand her a spoon and sit close to her, my thigh bumping her crossed legs that are still facing me. Opening the carton and passing it, I clink my spoon to hers in cheers.

"I think I can handle it," I say with a smile. And I can. Food? Definitely my specialty.

I'm mentally running through a list of restaurants to get her takeout from when Ellie puts a spoonful of ice cream in her mouth. She leaves the spoon in there, upside down, causing her lips to form an involuntary frown. It reminds me of Saturday's conversation again and brings a question to my mind that might be better left unasked.

Ellie scoops more ice cream from the carton she's holding.

"So what made you agree to...this?" I ask, gesturing between our two bodies with a spoon.

She puts the ice cream in her mouth and smiles around

the spoon, shrugging. "The sexth wath really good," she says, mouth still full.

I laugh and take the carton from her, getting myself a spoonful. Ellie leans forward to set her spoon on the napkin on the table and grabs the remote. She sits back and looks at me.

"I liked hanging out with you on Thursday," she says with a shrug. "You handled my proposition better than I imagined, honestly. Kinder than most people would have." She pauses and smiles at me. "I mean, the sex was really good, yeah, but the chatting and your little alien movie were really good too."

I balk at her calling one of my favorite films a *little alien movie*, but let her continue. At least she enjoyed it.

"I finished it this weekend, since we fell asleep with a little bit left." Ellie looks at my arm on the back of the couch before refocusing on me. "You were also a very comfortable pillow that night." She ends with a shy smile, a blush tinting her cheeks.

"I liked hanging out with you too," I tell her. "And I'm glad you liked the movie."

Ellie looks between my eyes, passing the remote from hand to hand. "So how come you're single?"

I hesitate, both out of shock at the question and because I'm not sure why she's asking. "What do you mean?"

"Are we fishing for compliments again?" Ellie raises a brow and I laugh.

"Hockey, I guess," I admit. Dumb as it sounds.

"Doesn't that get you a lot of, uh, suitors? Don't try to tell me there aren't any. I won't believe you."

If she only knew. I withhold a shudder and think of how to sum it up. "It's more my schedule and...priorities?"

Ellie's brow wrinkles. "Aren't a lot of hockey players

married? I'm sure there's lots of people who would understand the schedule and demands of your job."

Diving into how my relationships have ended and what could eventually end this one is not really what I wanted to talk about this soon. But maybe being transparent is best so she can set her expectations? The thought depresses me.

Then I remember how I felt leaving her on Friday first thing in the morning and then later in the day too. I didn't want to leave. Wasn't itching to get to the arena like I normally am. And that was certainly different from before with previous girlfriends, shitty as it sounds. Maybe that's a good sign?

I try to word this carefully. "Yeah, a lot are. Happily too. I guess what I meant was that for me, I wasn't able to prioritize my relationships over hockey. Or didn't want to, really," I amend, withholding a cringe. "Which wasn't fair to them obviously and is the reason most of them didn't work out."

Ellie seems to mull that over. "What's most?"

"Like how many?"

"Yeah."

"Three, I guess? It might depend on if we're talking length of relationship or seriousness."

"Those aren't the same?" Her brow dips low.

"I'd like to think not."

Ellie tilts her head to the side. "Wouldn't you say all long relationships are serious? I get that some shorter ones could still be significant."

"Well, I had a longer relationship with someone, but I think we both knew it wasn't going anywhere. She had different long-term plans than I did. It was convenient, I guess, since we were both content keeping it at that level and ending it when we were ready for something different. Then the other two varied in length but were more serious. I thought they might go somewhere eventually, but like I said, my priorities weren't really in line with theirs, so it didn't work out."

I set myself up here for Ellie to ask about long-term plans. And while I don't want to end things before they've begun, I also won't lie to her. Marriage and kids have always been things I figured I'd get to after hockey, if at all. Which could be soon, but also may not be. I realize I'm holding my breath when Ellie asks another question.

"Only three, huh?"

I nod, unsure where she's going with this. That seems to often be the case with Ellie.

She hums and fiddles with the remote some more. "What about more short-term things?"

"Hookups?"

Ellie nods this time and looks at me expectantly.

"When I first got drafted, I kept things really casual for a few years. But everyone's warnings from before I joined the league rang true, and those hookups felt... I was going to say shallow, but it was more than that. I mean, hookups are often shallow by nature, but I guess these felt almost transactional? Like they wanted to say they hooked up with Matt Anderson and that was it. I know it makes me sound naïve, but I just didn't like how that felt, I guess. I suppose the opposite end of the spectrum was more terrifying ultimately."

I eat some more ice cream and then set it on the coffee table.

"Terrifying?"

"As a rookie, a lot of the veteran players talked to me about how to handle the spotlight and specifically relationships. They said there are going to be a lot of people that just want the *trophy*"—I use air quotes—"of saying they hooked up with a professional hockey player. And then there were also the more ambitious types who would be looking to...you know, secure their future."

Ellie gasps. "You're talking about girls trying to get pregnant?" she asks with mild horror.

"Yep." I pop the *p*, still in disbelief myself that those people exist.

"Is that...something you also dealt with?" Ellie looks distraught at that thought.

"Just once," I clip out, not wanting to delve into that shit show. The only reason I left that condom in Ellie's trash can the other day was knowing she didn't know who I was yet. "So, yeah, as you can imagine, the hookups felt insincere and the other stuff was...paralyzing to think about. That's when I decided I'd listen to everyone's advice and stick to mutual friends for any kind of romantic involvement."

"I see," Ellie says. She looks deep in thought.

I grab the ice cream and take one more bite, noticing how melted it all is now. I should put it in the freezer. I'm licking a drop off my lip when I notice Ellie track the movement with her eyes. That small glance should *not* cause blood to rush to my dick the way it is.

"Do you want to watch another movie? You've earned enough cred to pick again," she says, jiggling the remote in her hand.

I shake my head slowly in answer, deciding it's my turn to look at *her* lips. They're pink and a little swollen, probably from the spicy salsa earlier. They part just before she speaks.

"Oh," she breathes, "something else then?"

She darts her tongue out over them and my resolve *snaps*. I want to taste those lips again. I move my hand to her face and press my thumb into her plump bottom lip. *Fuck.*

I grab the remote from her and place that and the ice

cream on the coffee table, freezer forgotten. I can buy her more next time. Because there *will* be a next time.

I lean over and gently bite her lower lip, giving in to temptation. I hold back a groan at her quick intake of breath. Releasing her and sitting back, I wait to see what Ellie wants.

# CHAPTER THIRTEEN

## *matt*

My back hasn't even touched the couch when Ellie scrambles out of her position and straddles my lap. I fail to stifle my groan this time as she rocks this way and that, getting settled right on top of my now aching cock. I instinctively grab her hips to still the movement.

Ellie looks down and squirms despite my grip on her. "I love your quads," she muses.

"My quads?" I laugh.

"Mhm," she hums as she looks back at me, her gaze above mine in this position. "Did you know your muscles here"—she rocks against my thighs again and looks down at them—"actually contain more mass than any other muscle group in your body? And the name is a misnomer now because they discovered it's actually five muscles, not four. You must use yours a lot. Obviously." She looks up and blushes, clearing her throat. "Can I kiss you now?"

*So fucking cute.*

I smile at her explanation and nod, eager for her lips on mine. We do get a lot of anatomy and physiology information from our trainers, but I'd let Ellie talk about it for hours just to listen to her voice.

"Whenever you want," I tell her. And I mean it.

Ellie's soft lips capture mine and I do my best to let her have control. She's slightly tentative and extremely sweet and I force my hands to maintain their relatively relaxed position instead of squeezing her the way they want to. Her tongue dips into my mouth, and the taste of vanilla ice cream and *her* breaks the control I had over myself. I grip her hips and pull them forward, my loose sweatpants hardly dulling the sensation of Ellie's core moving over me.

I take over and move my hands from her hips to her waist, finally touching her bare skin. A shudder passes through me at the goose bumps my fingers run over. I break our mouths apart to pull her shirt over her head and then sit back to the most perfect sight in the world.

Ellie's wearing a thin black cotton bra that cuts straight across her chest with tiny straps over her shoulders. Despite the enticing swell of her cleavage visible above the bra, my eyes catch on the large scar cutting across her collarbone and stay there. I remember seeing it last time and thinking it must have been a gnarly accident to leave such a prominent mark. I wonder—

"Matt."

My head jerks up at her voice.

"I know it's kind of...hard to ignore, but can we not do the whole sad scar thing right now? I can tell you about it some other time."

I school my expression in an attempt not to ruin the moment. And even though I know I won't like the story, I get a small thrill from her promise to share something important with me.

"Sorry," I say with a nod and kiss her softly, dipping my tongue inside to tangle with hers. I reluctantly pull back and then focus on her chest again. I exhale heavily as I study her taut nipples, visible through her thin bra. Following the curve of her breasts outlined by the dark fabric, I'm drawn to the few freckles I can see dotting her cleavage right above. I lean forward and run my nose along the small specks, skimming the soft skin there and inhaling Ellie's natural scent. *Fuck, she smells good.* I pull back slightly to see her already pebbled nipples even more pronounced through the fabric. I capture one in my mouth, pulling it with my teeth.

Ellie inhales sharply and arches her back to give me better access. I run one hand up her spine until I slide under her claspless bra, pulling her toward me. When her chest gets closer to my face, I suck her nipple into my mouth and slide my other hand up under the front of her bra to tease the other.

*Perfect fucking tits.*

I pop my mouth off the wet material and use my teeth to tug her bra up, exposing both nipples to the cooler air. They're dusty pink and perfectly taut, making my mouth water and my dick throb where it's trapped beneath her. With her bra out of the way, I lean back and drag her to me to capture more of her in my mouth. I want to play with her tits *all* day. I pinch and pluck her other nipple and then switch sides.

Ellie's chest is heaving under my thorough attention and it's making my cock painfully stiff. I pull my mouth off the other side and lean back, bringing both hands forward. I squeeze each nipple between my forefinger and thumb and look up at Ellie's face. Her hooded eyes are out of focus on me, mouth slightly parted on heavy pants.

I take a mental snapshot.

"I love these," I tell her, my voice sounding deeper than normal. I pluck and release her nipples, unable to stop myself from repeating the action a few times. "I'd like to fuck them one day."

She nods and pushes her chest into my hands. "Okay." It comes out breathy and sends a jolt straight down my cock, which automatically flexes against her. Ellie rocks forward onto me and I think I might come in my pants like a high schooler if I don't get inside her soon.

"Off off off," Ellie breathes.

I freeze what I'm doing for a moment until I realize she's moving her hips and using her hands to try and push her leggings down. *Don't have to ask me twice.*

I lift her off my lap and stand her in front of me, whipping my own shirt off first and then hooking my fingers in her leggings and underwear to drag them down. I come back up to an unhindered view of her pretty pussy. *God bless a low-sitting couch.*

I lean down and lick up her center until I get to her clit. Running my tongue in circles around it, I hear Ellie's breath catch and decide to suck it into my mouth. My hand is sliding up the back of her leg for leverage when I reach wetness up high on her inner thigh. She's fucking *dripping*. I groan at that and maneuver my hand under her ass so I can dip my finger into her from behind.

I add another finger and Ellie moans loudly at that, making me nearly drag her straight onto my cock before I realize I'm still wearing pants. I sit back and admire the sight of her soaked cunt. *Mine.*

"Condom?" Ellie asks me on a pant.

*Shit.* Condoms were so far from my mind I would've

dragged her onto me without a second thought. I don't think that's ever happened before.

I'm still staring between Ellie's legs when she removes her bra, bunched up high on her chest, and turns to go to the bathroom. I swallow at the sight of her naked form walking away from me and palm my cock through my pants. I need to get a grip or I won't last long.

She comes back holding a foil packet and drops it on the couch next to me. I did bring condoms, but I didn't remember them in time to save her the trip. I lift my hips from the couch to slide my sweats and briefs off, pulling them down until I can kick them off my feet. Ellie straddles my legs again and leans forward to kiss me. I grunt at the contact and blindly feel around for the condom she dropped beside us. I find it and rip it open, desperate to get inside her.

Ellie breaks off at the sound of the wrapper tearing and watches with those heavy eyes as I roll it over my painfully rigid cock. I grip the base once I have it on and let her move toward me to line herself up. Before she can raise herself above me, I use my hold to drag the tip from her clit down through her wetness until I feel myself in the right spot to get inside her. *Fuck*. Memories from last week come back and I can hardly resist slamming up into her.

I look to her face and watch her lick her lips as I feel her raise her hips to adjust the angle. It feels like my heart skips a beat as she sinks down, one inch at a time.

*Ohmotherfuck.*

Ellie bites her lip and the sight *almost* keeps me from watching my cock sink inside her. I can't fight my instincts though, and look down just in time to see myself disappear as she fully seats herself.

"Oh god," Ellie moans. She's squeezing my cock like a

fucking vise and I think I might black out. Nothing should feel this good.

Ellie flexes her inner muscles like last time and I groan, fighting to make sure I can last long enough to get her off first.

I lean in and lick a path up her tit, sucking on the tight bud there as Ellie starts to move. She rocks forward, lifting up a bit before sinking back down. As she arches her chest farther into my face, hands moving to rest behind her against my thighs, she angles herself backward and repeats the same motion.

"Oh," she breathes out.

I pull back and release her nipple, letting it pop out of my mouth. Ellie moans again, making it clear this is working for her. I grab her hips and take charge, moving her up and down at a constant, torturous pace. As her muscles tighten around me, I try to think of anything else so I don't blow this—pun fully intended.

"Please. Don't. Stop," Ellie says between each thrust.

I don't think I could even if I wanted to.

Her lightly bouncing tits in front of me are straight out of a porn scene and I think if I don't come soon I might actually die. I lean in and carefully use my teeth to latch onto one of her nipples, tugging it toward myself. I add pressure to my bite as I pick up the pace of my thrusts.

"Matt," she moans, dragging my name out as she drops her head back.

I feel her flutter and then pulse around me, muscles squeezing my cock harder than I remember from the last time. As her orgasm takes over, I release her nipple and bury my face between her tits as I feel my own rip through me. I hold her hips down as I come, wanting to stay like this for the rest of my life.

"Fuck, Ellie," I say between pants, letting the last of the pulsing pleasure run its course.

I lean back against the couch to get more air and feel Ellie slump forward. Wrapping my arms around her back, I soak in the divine pleasure that is holding a satisfied, naked Ellie. Our heavy breathing is all I can hear.

"See?" Her voice is muffled from where her head rests against my neck and shoulder.

"See what?" I ask her, still working to catch my breath.

"The sex is really good," she says.

I'd normally chuckle at that, but there's something so real about it that I find myself transfixed at the thought. The sex is *really* good. Like *the best I've ever had* good. I'm fucking thirty-six and I didn't know it could get better still.

I feel Ellie swallow. "Well, for me anyway," she says quietly.

It takes me far too long to realize I never replied to her previous comment.

"Hey," I tell her, tugging her off me enough so I can look at her. She responds and sits up, her pretty, flushed face making my heart give a heavy thump. "It's literally the best sex I've ever had," I tell her. "I was just thinking about that instead of telling you, like a dumbass."

Ellie smiles at my declaration and leans in to kiss me. I pull her into me with my hand in her hair and do my best not to get carried away. I need to dispose of this condom before we run into anything risky. I gently pull her head back and peck her lips once more before gripping the base of the condom on my cock and letting Ellie lift herself off me. I grab my sweatpants from the floor and head to the bathroom.

Despite my earlier musings, I tie the condom off and drop it in her trash again, feeling distinctly unworried about her pulling anything crazy. I grab a towel before heading back.

She's by the couch putting her shirt back on without her bra. I admire the view until she sees me standing there, staring at the perfection that is post-sex Ellie. Her hair is mussed and her pink cheeks highlight the sprinkling of freckles I love so much. Her bright caramel eyes are looking at me fondly.

*How did I find her?* I guess she kind of found me.

"That for me?" She points to the towel I had forgotten about in my hand.

I nod and walk the rest of the way over to her, dropping to my knees and using it to clean her up. I stand and bring it back to the bathroom where I saw an empty hamper before. I smile as I pass Ellie's bedroom door that's cracked. The room has clothes *littering* the floor. It looks like it was ransacked.

Ellie is definitely not a neat freak. And she didn't clean for me.

The signs have been obvious, but it's really hitting me now that Ellie doesn't care about impressing me. It slightly contrasts her shyness that peeks out sometimes, but ultimately fits with her confidence in herself I've picked up on. Ellie likes who she is. *That makes two of us.*

When I get back to the living room, she's sitting on her hands, looking at me.

"You said you have a game tomorrow?" Her nose scrunches at the question.

I nod and tell her the game time. It's an evening game, as most weekday ones are, but between the team meeting and everything else I do on game days I don't actually have much free time. I know Ellie has the day off, so the schedule is definitely not ideal for trying to see her. Unless I can come over afterward...

I try not to get ahead of myself. Two nights in a row might be pushing my luck.

"So you have to be up early for your meeting thing?" Ellie's face remains neutral, but I think I pick up some disappointment in her voice. I glance at my backpack by the door and decide to take a shot.

"Unfortunately, yes, but I brought my bag to stay over if you don't mind my alarm going off at eight. It's not too loud," I tell her. I wasn't going to invite myself to stay over originally, but she did mention that I was a good pillow earlier.

Ellie perks up. "Oh, I don't mind, I'm just gonna—" She points toward her room as she stands and darts that way.

"I already saw all your clothes," I call out.

She pauses at her bedroom door and turns back to me.

"I don't want you to clean for me," I say, raising an eyebrow at her and smiling.

She stares at me for a minute, then finally lets out a *harrumph* and goes to the bathroom instead. I hear the sink turn on and go to grab my own toothbrush from my bag. When I get to the half-open door, I can see Ellie bent over the counter, bare ass peeking out under her T-shirt. I feel my cock thicken at the sight and tell myself to calm the fuck down. At least until we get in bed.

Yeah, I could definitely get used to sleepovers at Ellie's.

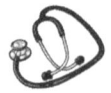

# CHAPTER FOURTEEN
## *ellie*

*Today 11:43AM*

ZOEY

Please tell me you're coming home for Chandler's baby shower 🙏 I am willing to beg. On my knees. I miss your face.

ELLIE

I was literally just checking flights again to see if something could work. I don't think I am going to be able to swing it 😭 between work and the $$

I'll send you a selfie

ZOEY

BOO

What if I promise to find a suitable Band-Aid-ripper here? It's like the perfect set up since you'd only be visiting.

Graham is going to a new gym and some of the guys are 😍. I feel like a super jacked dude would be hottt.

Imagine the stamina.

ELLIE

about that

we need to FaceTime soon

ZOEY

…

Tell me right now or I'll scream.

ELLIE

I'm pretty sure if you scream at work you'll scare the kids... maybe even get fired lol

ZOEY

Nothing scares these heathens, Ellie.

And it's lunchtime anyway.

TELL ME

ELLIE

fine

I may have found a proper suitor and done the deed

ZOEY

OMG ELLIE BELLIE!!!!!!!

Fuck yes

I'm so proud

How was it?? Tell me everything

ELLIE

so good! ya girl got herself a fuck buddy

ZOEY

Shut the actual fuck up you DID NOT!!!

You can't see me, but I'm crying happy tears for you. My little baby is all grown up with her own fuck buddy. *sobs*

ELLIE

please reread that text and remember your job is to teach kids

ZOEY

Ugh, don't remind me. I have to quit texting because of said job. The heathens are back from lunch.

Expect a FaceTime this weekend and be prepared with details!

I'll have a list of questions 🤍

BYE I LOVE YOU

ELLIE

love you more 🤍

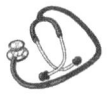

# CHAPTER FIFTEEN

*ellie*

"Something's different."

I look up to see Dev's eyes narrowed at me, running over my face and outfit. It's Saturday and we're sitting at a high-top table at an upscale bar walking distance from my apartment—my only actual requirement when we go out. The bar has trendy purple lighting that's giving Dev's dark hair an amethyst-like sheen. It's longer than mine, coming to her chest in subtle waves. Her makeup is annoyingly perfect, as always, and her dark eyes are looking almost black. She's only two years older than me, but she's really working the stare-down I imagine older siblings excel at. Not that I would know.

"What?" I ask her. I look down at my short black corduroy overall dress and white turtleneck she's checking out. I think it's cute. And paired with my sheer black tights and boots? I was really proud of this outfit. I look back at her in confusion, wondering what she's talking about.

"You're not trying to get laid tonight," she states, louder than I'd like.

I look around us to make sure no one overheard my loud-as-shit friend. My instinct is to tell her she's wrong. I'm actually totally looking to get laid tonight. But I happen to already know who I'm getting laid by and he's definitely not at this bar. He's at the hockey arena, close to finishing his game against who knows what team. I check the time on my phone—he should be at my place in an hour or so unless the game goes into overtime.

I think back to Dev's assessment of my look tonight and give her an insulted glare. I know my outfit doesn't scream *come and get it*, but I still think I look good enough to get hit on. "Are you saying I don't look hot? I love this outfit! And I'm sitting, but my butt looks good in this dress, I swear," I tell her. *It does.*

Dev rolls her eyes and sips her drink. We're having French 75s tonight, playing into the fancy vibes of the place. I love me some champagne.

"Oh stop, you always look hot. You know what I'm saying," Dev says as she sets her drink back down.

I do know what she's saying, but I'm not trying to admit anything tonight. I also hate lying. Which reminds me I still have to figure out what to tell Zoey when we FaceTime before work tomorrow.

"Fine. You're right, I'm not looking to pick a guy up from here," I say, waving my hands at the bar around us.

"So you're giving up on your Band-Aid sex?" she asks me.

I am seriously regretting sharing that information with her. Zoey too, honestly.

I feel my face heat, both in slight embarrassment at the topic and also at the memory of said sex. Who knew ripping a Band-Aid could be hot? Honestly, all of our hookups have been. And I can't imagine tonight will be any different. Unless Matt's tired from his game? This is the first time we are hanging out after one. I hadn't thought about that. He was the one who asked to come over though...

We hadn't been able to meet up this week and I think he wanted to set something up before I start my work week tomorrow.

Maybe we can try a position that's not too tiring for him?

My thighs clench at the thought and I shake my head to clear it. What am I going to say to Dev?

"I'm..." I pause, hesitating. I should've planned this out. I look at my drink and spin it slowly on its napkin. *Damn it.* "I'm not giving up, I just...kind of...did it already," I finish quickly, bringing my glass up to drink and hide my red face.

Dev's mouth pops open.

"What!" Her near-yell comes out more like a statement than a question.

I set my glass down quickly and lean into her across the table. "For the love of— Can you keep your freaking voice down?" I implore her in a whisper-shout.

"When? Where? With who? I know you didn't pick someone up when we went out! I left with you! Did you go out without me?" Dev pouts at me dramatically and I want to roll my eyes.

"Oh my god," I mumble, putting my face in my hands. "I didn't go out without you. I don't have any other friends! You know that." I look up at her face.

She's giving me a "go on" gesture. *Goddammit.*

"I ran into someone on my walk home after we went out last time," I tell her quietly.

"Ellie! That was weeks ago! Wait, you picked someone up off the streets?!" Dev's screech could be heard from outside.

I give her wide eyes and look around the room at all the gazes on us. *Great.*

"Sorry," she whispers and winces. "How about we go to your place?" Dev flutters her eyelashes at me and gives me an innocent smile.

*Why is it so hard to say no to her?* I hesitate for a minute and then cave. "Fine, one bowl of ice cream."

Dev claps her hands and hops off her chair, putting her jacket and gloves on faster than I've ever seen.

*Crap*, how am I going to get her out of there before Matt shows up? And what am I going to say? That eager energy she's sporting is not going to be easy to stamp out. Good practice for Zoey, I guess.

I grab my own jacket and fish out some cash to leave on the table for a tip since we already closed our tabs. We bundle up and start the short walk to my place. Thankfully it's too cold for conversation, both of us burying our faces as far into our jacket collars as we can with our hands shoved deep in our pockets.

When we reach my apartment I quickly open the main door and then trudge up the stairs. I feel Dev behind me and all of that eager energy she's still giving off. *Ugh.*

I've barely opened my door when Dev starts in on the questions again.

"So, on your walk home? Please tell me you didn't pay someone."

I give her a flat look and hang up my stuff before grabbing the ice cream and bowls. I hand her the scoop and go get our spoons. Thankfully I had strawberry ice cream still in my freezer, so I don't have to share my stash of Matt Vanilla.

"Obviously I didn't pay anyone, you freak. I can't believe you thought I picked up some stranger outside."

At least she looks contrite. "It just popped out," she says with a guilty smile, shoveling a bite of ice cream in her mouth.

I lean on the counter and start to eat my own. Best not to get comfortable—I need her out of here in the next twenty minutes.

"So if you didn't pick up someone random on your walk..." Dev leads, eyebrows wiggling at me.

"Fine. I ran into this guy I had met back in January. He was actually at the same bar where I first met him. So he came out to say hi and..." I shrug, desperate for that to be enough information.

"And you said 'Do you want to have sex with me?'"

Fucking Dev.

"I mean, kind of? We chatted first, obviously, and I invited him in. Then I asked."

"Hell yeah, get it girl," she says, holding up her hand for a high five.

I ignore her hand. "Why are you like this?" I mutter.

She laughs and eats more ice cream. "So what's his name? Are you going to see him again?"

I feel my blush take over and curse my complexion for making me so transparent.

"I...may have seen him again already. A few times. We kind of agreed to be fuck buddies. But it's new and I don't know if I'm ready to share more yet," I tell her with an apologetic look.

Her face sobers and she gives me a smile. "Understood," she says with a subtle nod. "You'll talk to me when you're ready?"

"Of course," I promise. I look at the door and back to our ice cream.

"He's coming over tonight, isn't he?" Dev's smile grows but maintains that soft edge that promises she gets my hesitance and won't push.

"Mayb—" My voice is cut off by a knock at my door. I drop my spoon and look from Dev to the door and back.

*Shit, he's early.*

My wide eyes must betray my panic, because Dev squeezes my hand before dropping her bowl in the sink. She quickly grabs her jacket and gloves and walks back over to me. "I'll be cool, promise. Sorry for inviting myself over," she says as she gives me a fast, tight hug.

I force my body to unfreeze and squeeze her back, releasing her and then walking to the door. I check the peephole to be sure and feel my breath catch at Matt's appearance.

His hair is wet and face flushed, black sweatshirt matching his black backward hat and black shorts.

He looks edible.

And I think I know Matt's favorite color. Also, how the hell did he get through the building door again?

I open the door and offer an apologetic look. His smile falters at that and then freezes when he presumably sees Dev. I turn to look at her and her mouth is hanging wide open.

*Way to play it cool.* Dev's a true Minnesotan, so she likely knows who he is. Or maybe she's stunned at how hot he is. Either feels feasible.

Thankfully she recovers, giving Matt a polite smile. "Hi, sorry, I'm just heading out. I'll see you tomorrow, Ellie?" she asks, looking over to me.

"Yeah, of course," I tell her on a nod. "Text when you get home?"

She nods back at me and smiles again at Matt, who turns sideways to let her pass by out the door, returning her polite smile.

He faces me and raises both eyebrows. I sigh and turn

around to put the ice cream away, Matt's low chuckle clear behind me as he follows and shuts the door.

*Dev is going to have so many questions.*

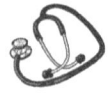

# CHAPTER SIXTEEN
*ellie*

"It's not that funny," Matt grumbles from where his head is resting on my stomach. My stomach which is shaking with laughter. "What's your next question?"

I just discovered Matt's full name is Matthew Benjamin Anderson, making his initials MBA. It's *not* that funny, obviously, but for some reason it's making me giggle. Matt didn't even go to college.

I try to get my laughter under control, running my fingers through his hair. Not too long ago I had one hand firmly gripping the short, inky strands, the other on my headboard as I rode his face. Yep, Matt asked me to sit on his face tonight and now I can officially say each hookup has been hotter than the last. Thinking about his large hands clamped around my hips, holding me down, makes my abs clench. He literally had me grinding myself against his tongue. A slight shudder passes through me, causing Matt to lift his head and look at me.

"Cold?" he asks.

I shake my head and definitely blush, forever at the mercy of the involuntary reaction. One time I even looked up if how often I deal with it would be considered severe. That made me thankful for the relatively small amount of blushing I have in comparison to legitimate medical cases.

Hmm, what's my next question? I decided tonight was get-to-know-Matt night. I've already asked about his favorite food (tacos), if he prefers movies or TV shows (movies), and what sport, other than hockey, he likes to watch the most (soccer, which apparently his younger brother Connor played up through college). I think that's the sport he was watching that first day at the bar. Oh, that reminds me...

"What's the name of the bar?" I ask him.

"The Bar."

"Yeah, the one you own with Nate. What's it called? There's no sign out front. I only knew to go inside for a drink because I looked in the window."

Now Matt is laughing.

"Is it a dumb name? I won't make fun," I promise. I'll *try* not to make fun, I amend in my head.

"I think if I make a *Who's on First* reference, I'll just end up aging myself," Matt says on a sigh, still smiling.

What the heck is he talking about? "That ship has sailed, Mr. MBA. Have you seen the way you text?" I give him a sweet smile.

He nips my hip bone at that and I hold in my yelp.

"The bar is called 'The Bar,'" he tells me. "At first we couldn't come up with anything, so that was our stand-in name. Then it just kind of stuck. Now it's been around long enough it's actually decently well-known with the locals and I think they like it. Obviously it leads to conversations like this sometimes, but I think that's part of the charm."

*The Bar.* Huh, I actually like that a lot. And it makes me feel like a local for knowing about it.

"I like it. It's simple," I tell him. "Was it your idea or Nate's to open it?"

Matt gets up from his position sprawled across me, maneuvering himself next to me so our heads are both resting on the pillows and facing up toward the ceiling. I just have one lamp on in my room so the lighting is dim and soft. I grab the comforter and pull it up to cover us now that I don't have the heat of Matt's body on mine.

"It was my idea. I think I told you Nate moved here with me from our town in upstate New York? Well, he was a bartender for a few years just to have a job, but then he actually seemed to really like it, so it felt like a good idea," he explains.

I think about Nate moving with Matt at such a young age —they must have been just barely eighteen. I'm glad they had each other, but I can't imagine doing something like that without the environment of college and other kids my age around. I roll myself toward Matt so I'm facing him.

"Why'd Nate move with you? Didn't he want to go to school or anything? It must have been hard moving away from his family, right?"

Now that I'm facing Matt, I wish I could take my questions back. His eyes are closed and he looks so at ease.

"We can go to sleep," I whisper to him.

At that, he opens his eyes and smiles at me. "Nah, I prefer talking to you." He leans over and pecks my lips before he sits up and switches off the lamp on the bedside table near him. He faces back to me. "But I wouldn't mind a cuddle. Turn over," he says, nodding his head toward the windows. I smile and quickly rearrange myself.

Matt slides his arm under my neck and gently wraps the other around my torso. He pulls me backward until I'm snug against his warm body, his nose tracing the shell of my ear. I feel his deep exhale against my neck as his body eases against mine.

I'm not teeny-tiny, but Matt makes me feel that way. It's not that he's a giant or anything. He just has a way of maneuvering me and taking charge that I feel so...safe? Yeah, safe. I wiggle back into him and feel myself relax.

"Nate moved with me because pretty much any situation would have been better than what he was dealing with at home. If I hadn't been signed, we would've still left together somehow," Matt says quietly.

That sounds...bad. I think of Nate and his easy smile, that curling blond hair and those crinkling eyes. I hesitate, unsure how much to pry. I don't want Matt to feel pressured to share —especially if it's not even his story to tell.

Before I can make a decision, I feel his body relax in a way only sleep can bring. His arm becomes heavier than before and his breathing a little slower. I revel in the vulnerability of this moment, holding tight to Matt's arm around me and this feeling of deep contentment I get from being snuggled close to him.

*I could get used to this.* The thought surprises me, like my body sent the message to my brain without permission.

I trace his fingers with mine and think of how tired he seemed all night. Matt mentioned tonight how nice it was to drive five minutes to my place after his game instead of the twenty-five it normally takes him to get to his house. His house which I know I should eventually go to, instead of making him come to my smaller apartment and smaller *bed*. But that means driving, ugh. And he hasn't complained about being here. Not that he would, I guess. I get the vibe that he likes my apartment just fine.

It worked out well tonight since I was off, but I know he has games on nights when I'm at work, so I wouldn't be able to let him in on those days. Man, being fuck buddies takes some serious coordination with two demanding jobs.

I feel my mind start to drift as the day's activities catch up with me. I fall asleep thinking of warm cuddles and logistics.

# CHAPTER SEVENTEEN

## *matt*

Aside from the endless plane rides and inconvenient travel hours, I used to love away games. There's something about playing without home ice advantage that puts me on edge in the best way. They expect you to play worse without your familiar arena and screaming fans and I love that unspoken challenge.

But as we sit in the guest locker room in D.C., debriefing on our close-call win, I'm hit with a new feeling—*I want to go home*. And it's not because I want to sleep in my custom bed or wake up to the view of the lake. Not because I miss my favorite regular food joints or because I want to grab a beer with Nate and watch tonight's soccer match. And although I *do* want all of those things, they've never been the reason for me to want to go home prematurely. And they aren't factors now.

I've been texting Ellie on and off since we left yesterday morning, but it's Saturday now and her texts abruptly stopped a couple hours before the game started. I know she isn't working, so a little part of me wonders why—especially because we were mid-conversation. She normally texts back pretty quickly and hasn't ever left a conversation unfinished. I'm trying not to overthink it or worry too much and come across clingy by checking in. The fact that I'm even referring to myself as potentially *clingy* is really something.

But being just *fuck buddies* is really *fucking* with my head. *Shit*. Confidential ones at that.

Despite the sting of the situation, I catch myself smiling at her silly term for us. I quickly work to wipe the expression off my face in case it makes it obvious I'm not listening to Coach. I try to tune in to his postgame speech for the third time...

"...which is fine, but I need you guys to keep the momentum going in New Jersey Monday night. We know what their game is, and if we play like we did tonight, we'll give them a run for their money. I'm proud of how you guys played, so keep it up. All right, Alex, you're up," Coach Dan finishes, handing an old, worn helmet to Alex for our player of the night ritual.

Alex scored two goals at our previous game, which earned him our silly trophy. It'll now be his job to decide who earned it tonight.

It's always fun watching the rookies' excitement over one of our casual locker room traditions that has long since lost some of its luster for us vets. Sometimes the little things can make a big difference in team camaraderie though, so we make sure we do this after every win.

"Hey, guys, awesome job tonight. I think there are a few people that could wear this, but I'm gonna give it to Mikey. You killed it, man," Alex says as he hands the helmet to our goalie tonight and gives him a quick slap on the back.

We all give a quick applause with some shouts mixed in as Mikey puts the helmet loosely on his head.

"Great win, boys. Let's get another Monday," he says

simply, whoops and hollers from the team drowning out his last words.

I smile at the infectious atmosphere and finish packing up my things, putting my baseball cap on and grabbing my phone. I know there's probably nothing new, but I check it just to be sure.

"Everything good?" Niko's elbow catches me in the side as he looks from my face to my phone.

I pocket the offensively quiet device and try to put it out of my mind. She's probably just busy on her day off, I reassure myself. Could she be busy with someone else?

We haven't talked about being *exclusive* fuck buddies, and that sudden realization hits me like a ton of bricks. *Fuck*. Things seem to be going well, but so far I've initiated every date-slash-hookup. And she was the one reluctant to be with me to begin with…so it's hard to know where she's at with everything.

This feeling of being so *unsure* is foreign to me and I'm not sure how to handle it. I almost wish I could talk to Niko about it. But one, that wouldn't be very *confidential* of me. And two, he'd probably call me a pussy or something else rude for being so uncharacteristically antsy about all of this. Best to keep things to myself for now.

"Yeah, all good. Save me a seat near the front?"

For whatever reason, Niko is always one of the first on the plane. Maybe a superstition he's not willing to admit to. Maybe he just likes to be close to the bathroom. Whatever it is, it means I usually get a good seat too, so I can't complain. "You got it, man."

As he turns to leave, I take out my phone one more time. I just can't quite curb the reflex to keep checking.

Ironically, I used to let my phone die all the time. My

friends and family would beg me to be better about it so they could reach me. Now here I am, staring at zero notifications, knowing without a doubt I'm keeping it charged twenty-four seven so there's no chance I miss a text from Ellie.

Is there a term for this feeling? My mood being so tied up in even the most trivial communication—or lack thereof? It's both exciting and scary, feelings I haven't really experienced with dating in a long time. Maybe ever, if I'm being honest.

I think back to Ellie's proclamation that I'd be safe with her. She was making a joke, but I believed the sentiment then and I want to believe it now. Remembering that early conversation seems to calm some of the anxious energy I have.

I reach down for my bag on the floor and shoulder it before heading out the door. I'm feeling eager to get on the plane and get one step closer to home.

*One step closer to Ellie.*

To call or not to call.

Not quite a Shakespearean sentiment, but with the way this is weighing on me, you'd think as much was at stake.

There are a few possibilities I've come up with for why I haven't heard back from Ellie, and in most of them she's obviously totally fine. But my keyed-up post-win brain can't totally count out the idea that she's not. I'm not sure when I got so attached to this pretty girl from Boston, but I'm so desperate to know that she's at least safe, I think I'm willing to look a little needy.

Sitting on the bed in my hotel room, I swipe to her contact and hover over the call button, giving myself one last chance to back out. I'm committed to hitting the button when the screen changes to show an incoming call.

*Confidential Fuck Buddy.*

With the speed I accept it, I'd be surprised if it even rang on her end.

"Hey," I exhale.

"Hi! Oh shoot, did I wake you up? I was just going to leave a voicemail."

The relief I physically experience from hearing Ellie's voice should be studied. I lie back against the headboard and close my eyes, feeling both relaxed enough to sleep and too happy about talking to her to let that happen.

"No, I was actually just thinking of calling you to check in. Is everything okay? Why a voicemail?"

"Oh, phew. Yes, ugh, I feel so bad. I didn't mean to leave you hanging today. I was with Dev and she wanted to look at something on my phone so I set it to Do Not Disturb. Didn't really trust her nosy butt to not click on a text notification from you. Anyway, I totally forgot I did that so I never saw your texts until a few minutes ago. They really need to give you regular reminders so you don't accidentally leave it on all day," Ellie huffs. "I was going to call to apologize and explain that instead of texting you an essay," she adds sheepishly. "Did your game go okay?"

A rambling Ellie will always make me smile. "I'll be sure to file a complaint on your behalf," I tease. "How was your time with Dev? Has she grilled you yet?"

"When she didn't say much at any of our shifts this week, I thought I was in the clear. Boy, was I wrong. It was something all right. Felt like I was on trial with the level of interrogation she launched at me," she laughs. "Thankfully she's satisfied now and will *hopefully* be chill."

"I take it she recognized me?" I guess. I remember the look on her face when she saw me outside Ellie's door.

"Oh yeah. She said she had secondhand embarrassment that I propositioned someone famous with my Band-Aid sex idea. So that was nice."

I laugh out loud at that. "Well you can tell her I found it incredibly endearing so she has nothing to worry about."

"I'll let her know," she says quietly. It sounds like she's smiling, but I guess I can't be sure. "So did you guys win or what?"

"Oh yeah, we did. In overtime, actually. Kind of a close one, but we pulled it out."

Ellie would have no way to know this, but I can't remember the last time I spoke to someone who didn't already know the results of the game. Family, friends, girlfriends...They were always watching either on TV or in person. Or were at least invested enough to check the stats online.

There's something oddly refreshing about that *not* being an assumption with Ellie. In fact, I think it'd be safer to assume the opposite.

If I get caught up thinking in the long term, I can admit it might worry me a little that she doesn't have any interest in something that makes up my whole life. But I still feel like we always have plenty to talk about without hockey. And ultimately, having a relationship *not* built around that seems like it might be better. After all, my career here isn't going to last forever...

"Showed those losers who's boss," she declares, graciously interrupting my almost thought spiral.

I hold back my chuckle. I don't think she even knows what team we played.

"Why aren't you out celebrating? Isn't that what you guys do?" she asks, an odd tone to her voice.

"Sometimes, I guess? Depends on the situation. Some of the team is out having a celebratory drink though, yeah. We got into Jersey a little bit ago and don't play until Monday. I'm sure some of the guys are taking that as a pass for getting drunk."

"You didn't want to join them?"

"Not really my scene. And I was kind of hoping to chat with someone on the phone," I add.

"Just someone?" Her light tone is back, making me think I heard incorrectly before.

"Someone really specific, actually," I tell her. "She's kind of a secret though, so that's all I can say."

Ellie laughs and I wish I could bottle the melodic sound for a rainy day. It's not jarring or silly—it's the type that makes you smile and desperately want to be in on the joke.

"I hope that works out for you," she says.

"Things are looking pretty good. Are you headed to bed or can I pitch an idea to you?"

"Well, even if I was going to bed, I'm definitely staying for this pitch. It does seem to be our thing."

I chuckle and hope my dumb idea isn't actually going to keep her from sleeping, if that's what she wanted to do. "Okay, I probably oversold this. I was just going to propose we play twenty questions."

"Like the game where you're trying to guess a person, place, or thing?" she asks, a hint of confusion in her voice. I can almost picture the little nose wrinkle that'd accompany the question.

"Oh, well, shit. No? Is that what that game means?" I laugh. "I was imagining us asking each other random questions, like ten each, but alternating back and forth. Just for fun."

"I don't think that's a game," she says as she giggles. "But lucky for you, this sounds way better than twenty questions, which I might have bailed on in favor of sleep. You go first."

The anticipation of getting more Ellie-knowledge has me propping myself up higher against the headboard. "Let's see. Steak or sushi?"

"Sushi. You? Wait, does that count as my question?"

"Also sushi, and nah. You're up."

"Hmm. What's something you're really bad at?"

*Summoning the balls to ask if we are exclusive. Hence this game.*

"Snowboarding," I offer instead.

"Ugh. Why do I feel like your *bad* is still way better than most people's *passable*?"

"I promise I'm bad," I say on a laugh. "More of a skier. Do you do either?"

"Define 'do,'" Ellie jokes. "I *have* skied. I'll make it down the mountain, but I'm not going to impress anyone. And I might eat it a few times."

"We can work on it," I assure her. "If you want to, I mean. Okay, my turn...What would you give a TED Talk about?"

"Like a presentation?"

"Right, just something you could talk about for a while to a large group."

"First of all, that sounds like a nightmare. Please don't ever make me do that. Hmm, this is boring, but I think I could go through how to triage with my eyes closed. So maybe that."

"That is not boring and it's way more useful than anything I could come up with."

"It's just my job. I'm sure you could talk about yours the same way," she says.

"I guess, but I feel like between interviews and random league things, everyone has already heard everything I could come up with on that topic. Maybe I could give one on my *little alien movies*," I quip, holding back a chuckle.

"That wasn't a diss! I just couldn't remember the name, I swear. It was a good movie. I told you I'd watch another."

"I'm just messing with you. I will gladly introduce you to all of my little alien movies," I promise.

"Okay, good. Hmm, my turn." Ellie pauses for what feels like a full minute. "When you said you were hoping to chat tonight, did you mean phone sex?"

If I had a drink in my mouth I would've spit it out. Instead, I'm choking on air over here.

"What?" It comes out like a shout. I try to lower my voice. "No, why'd you think that?"

"Well we're fuck buddies, right? I thought that's the idea you were going to pitch!" she exclaims.

Maybe one day I'll be able to predict what she's going to say, but today is not that day. I groan, mind fully where I don't want it to be, given that I'm literally states away from her. A shared hotel room is not exactly where I want to get myself off solo either.

"I'm definitely not opposed to phone sex, to be clear, but that's not why I called. And unfortunately, there was a mix-up at the hotel and I offered to share a room with Niko, so I think it's off the table. I'm guessing he'll be back shortly," I grumble, regretting that decision. "Did *you* want to have phone sex?" She did say she was intrigued when I mentioned pitching an idea.

"I don't know. I've never done it before. I think I'd be awkward."

"I seriously doubt that," I mutter, fisting my hand to keep from palming my semihard dick. "Okay we gotta change the subject, Ellie. Is it my turn? I think it's my turn." I hum and try to think about anything other than getting her off over the phone.

She did mention fuck buddies again. Guess this is my opportunity. "Alright, I got one. Have you propositioned anyone else recently?"

"Propositioned... Propositioned like I did you?" She sounds surprised.

"Right." Am I holding my breath?

"Oh," Ellie says. She's quiet for a minute.

Fuck, is she going to say yes? That's what I get for not having this conversation sooner. *Shit.*

"Are we not—" Ellie clears her throat. "I guess fuck buddies means not exclusive?"

Her voice is quieter than before and I'm trying to decipher why. I play what she said back in my mind. *Oh.* Shit.

"I'm not hanging out or sleeping with anyone else, Ellie. You're my exclusive confidential fuck buddy. I just wasn't sure if you'd want that too, since we didn't really talk about it," I hurry to tell her. Then hesitate before asking, "Does that mean you haven't propositioned anyone else?"

"Correct," Ellie says, less quiet than before.

"Do you plan to proposition anyone else?"

"Definitely not." *Thank fuck.* "No need to embarrass myself again when I have my very own CFB, right? Plenty of practice happening here," she adds cheerily.

*Okay, phew.* The mention of *practice* stings a little, but I remind myself this is what I signed up for. And, honestly, I can admit that *some* Ellie is better than *no* Ellie. Hopefully time will change her mind about us being only CFBs, but for now I just have to accept my role if it means spending time with her. And if what we're doing is making her happy, I can't complain too much.

"It's my turn, right?" Ellie asks, a yawn taking over on the last word. I pull the phone away to check the time—just after midnight.

"How about one more and then we can resume next time?" I ask her.

"Deal. I actually thought of a really important one. Would you rather become a werewolf or a vampire?"

I think I laugh loud enough to wake up the unlucky guests above me.

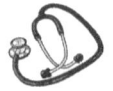

# CHAPTER EIGHTEEN
## *ellie*

WORKING THE ER WILL BREAK YOUR HEART. THE WORDS FROM MY old charge nurse in Boston are ringing true in my head on this shitty Monday.

One of my patients died this evening. He was only thirty-seven. I want to forget him right now so I can focus on my current patient, but I already know she just has the flu and it's not taking up enough mental capacity to banish the memories of that damn flatline tone. It's not that we got particularly close; he wasn't here very long. But he was in a car accident and those cases are always particularly poignant for me.

The dull tone of a flatline is not all that different from that ringing noise you get in your ears. It's hard to describe and yet everyone knows exactly what it sounds like. Sometimes I feel like I hear phantom flatlines when I'm not at work. They don't happen frequently, but this is the biggest hospital with the best emergency department in Minnesota, and just based on the sheer quantity of patients, we see a lot of death.

And like everything else in the world, flatlines are really nothing like the movies. Hollywood always depicts them as quite dramatic, obviously—that terrifying tone coming out of nowhere, followed by doctors desperately trying to shock the flatlined patient back to life.

The one thing they *do* get right? The chaos. That's totally real. It's organized and efficient, but chaos nonetheless. And sometimes we are *terrified* to hear that tone.

But that's because it usually means we're too late.

Flatlines don't just come out of nowhere. Hearts don't just stop. They struggle and they fight, the electrical impulses firing away until the very end. It's during that struggle and fight that *sometimes* we use a defibrillator to "reboot" the heartbeat and try to get it back to normal. But you can't reboot something that's gone.

So when you do see that final flatline? There is no fight left. There's nothing to shock to life, nothing to fix. It's irreversible.

And it's haunting.

We're desensitized for the most part. But sometimes that *noise* just stays with you. Follows you around all day. Memories of the patient and their *fight* replay in your head like some traumatizing movie reel.

My therapist back in Boston wasn't sure going into emergency medicine was the best path for me. And honestly? She had good reason to think that.

She was worried it might keep my trauma too fresh, being in that environment—like a scab you keep picking at and won't let heal. She smartly encouraged me to do my research and talk to other nurses.

And everyone said the same thing. Warned, really. *When you get into this field, it is going to take a toll on your mental health.*

They said it's traumatizing and often thankless. It's chaotic and impossible to feel caught up. That it's draining and easily turns that desire to help people into a disdain for the healthcare system. They said you're likely to burn out—most people do.

And with all those things listed out? I can admit I was intimidated. Who wouldn't be? It *does* sound rough. But some things they shared as hardships of the job I only saw as reasons why it was perfect for me.

Because I'd been an ER patient and had lost a *lot*. So I knew what I wanted out of my job. What I needed.

First? The lack of downtime. I've talked about this before and I'll continue to preach it: having a job that doesn't allow for a wandering mind is really, really great for someone who doesn't want to get lost in their thoughts. Maybe someday this will change, but when I was picking a specialty? And even now? I crave the utter focus my job requires.

The days I go to work are often my best mental health days, despite the trauma that so regularly comes through those doors. Sure, the reminder of my own can hit me like a wall, but just as quickly I'm swept away in the task of it all. I'm just *working* and *helping* and *passing time* faster than anything I've ever experienced. For the most part, I don't even think much about my work day once I'm home. Which leads me to the next thing on the list.

Emergency room patients are in and out. And you know what that means? No long-term relationships. This one is a major downside for most people getting into nursing. You hear the stories of the angel nurses that patients connect with and how they become almost like family. How they kept in touch over the years because of how much time they spent together in the hospital. And don't get me wrong, I *love* those stories. I do. I fell in love with nursing because of those stories.

But after the accident, the idea of forming meaningful, lasting relationships with patients scared the shit out of me. I didn't even want new friends or a boyfriend for nearly two years after my mom died. So the idea of having a constant influx of people to get attached to? No, thank you. Getting attached is all fine and good until your patient dies. And then not only is your patient dead (shitty), but you're way more heartbroken because you *knew* them and now they are gone (ultra, ultra shitty). I'm not going to say it's a matter of quantity over quality, because that's a gross oversimplification (and probably makes it sound like I don't deeply care about helping my patients), but you get the picture. I have to care without getting attached. Because in the ER, you just don't have the *time*. And that works in my favor.

The next two things were just...things I couldn't get out of my head. Things that really stuck with me since *my* day in the ER.

When I was a patient there, a lot of it was a blur. Not really in a metaphorical way either. I was in and out of consciousness and often I'd open my eyes to bright, unfocused light. The noise was not loud, but it was jarring all the same. I was lost and confused. I was hurting. And I was *scared*.

I must have said it out loud at some point, because despite the blur, I have a very clear memory of one of those aforementioned angel nurses.

She said it was okay to be scared because she wasn't.

She held my hand a lot and talked me through what was happening. When she found out I was in school to be a nurse she got more detailed in her descriptions of various procedures—more technical. I still remember her voice and how calm she was. How she made me less scared just by the simple fact that she wasn't. There was something so comforting about that.

I so badly wanted to have that type of impact on my

patients. To bring peace to an often chaotic place. Safety to somewhere people feel scared. *I can do that*, I remember thinking. And I hope I do. It's one of the main reasons I love my job and why I continue to do it.

Sometimes that's the main thing the doctor needs my help with, keeping the patient calm—getting them to focus on something as simple as breathing. And I was doing that today, using my normal script and holding his hand, when I noticed his nails were messily painted bright purple. The edges were uneven and some smudges of the polish were on his fingers. I asked him where he got his manicure.

"My five-year-old," he rasped. "Little girl."

I should've seen that coming—the adorably sloppy job had tiny human written all over it—but that sentiment left me reeling. I knew from the doctor and my own read on things that his chest injuries were causing a rapid decline. He wasn't going to make it. He wasn't going to see his daughter again. And she wasn't going to see him.

It's a shitty club: the dead parent club. I wish so badly that little girl didn't have to join it. I think it'll be a while before I can get him—and her—out of my head.

And that brings me to the main reason I wanted this job. The reason I've been stuck on this path ever since the worst day of my life.

I would do *anything* to keep someone from being in my shoes.

I will keep going and going and going so that maybe, *maybe* I can save someone from having to live without their mom or dad.

I couldn't be that person for that little girl today, but I'll never stop trying.

# CHAPTER NINETEEN

## *matt*

"How do you do that?" Alex squirts water into his mouth and drops heavily on the bench next to me, taking a breather during the commercial break.

"Do what?" I respond.

"Ignore these fuckers. They're on you like goddamn rabid dogs and you don't even look bothered."

"I'm bothered," I laugh. "But they're just doing their job."

"I mean, yeah, but don't you want to defend yourself? Pretty sure you could take them."

"If they're able to get to me that easily, then they're doing their job better than I'm doing mine." I knock my padded leg against his and grab my own water. "It got easier over time for me."

Alex sighs. "I don't know, dude. I feel like you just have a long fuse."

I swallow my water and set the bottle down in front of me, tilting my head back and forth as I think about that. "Maybe now," I concede. "But it took me a while to figure out how to not just *react*. I had to constantly remind myself that if they draw a penalty, I've lost. And I fucking hate losing."

He shakes his head and laughs. I raise my eyebrows in question at him.

"I just can't believe this is my life sometimes, getting to talk hockey with you. I had your jersey before it had a C on it. I'm definitely making you sign that shit before you retire," he jokes.

"Yeah, yeah, I'm old," I grumble. I push his last comment aside and focus on the rest. Shit like that is part of what I love about my job these days. Getting to help the next generation of players—people who watched me play as they grew up—is flattering and rewarding. The fact that they think I can help them is no small compliment either. Some of these guys are destined to be great. Some already are. "You're killin' it, man. This kind of shit will come with time. Just don't forget to focus on your game. Set up plays and find quiet ice. Put the puck on frame. The rest is noise."

"Noise," Alex repeats, nodding slowly.

I turn to look up at the scoreboard as the game is about to resume and I grimace.

There's three minutes and twenty-two seconds left on the clock and we're down by one. It's enough time to score, but their defense has been on point all damn night. And ours has been...less than stellar. I sigh and look away from the score, focusing back on the ice and the face-off that's about to happen. I'm determined to do my best to tie it up when I get in there, and keeping a read on the other team's lines is crucial. Who am I up against and what are their strengths? Their weaknesses?

I watch our guys lose the face-off and try not to curse. More often than not, I'm itching to get off the bench and back on the ice. When we're down by one with only a couple of minutes left? The pull to hop the boards feels like an impulse I can hardly control.

We're finally back in possession of the puck and I see our third line guys making their move for the bench. I sigh in relief at being able to get out there and quickly hop up for the change, Alex and Niko following suit. Mikey sends the puck to me from near our goal and I quickly maneuver between two players to get down the ice. Niko's waiting off to my right, ready for a pass. I see a defenseman covering him so I fake like I'm going to shoot, keeping my eyes on the goal. At the very last second I pivot so my stick sends the puck over to Niko, relieved to see he's more open now. I hold my breath as he goes for a one-timer—

Their goalie deflects it off his stick and New Jersey scoops the puck up to head back toward our goal. *Damn.* I'm racing to catch up, but their fastest player breaks away for a one-on-one. I watch helplessly as he shoots...and scores. *Fuck.*

It's a hell of a lot harder to score two goals in two minutes than just one. I circle around and line up for a face-off at center ice, determined to keep my head in the game even with the odds against us. Feeling defeated serves no purpose, and as much as I hate losing, I hate giving up even more. I look around and check that my teammates are focused and then face forward, ready to fight to the end.

WE LOST. NOT THAT ANYONE WAS SURPRISED, OBVIOUSLY.

So no points for us and an increasingly worse record in the ongoing race for a playoff spot. *Great.*

The standings are tight this season and we're currently tied for a wild-card position in our division. Which means we could be a contender, or we could keep losing like tonight and just fall out of contention altogether. Every game it feels like the pressure rises. And I have a feeling it's going to come down to the wire for us.

I think of the different outcomes: making the playoffs and fighting our way through, or falling short and the season just... ending.

Every time we don't make the playoffs—or make the playoffs, but don't win the Cup—I feel like some seasoned gambling addict that can't quite quit. *Maybe just one more season will do the trick.* It's so easy to convince yourself to try again.

But if I'm being honest, our last few seasons have either gone downhill or kind of plateaued. So unless something drastic changes, I don't see us miraculously having a way more competitive team next year. We're *good*, but we haven't been great in a while. I know we have Alex now and some young talent in the pipeline, but it usually takes new guys a few years to make a difference. It probably wouldn't be enough for next year.

*It could be though...*

This is how it always goes in my mind. I'll wonder if retiring after the season is the move and then find a way to convince myself *one* more season won't hurt. It's been like that for the past few years and I'm getting a little sick of the predictable cycle. I know I should just make a decision. But I genuinely don't know what to do with myself when it's over. And just the *idea* of another Cup is so goddamn appealing. It really does feel like an addiction.

So where does that addiction to compete go when you stop playing? What do I do with that drive that's been my life's purpose for as long as I can remember? I've spent my entire life *playing a game*, for fuck's sake. It's like I've lived my life through the lens of competition—something that's shaped how I face nearly everything.

I know some guys get into golf when they retire just to find an outlet for that innate drive to compete. But golf? I'd rather take a puck to the knee.

People recommend coaching, becoming involved with the team, starting up a new sport or hobby...the list goes on. I *know* there are options. But nothing feels right. Nothing sounds fulfilling.

I think of Ellie and her job. Her selfless, stressful, make-the-world-better job. She fucking saves lives and I play a game for a living. God, sometimes I want to punch myself. Poor me and my very hard decision on whether I should retire or not. From my extremely well-paying job doing something objectively fun.

The perspective is a welcome wet blanket on my pity party.

Whenever I find myself in this vicious cycle of self-loathing, I know it's time to take a step back and focus on something important. Something that matters. And little matters more than giving back to this community that's given so much to me.

As my mind drifts back to Ellie and her job, I realize I know exactly what I want to do. It's been a few months since I've been there and nothing recharges me quite like those little kids and their not-so-little hearts.

We travel home tonight and I know precisely how I'm spending my day off tomorrow.

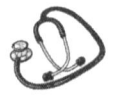

# CHAPTER TWENTY
## *ellie*

I haven't seen Matt in almost a week. I *know* that's not that long, and I did talk to him on Saturday at least, but I'm getting addicted. Fuck buddies was a great idea.

I think he gets back from his away games today...or maybe last night? So hopefully I can see him soon. It's been nearly impossible to meet up on the days I work, but maybe that will change soon when I give him his present.

My half-eaten turkey sandwich is midway to my mouth when a commotion at the other end of the cafeteria catches my attention. I pause my eating and scan the small crowd that's gathered there to see what the fuss is about.

I feel a swoop in my belly when my eyes land on a familiar black baseball hat resting on a tall figure. Is Matt at the hospital? Do I have magical manifesting powers? I put my sandwich down and watch as, yes, *the* Matt Anderson politely engages with his growing entourage, all the while discreetly peering around.

His eyes eventually land on mine and stop. The swoop turns into full-fledged butterflies. He's criminally handsome.

And he's at my hospital.

Looking at me.

I wonder what he's here for. Maybe some publicity thing? That's probably it, as much as eleven-year-old me believed in having magical powers. It is almost nine p.m. though, which is past normal visiting hours, professional or otherwise.

Matt's still chatting with the staff as I gather my leftovers and trash. I check my watch and calculate I have eighteen minutes left on my break. Perfect. I thank my lucky stars the ER is having a slow night, otherwise I wouldn't have been on a break at all. And bless Maggie, our charge nurse, for encouraging us to take them. I probably would've eaten my sandwich at the nurses' station like I normally do otherwise.

I give Matt a quick, secret smile across the room when I see his eyes still on me and casually walk my way past him down the hallway that leads to the ER. I look over at him once before letting myself into a private exam room on my right. I shut the door behind me and wait.

In the movies, he would instantly understand the assignment, give people an excuse, and follow me in here, but in real life I'm not sure if I was obvious enough. He might just think I went back to work. *Shit.* He might not even know what kind of room I walked into. Oh god, he might think I went to the freaking bathroom. Maybe I should peek my head out to give him—

"Hey." Matt's voice startles me out of my spiral. I turn around to face him and, like a mirror image, I watch his smile stretch across his face at the exact same pace as mine until we're both cheesing at each other like idiots. Matt pockets his phone and then backs up a step to shut the door behind him with his body, looking down quickly to flip the lock before facing me again. Cheesy smile still in place.

*Criminally* handsome.

"Hi," I say back to him through my own smile, fighting the surge of shyness that just washed over me. How is someone this good-looking smiling at me like *that*?

"C'mere." Matt gives a little head jerk.

I walk over until I'm right in front of him, looking up at that perfect face. Matt grabs my wrists and puts them up and over his shoulders before bending slightly and wrapping his arms tightly around me. His big frame envelops mine as he buries his face in my neck and takes a deep breath, lifting me so I'm resting on my toes. I push up as far as I can to hug him tighter and hopefully lessen any strain on his back.

"I missed you," he breathes against my neck.

I think I might legitimately swoon if it weren't for Matt's arms holding me snug against him. I inhale his scent and close my eyes, content to stay like this for...as long as I can. Maybe longer.

There's something about the way he smells that simultaneously puts me at ease *and* excites me. It's an addictive combination. Is this what the hard drugs feel like? Because if so, I get it. I would huff Matt's scent all day if I could without looking like a freak. I'd like to be high on this feeling twenty-four seven.

"You saw me like a week ago," I tease, as if I haven't missed him too. "And we talked on the phone. How was the road?"

Matt drops a kiss on my neck before pulling back to look at me. "It was fine. Long," he says. I feel his shrug under my arms that are still looped around his neck. His eyes are bouncing around my face, cataloging who knows what.

"Why are you at the hospital?"

"I had the day off, so I was just doing some visits to the kids over in oncology. They let me come past visiting hours to avoid making more of a scene. And selfishly, I was hoping I'd get to see you. I feel like my eyes have a slight strain from constantly looking for you everywhere I went," he adds with a smile and barely visible blush tinting his cheeks. "Had to fake a phone call to follow you in here."

"You just came here on your day off?" I ask him, mouth ajar.

He nods.

"To visit sick kids?"

Another nod. Redder cheeks.

Matt Anderson is visiting tiny humans with cancer. On his day off. Voluntarily. It's not even some contractually obligated publicity thing.

That is so...I don't even know. An act like that is kryptonite to us healthcare workers. Something almost painful squeezes the heart in my chest. Something new.

I swallow the lump in my throat and push the scary feelings away for now. We've only known each other for a little over a month. Time to distract myself with something else—something I've been wanting to do with Matt, but haven't mustered the nerve for. I kiss him quickly on the lips and then unhook my hands behind his neck and drop down to my knees.

"What are you doing?" he asks me with...alarm?

I grin up at him from the floor. "Taking a page out of the Matt Anderson handbook—being selfless." I stick my tongue out at him and then start slowly undoing the perfectly tied drawstring on his joggers.

"Ellie," Matt warns. "I don't think this is a good idea. Don't you have to get back to work?" He looks behind him at the door and then back to me.

I stare at the growing bulge clearly visible in his briefs and lick my lips. Then I pull them down shakily, letting his rapidly hardening cock bounce up toward his stomach.

"I have..." I look at my watch. "Eleven minutes." I grab his thick length and lean forward to swipe my tongue across the drop of pre-cum in front of me. I hum at the taste—not bad.

"Fuck." I hear a thud as Matt's head hits the door behind him.

I move my hand up and down twice before licking from the base up to the tip. Then I guide him into my mouth and swirl my tongue, slowly taking him deeper. Matt's hand works its way to the side of my face, his thumb resting on my cheek, fingers reaching behind my ear into my pulled-back hair.

I look up at his face and see his jaw is clenched and his eyes are closed. *Hmm. That won't do.* I pause and move back to release him, hearing a soft pop as he bobs out of my mouth. I rest back on my heels.

"You don't want to watch?" I try really hard to keep the disappointment out of my voice. But isn't that part of what makes it so hot for guys? I look down at my teal blue scrubs. They aren't exactly sexy, but I didn't think they were offensive. Heck, I find them kind of cute. "Is it the scrubs?" I ask him, face twisting to the side.

Matt groans. "Ellie, whatever you're thinking, stop. I love your scrubs." He sighs and starts again. "If I try to look at you down there on your fucking knees, pretty eyes focused on me, I'm going to finish in fifteen seconds."

Oh. *Oh.*

"That's okay. We're on the clock anyway." I push back to my knees and lick my lips again before leaning forward to take him in my mouth.

I look up to see his Adam's apple bob on a rough swallow. On my second pass, I make sure to hollow my cheeks and suck, moving my hand in unison with my mouth. Up and down, adding pressure with my firm grip on him. I don't really have a *ton* of expertise, but I take him as far as I can each time, letting my eyes water at the gagging sensation. I'm getting lost in the act, feeling a heavy desire pool low in my belly, when I'm abruptly pulled off Matt and up to my feet.

An involuntary pout takes over my face as I look down at his now slick cock.

"Go bend over that table." Matt chucks my chin up toward him, his chest heaving and pupils blown.

*Oh shit, that's hot.*

I scamper over to the exam table and try to assess how to bend over it. Do I lean forward, resting on my palms? Do I go on my elbows? I'm standing there, still staring, when I feel a hand press against my back, pushing it down until my entire front is flush against the table's surface. *Oh, fuck, I like that.*

Matt reaches a hand in front of my hips to untie my scrubs. He hooks his thumbs under the waistband to my underwear and tugs them down over my butt. Matt slowly smooths his hands up over my ass to my hips, where he grips the dip of my waist and pauses.

"You said you have an IUD?" he asks, remembering what I told him during a recent hookup.

I nod. "I just got a new one when I moved here," I tell him over my shoulder.

"Are you okay without a condom? I don't have any with me," he says a bit reluctantly.

I think of his past and know this is not a minor concession for him—offering to go without. I also think of the hospital's stock of condoms and how there are probably even some in this room somewhere.

Then I think of why Matt's here today and our exclusivity

conversation on Saturday and how much I realize I just...trust him. So I give him another nod. "Are *you* okay without one?"

I feel him flex his fingers on my waist. He's so quiet I'm debating telling him I can go try and find some. I don't really want to get up though. And my break is almost over...

I wiggle my butt in impatience and am startled when Matt's finger swipes the wetness from my center up to my clit and back again. He dips it inside then and I have to bite my lip to stifle my moan. He groans and grips my hip tighter with the hand that's left there.

"So wet for me," he says under his breath. "Can you spread your legs a bit, pretty girl?"

My heart thumps at the endearment and the anticipation. I step my legs farther apart and almost immediately feel him push into me. There's a quick bite of pain from the sudden intrusion that shifts to pleasure almost instantly. *Fuckkk*, that feels good.

"Fucking perfect," Matt grits out.

I grip the edge of the table in front of me as he pulls out and then *slams* back in.

Oh god, *yes*.

"Okay?" he asks, stilling his movements.

"*Yes*, please don't stop."

Matt grunts and then starts fucking me. Matt is *fucking me* at *work*. And I'm getting absolutely, deliciously wrecked with every slam into this exam table. I hope my hips bruise so I have some tangible proof this happened.

Matt's hand slides from my hip to my ponytail, which he grasps firmly before using it to gently angle my head to the side.

"Gonna come for me, Ellie?"

I nod and feel a tug on my hair from the movement. My vision starts to tunnel as my climax closes in, the pleasure literally taking over my sight. Matt's grip on my other hip disappears and then I'm hit with a drugging pulse of sensation as he presses firmly on my clit. Waves of pleasure radiate through me as my release slams into me, forcing an involuntary moan to slip out.

It's quickly cut off as Matt lets go of my hair and presses his hand over my mouth, muffling any more sounds. He groans quietly as he finishes, falling forward heavily and pushing me farther into the table.

Gently smothered by post-sex Matt might be my preferred method to die one day.

What's the saying? *My ideal weight is Matt Anderson on top of me.* I smile and give his palm a quick nip. He removes it, using it to lift himself up. *And* unveiling my embarrassingly heavy breathing. I need to work out more. Or just at all. I should ask Zoey what she suggests for being in shape enough for hot sex. She'd get a kick out of that. She'd also get a kick out of my having sex at *work*.

"I can't believe we just did that," I pant out.

"I can't believe you got on your knees for me." He groans as he starts to straighten up. "It's going to live rent free in my head for the rest of my life."

*Success.* I smile and look at my watch. *Shit.* I hurry to push off the table and pull my pants up. Ugh, I'm going to have to wear my wet underwear until I can change them. I undo my loose ponytail and retie it, surveying the room. We didn't leave a mess, but this room is definitely not patient-ready anymore. I start to pull out random items here and there, leaving a small chaos in my wake.

"Ellie?"

"Hmm?" I finish dropping a few clean swabs on the counter and turn to look at him.

He's fully dressed again and has his hands in his pockets, smiling at me indulgently. "What are you doing?"

I glance around the room at my new mess and feel satisfied with the result. "No one will accidentally use this room thinking it's clean now," I tell him.

Matt laughs and shakes his head. He mutters something, but I don't catch it.

I step over to him and place my hand on his chest as I lean in for a kiss. "I have to get back to work, but can you wait here for a few minutes? I want to grab something for you," I tell him.

Matt gives me a curious look as he nods. I bolt out of the room and do my best to speed walk to my locker. No need to cause a panic if people see me running. I hastily put in my code and unlock it, pulling it open to grab the envelope from inside my bag. I feel doubt creep in as the heavy item sits in my palm. But I remind myself of the trust I felt before and the reason I wanted to do this in the first place—cuddles and logistics. And more sex.

I rush back to the room and find Matt where I left him, patient as can be. He smiles big at me and the earlier doubt seeps out of my body, replaced with giddy excitement.

I hold out my hand, palm up, in front of him. "For you."

Matt slowly grabs the envelope and gives me his narrowed gaze, probably due to the weight of it. He opens the flap and pours the metal key and keychain onto his other palm.

I look from him to the key. And back. He isn't doing anything. Or saying anything. My heart rate picks up as I realize this may have been a bad idea. What if he thinks I'm being weird? Oh god, what if he thinks I'm asking him to move in to my tiny apartment?

"It's so you can let yourself in after a game night. When I'm at work. If you want to sleep sooner," I rush to explain. "You said your house was like almost a half hour away, right? So I thought, you know, if you're tired after a game and I'm busy, you could just let yourself in to sleep. If you want."

Matt swallows and closes his fingers over the key slowly, finally angling his head up to look at me. "You got me a key?"

I nod, unsure how he's taking this.

"You got me a key to your apartment so I could sleep more?"

I nod again.

"That's…" Matt drops his head and lets out a huff. He looks up and moves his hand to cup my cheek. "Thank you, Ellie. I don't even know what to say."

I smile wide at him and lean into his hand. I think my subconscious is doing jazz hands. "That's okay, I have to go anyway," I tell him, letting my smile turn into a pout.

He smiles at my dramatics and leans in to give me a soft kiss. I back up toward the door until I feel the handle behind me.

Pointing at him, I instruct, "Wait at least two minutes before you leave. And don't forget to look at the other side of the key."

"Yes, ma'am," Matt says with a serious nod.

His smile is the last thing I see before I shut the door and head back to work.

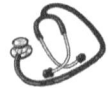

# CHAPTER TWENTY-ONE
## ellie

*Today 2:17PM*

**DEV**
I have an idea…

**ELLIE**
hit me

**DEV**
We should go to a game together!

I know you said your situationship is on the DL, but we can get nosebleed seats and be quiet supporters (not literally of course, I will be loud as shit but you know what I mean)

You can borrow one of my Bears shirts

It'll be so fun!

What do you think?? They have a home game tomorrow, Saturday and Sunday and then they are playing away games for a bit

So I feel like Saturday would be perf?? I know you picked up a shift tomorrow

I can see those typing dots appearing and disappearing Ellie 🏛

Spit it out girlfriend. I could drag you there by force...

S̲HIT.

# CHAPTER TWENTY-TWO

## *matt*

"How are things with Ellie?"

If I thought I could play it cool with Nate, the smile I can't seem to stop from spreading across my face diminishes any semblance of that.

"That good, huh?"

I stop fidgeting with my new favorite piece of hardware in my pocket, clasping it in my palm and then letting it go. It has *CFB* engraved on one side. So fucking cute. She even attached a vintage Bears keychain—something I wouldn't expect from someone who doesn't seem to have any interest in hockey. I didn't expect a key either, though, I guess. Ellie and her sweet unpredictability. My smile grows.

"She got me a key," I tell him. I look up from my food and glance at his face. His eyebrows are nearly at his hairline.

"And you're not freaking out? Wow, man. Talk about growth," he says on a laugh.

I roll my eyes at his antics and try not to think about how cringeworthy my reaction to a similar situation was last time. To be fair, Sabrina, my ex, was purely looking for me to offer *her* a key in return. And that wasn't going to happen. If I'm being completely honest though, I think I *would* give Ellie a key to my house if I thought she'd want it.

"So things are getting serious?" Nate asks genuinely, leaning back in his chair.

We're at one of our favorite burger joints not too far from The Bar. Normally I'd eat a quick lunch with Niko on game days, but he's got family in town right now. Because it's a Thursday I was hoping I could actually have lunch with Ellie—not that I'd tell Nate he was my second choice. Turns out she's covering for someone at the hospital today.

"I don't think she meant for the key to be a sign of any significance really, if I had to guess, but I do hope it's getting more serious, yeah. She still seems to want to keep it under wraps though, and she turned down my offer of tickets to a game."

Nate hums at that and takes a sip of his drink. "Did she say why? Maybe she was just busy."

I wince a bit at the reminder of the text conversation, still not entirely sure how to interpret it. I grab my phone and find the texts, sliding it over to Nate across from me so he can see for himself.

*Yesterday 1:16PM*

MATT
Could I convince you to come watch a game sometime soon?

CONFIDENTIAL FUCK BUDDY
and blow our cover? I think not 😜

MATT
No one has to know I got you the tickets ;)

**CONFIDENTIAL FUCK BUDDY**

ah, sure sure. thanks for the offer, but I'm not so into the crowds and all that. more of a "watch from the comfort of my cozy couch" gal. when's your next game?

**MATT**

What a lucky couch. I've got a game tomorrow night at 7pm.

**CONFIDENTIAL FUCK BUDDY**

drat. I'm covering a shift at the hospital. you could break in your new hardware though...

**MATT**

Say less

"Confidential Fu— Never mind, I don't want to know." Nate passes my phone back and leans forward with his elbows on the table, resting his chin in his hands. "Huh. Maybe she gets claustrophobic? Or she might just not like hockey, man. Or sports? That could be rough," he says with a slight grimace. At whatever face I make he quickly continues. "Orrr it could be perfect. You need a life outside of hockey, right?"

I never told Nate about Ellie's reaction when I asked if her ex had played hockey. I've tried to mostly forget about it myself. But I can't help wondering why she reacted that way and if she has something against hockey specifically. Or doesn't like sports, maybe, like Nate said. She hasn't made any other notable comments. She also hasn't asked much about it though.

I *know* I could just ask her, but I think I'm afraid of what the answer might be. What if wherever her dislike comes from is big enough that it keeps her from wanting more with me? We've been hanging out and *practicing* and it just feels so right. I don't want to mess it up. I guess a large part of me is also hoping that whatever it is, I'm convincing her that hockey or athletes or being in the spotlight is okay. That it's possible for us to have a relationship, no matter what the hangups are.

"Yeah, I guess," I sigh.

"Speaking of hockey. You're closing in on a thousand assists—your parents swinging through soon?"

I nod. "End of the month. I didn't think I could hit it before then."

"I'm sure if you got close they'd make it out sooner. I'm excited to join them for some games, haven't seen them in a bit." He pauses. Smiles. "You gonna introduce them to Ellie?"

"I want to, yeah. I'm nervous to ask though. And I feel like a game would have been the perfect time for a casual first meeting. But based on that conversation, I'm guessing she wouldn't want that."

Nate hums and starts cleaning our table—a habit he can't seem to shake from working the bar so often. "Well, for what it's worth, I really do think it's okay that she doesn't seem interested in hockey, man. I mean, imagine the opposite. That could be a hella big red flag, I think. And Shirley and Peter are super chill. Any type of meeting will go great if she's up for it."

I palm the key again and think about what he said. I do think my parents will be great around Ellie no matter where it happens. I just hope she'll want to meet them. And while I agree it's okay if she doesn't like hockey, selfishly I do wish she could be at my games. Her support as we get closer to making (or not making) the playoffs sounds...better than having anyone else's, honestly. But maybe that will come with time.

Nate starts to grab at my plate and I shoo him away, collecting my trash with my free hand before he tries again.

"She makes you happy, right?"

I huff. "Pretty sure I'm halfway in love with her already." I pull out the key from my pocket and look at it before sliding it back in. I should probably add it to the rest of my keys, but there is just something keeping me from lumping her gift with everything else. When I look up, Nate is grinning at me. "What?"

He laughs and shakes his head. "Nothing. I just don't think I've seen you this all-in before. I'm happy for you, man."

If *all-in* means obsessively looking at my new key and counting down the hours until I get to use it tonight, he's definitely right. T-minus…eleven hours, give or take.

Why does that feel like an eternity?

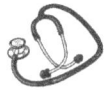

# CHAPTER TWENTY-THREE
## *ellie*

I HASTILY UNLOCK MY APARTMENT DOOR AND TOE OFF MY SHOES while I hang my coat on the hanger. Fuuuuudge I'm cold. The walk home at three in the morning is brutal when it's this temperature. And when it's snowing? Kind of makes me want to die. I might have to start driving. *Ugh.* I'm pretty sure we're supposed to get more snow this weekend. I should probably check the forecast before my next shift on Sunday.

Thinking about this weekend puts a tiny pit in my stomach. I was not prepared for Dev and Matt sending coincidental back-to-back texts trying to get me to go to a game. Talk about a double whammy. I'm not sure how realistic it is to keep this up...

I try to force it out of my mind for now. I'll cross that bridge later.

My scrubs land somewhere en route to my bedroom as I pull them off and drop them along the way. I go to turn the light on to find my warmer sweats for after my shower when I notice my bed is not empty.

I'm about to scream bloody murder when I see Matt's

backpack on the floor. And then I remember those texts from yesterday I was just thinking about.

Holy moly, I almost had a heart attack. Looks like he put his key to use. If my heart weren't already racing, I think I'd feel a swell of satisfaction over that.

I put my hand over my heart and slowly abandon my mission for sweats to head to the bathroom to brush my teeth and take the fastest shower humanly possible. Then I get to cuddle with my personal heater. *Heck yes.*

I try not to think too hard about how excited I am to not fuck my fuck buddy tonight. Fuck buddies cuddle, right? *After they fuck, maybe*, my subconscious says. I ignore her.

When I come back to my room, I see Matt's awake and looking at me with half-lidded eyes. I quickly grab and put on sleep shorts and a tank.

"Sorry if I woke you up," I whisper as I slide into bed and snuggle close to his warm, solid chest. Thanks to my quick and not very hot shower, I press my still frozen hands and feet against him and immediately feel them start to thaw. *Heaven.* My cold extremities must feel like ice, but Matt doesn't say anything. Are green flags a thing?

Matt presses a kiss to my forehead and hums. "Wanted to be woken up. How was work?" His sleepy voice makes it all sound like one long word. *Howwaswork.*

I hold back my laugh. "It was good. I'm actually glad I picked up the extra shift. Got to show off my suturing skills, since we were swamped," I tell him proudly on a yawn.

I *love* doing stitches. Usually the doctors do them, but sometimes, if we're busy enough, those of us who are trained can do them too. Sometimes suturing just needs to be efficient and it's less about perfection than getting the job done. When I have time to focus on that perfection though, that's what I'm obsessed with. There's something so peaceful and entrancing about putting your full focus into the task. Your mind can't wander or blur—you just have to be present. It feels like some magnificent combination of art and science. A tiny medical masterpiece.

"Not surprised you kicked ass," Matt says quietly, but more clearly now, interrupting my musing.

I smile at his sentiment and then sober as I watch his face. It's dark, but I can feel his eyes move to my collarbone as he starts to trace the raised scar there with the tip of his finger. It doesn't feel sexual in nature or conversely like some clinical exam. It's soft and slow, maybe sad.

"It was a car accident." My voice is quiet. Matt abruptly pauses his tracing and shifts his focus to my face.

I'm not sure why I haven't told him yet. I know he's wondered probably since he first saw it that night in the shower. It's not small or insignificant. The scar cuts diagonally across my collarbone on the left side, spanning a little more than four inches. I think about the thirty-two stitches the doctor had to carefully suture there over five years ago. I don't actually remember that part. They did a good job—some scars are just inevitable.

*A car accident* is usually as much information as I give people if they ask, if even that. But there's something about being cuddled up to Matt right now that makes me want to tell him more. He's so...solid. And not just in a physical sense. He feels so calming to be around, so peaceful. Like you could tell him the world was ending and he'd somehow make it not scary.

Matt Anderson is bombproof. *Safe*, my mind tells me again. I remember thinking that even early on. Funny how my original Superman comparison feels even more apt now.

The nerves that normally accompany this story aren't there. Instead I feel a sense of rightness. I think I want Matt to know me better. I'm not ready to think about what that might mean.

"This is from a piece of glass," I say, pointing to my collarbone.

Matt looks back to my scar and I hear a rough breath leave his nose. "From the car?" he asks in a low voice.

"They think the window, yeah." I swallow and try not to think of what I'm saying. "A drunk driver hit the driver's side of our car head-on. My...my mom was driving, so she had fatal injuries."

Matt's face crumples as he looks to me and I almost regret sharing. A sad Matt might break my already fragile heart.

I'm also sure he doesn't know what to say to me now. What *do* you say when you hear something like that? This is half the reason I never share with anyone. Death is awful and heartbreaking and happens *all the time*, and yet nothing feels right when it comes to comforting someone grieving. Especially when it's a tragic accident like this.

"I'm so sorry, Ellie." His hand still hovers near my scar. I put my own over his and give it a squeeze. I never know how to respond to that either.

I think about where his hand is and what led to this conversation. "I used to hate that scar so much. The visible reminder of everything. Like something I couldn't escape," I share with him, words just above a whisper. "I avoided so much for so long. The beach, gyms, tank tops...showers. Isn't that crazy?" I let out a humorless laugh. "I just couldn't handle seeing it or the questions it brought on. Sometimes when people asked about it, I'd pretend not to hear them. Or I'd tell them something fake—something less depressing."

Matt clears his throat. "And now?" His voice is deep and gravelly.

"Now…" I sigh. "Now I still don't like it. Still don't like the questions and the reminder of that day and my mom. But I also look at it now and see something kind of miraculous."

I use my hand to move Matt's tracing finger down two inches below my scar.

"If the glass had gone here"—I tap his finger to the spot—"it could've punctured my heart." I pull his finger back up slowly, moving it up and over my scar to a spot an inch above. "Here would've been my carotid artery." I pause and take a moment to let that reminder soak in. "I probably wouldn't have survived those," I breathe out.

I don't feel lighter or any less sad, really. But I'm flooded with that overwhelming sense of rightness again. Sharing with Matt feels *good*. I think deep down I knew it would.

I remove my hand from Matt's as I hear him swallow on my last few words. "So now I just try to balance it all. Feeling deeply unlucky and lucky at the same time. Accepting the ugliness of the scar while appreciating the incredible suturing the doctor did that day. Dreading seeing it in the mirror and also forcing myself to look and desensitize myself. Some days are easier than others," I finish quietly with a shrug.

Matt moves his hand up and cradles my face gently, thumb stroking my cheek. "The day I met you…"

"January eleventh." I pause and think about the day. Not the worst anniversary I've experienced, somewhat thanks to Matt. "That's the anniversary of the accident. I was trying to avoid thinking about it, hence the tequila."

Matt's thumb freezes on my face. "I wish I had known you then," he says sadly. "Not that I could've made it better, I know that. But I would've tried."

I place my hand over his. "You did," I tell him quietly. "You were 'Clark Kent.' A perfect momentary distraction. I remember thinking you were a little birthday gift from the universe on an otherwise crap day."

"Birthday?"

I cringe at the slipup and move my hand from its position against his. I did not intend to drop both of these tragedy bombs on Matt today. It's a pretty awful part of my life. Who wants to celebrate their birthday on the anniversary of their mom's death every year?

I've taken to just not sharing my birthday with new people and chalking it up to not liking being the center of attention. It's not a total lie but I used to love my birthday, and it stings knowing I'll never feel that way about it again. My mom wanted to buy me my first legal drink and now she won't ever celebrate a birthday with me again.

Obviously some people know, like my family and Josh. Zoey. *And now Matt.* You can't change the day you were born.

"That day at The Bar, that was your birthday?" There's an undercurrent to his voice, like he's putting together all these very sad puzzle pieces, the culmination of all of those events making for one tremendously horrible day.

He sounds so sad that I suddenly wish my life were different, if only to keep Matt from feeling that way. "It was actually a little easier this year, you know? Being away from home meant I didn't have to juggle the pain of my dad trying to figure out how to celebrate me and mourn my mom at the same time. Or watch my ex-boyfriend struggle with whether to plan something or even buy me a gift. Being alone was kind of…peaceful. Simple. I got to do my little tequila ritual without the burden of my loved ones' concern. I know that sounds bad, but dealing with my own grief is hard enough. Love can be complicated, and on that day..." I clear my throat. "On that day I just needed easy."

Matt moves his hand from its spot against my face to my hand between us. Sliding his underneath mine, he grasps it firmly and gives it a quick squeeze.

I think Matt's hand squeezes may cure diseases one day. I might be addicted to that gentle reassurance and support he literally presses into my palm. I *might* also be addicted to a little more than his hand squeezes. *Shit.*

I strain my eyes against the darkness to study his face. He's so handsome it makes my heart thump heavily in my chest. When I looked him up that day I found out he played hockey, I had the privilege of watching him grow up through press and game day pictures. He's always been cute, even when he was drafted at eighteen and still looked so boyish with his undefined jaw and floppy hair.

He's heart-stoppingly beautiful now, with his sharper lines and little imperfections.

I can't see them clearly now, but his dark green eyes have long been burned into my memory. They remind me of Christmas trees and my favorite threadbare evergreen cardigan hanging in my closet—a gift from my mom. His scars, so different from mine, I now know are from hockey, not a bar fight or an accident. And despite knowing their cause, I find them incredibly disarming.

I might petition for the saying "aged like fine wine" to be changed to "aged like Matt Anderson." People would understand.

I use my grip on his hand to pull myself closer. Gently touching my nose to the side of his, I angle myself to give him a soft kiss. Just a quick press of my lips to his. I feel his rough exhale as his hand tightens and pulls mine up behind his neck where he releases it. Using both arms, he tugs me flush against his body and wraps himself around me as he buries his face in my neck. They tighten behind my back and...*oh*. Matt is hugging me. I swallow the sudden lump in my throat and bring my other arm around to clasp my hands there and hold on tight.

Being wrapped in his arms is bringing me a sense of comfort and peace I haven't felt in a long time. I inhale his scent that's become so familiar so quickly, and close my eyes to soak in this moment.

I used to think home was Boston, Massachusetts. The familiar shitty roads and never-ending winters. The countless Dunkin' Donuts stops and autumn walks on Crane Beach with my parents. My mom's apple pie and my childhood bedroom filled with *Free Willy* and *Grey's Anatomy* paraphernalia. My dad's quiet support through nursing school and Josh's spontaneous train trips up the coast to try every lobster roll stand we could find.

But now home is already beginning to feel like my nights tucked close to Matt Anderson.

And I'm not sure how I feel about that.

# CHAPTER TWENTY-FOUR
## *matt*

I check the digital clock on the wall—eight twenty-eight.

I've been skating alone for two hours at the rink. And practice doesn't start for another thirty minutes. I think I only slept for three hours before Ellie got home last night. I'm going to be so fucking gassed when we run drills. I'm internally groaning at that, but even holding Ellie's warm sleeping form in bed couldn't keep my restless energy at bay after that conversation.

I just had to move. Had to think. And this has always been where I've felt most at ease.

*Until recently*, my subconscious reminds me.

I'm doing loose, unhurried figure-eights around the rink as my mind spins. Ellie's mom died—no, was killed—on her birthday five years ago. And she almost died too. It's the thought that's been occupying my mind since last night. I've never felt like this before. So deeply sad for someone else and so helpless to make a difference. It feels like my heart is no longer fully in my control—like some part of it is tied to hers.

And her heart has been truly, tragically broken.

I watch my stick as I glide a puck between some others I laid out on the ice earlier, the taped blade gripping it just so. I wish I could wrap Ellie's heart in so much of this stupid tape that nothing could crack it ever again.

Ellie's strong, I *know* that. She's been through hell and she's still...here. Living and helping other people. Being amazing and wonderful and so quickly my favorite person to be around now.

But I also remember that first day at The Bar and how fragile and broken she looked. Young. Lost too, maybe. I'm so terrified of anything or anyone hurting her.

And deep down I'm worried it's going to be me—and my job. Either my inability to prioritize her or the attention that comes with it. I have to assume that's why she asked all those questions in the beginning. It might even end up being a deal-breaker.

I suck in a breath at the thought.

The first thing I feel like I have some control over. Kind of. But the other? Not really.

I cringe as my mind runs through the possibilities. I know it's inevitable, no matter how hard I try to keep things private. Eventually it will get out. Someone on the team will say something or some picture will get taken. But I don't know if Ellie knows that and I don't know *why* she's so hell-bent on it not happening. I'm trying not to take it personally or read into what it means about our future, but I'm already having trouble envisioning a future without her.

I need to talk to her about it—I should have already. I'm just so nervous of what she might say. What if she doesn't want to hang out anymore? *Fuck.* I hate that phrase. *Hang out.* It sounds so casual, so impermanent. I want this to be on her terms though. I don't want to push her or rush something she's not ready for.

I can be patient and keep things private. I just don't know if the outside world will do the same.

I brace my stick across my thighs as I make my way to the rink exit. I need to take a break before the guys show up or this is going to be an embarrassing practice. I squirt some water in my mouth and drop to the bench. Hanging my head as the thoughts still spiral, I almost feel like getting right back up and skating some more.

What if Ellie's still only interested in *us* if it's a secret? Could I convince her it will be okay if our relationship becomes public? I wish I knew why she was so against it. I just can't—*won't*—be responsible for making Ellie unhappy or scared. I'd rather rip the damn heart out of my chest.

She deserves so much better than someone who doesn't put her first after the shit she's been through. She deserves to be the priority. She deserves everything.

I just hope I can be that for her.

Yep. I'm fucking gassed as shit.

My legs are nearly shaking as I sit heavily in the locker room to take my gear off. I'm untying my skates when I feel Niko sit beside me. I can sense him studying me, but with the whole team in here I'm not really in the mood to do any explaining. I know he knows something is up. I didn't exactly *embarrass* myself at practice, but I certainly didn't perform at my usual level. And right now I just want to go crash in Ellie's bed. Maybe I can even try bringing up the future. Maybe.

"Let's go get lunch." Niko's voice halts me as I reach for my bag.

"Aren't your parents still here?" I ask him, grabbing my phone to check for any notifications.

"Yeah, but they're shopping today. They're checking out the Mall of America even though I recommended other places."

"Good luck to them," I say on a laugh. "I was planning to just head home now. How about tomorrow before the game instead?"

"I wasn't asking." Niko shoulder-bumps me as he walks out of the locker room, calling "Let's go" from the door.

*Dammit.* I check the time on my phone—a little after ten-thirty. Ellie probably won't be up for another hour or so since she's off today. Maybe I can swing by later if she's not busy. We have back-to-back games this weekend, so it might be tricky to see her before her shift starts and then we head out of town next week.

I guess I have been slacking on my friendship duties lately. I sigh and grab my shit to follow Niko out the door, catching up to him in the hallway.

"You want to go to Geno's?" I ask as I fish my keys from my bag.

"Nah, let's go to your place. I'll pick up food on the way."

I narrow my eyes a bit at that, wondering why we wouldn't just go to our usual. *What exactly is he planning?*

I leave Niko at his car and head to mine, feeling apprehensive about what kind of inquisition I'm going to get when we meet up at my place. I spend most of my drive thinking through what I'm willing to share and what still feels...off-limits. Other than Nate, I haven't talked about Ellie with anyone.

The idea of sharing with Niko certainly carries some relief. And if I'm being really honest, not hiding her in general would be a big weight lifted. But there's something about her being just *mine* right now. I don't want to keep her a secret. I just love having her all to myself and our time together feels almost sacred. Special. Like I get the privilege of getting to know this amazing person without anyone else interfering.

And while I trust Niko, I know the more people I share with, the more likely it is our relationship won't be so secret anymore.

I park my car in my garage and head inside to wait for Niko. I wonder what Ellie would think of my house? I've made sure she knows we can always come here, but I think she believes it's riskier going to my house. Even though we'd just park in the garage and it's not like anyone would see us. Hopefully I can convince her to come soon.

I look around at my kitchen and living room, trying to imagine how she might see it. She'll probably think it looks empty. Maybe plain. Ellie's apartment is full of knickknacks and color and *her*. There's tons of pictures and random framed things, like a fortune cookie message and a Red Sox ticket. It's messy and adorable and special. Other than a few plants and hung-up memorabilia, my place is pretty plain and bare of detail like hers. I don't even have enough stuff to make it messy if I wanted to. Ellie has lived in her place for less than six months and it has way more personality than my home of twelve years.

I wonder what she'd change about this place? I think she'd like the old wood floors and floor-to-ceiling windows overlooking the lake. She'd definitely like the brick fireplace and all the trinkets she could put on the empty mantel there. She seems like the type who would put up a huge Christmas tree and decorate it within an inch of its life. I imagine her balancing on a step stool to place corny ornaments on it and feel an involuntary smile pull at my lips. I bet it would be all colorful and chaotic instead of the stylish catalogue-inspired trees my previous girlfriends were always aiming for.

My eyes catch on the white rug under the leather couch and the white walls behind it. She'd hate those. She'll probably want to paint or do some kind of wallpaper that's super elaborate. I'd probably pretend to be unsure, but obviously she could do anything she wanted here and I'm sure I'd love it just because it was her choice. Those few days off in between her shifts would help with having time to decorate and make it...hers.

My chest feels tight at the thought, so I try to bring myself back to reality. We've only been together for a little while. And it's all been in secret. She might not be interested beyond that. And she works downtown, so a commute from here would be brutal.

Now that I think about it, I'm not sure Ellie has a car. Or even drives? She mentioned walking to work before.

And then it hits me.

Ellie was in a car accident. A deadly one. Is that why she walks in the freezing cold to work? I know it's close to her apartment, but it gets really cold here...

I'm jolted from my spiral when I hear a knock at my front door. I force myself to save those questions for later and go to let Niko in.

Nikolai Kotov has been on the team with me for the last fifteen years. He's a few years younger than me and is known as "Koto" to the team and most fans, but to me he's always just been Niko. He's met my family a handful of times and I've even been to Russia to visit his twice. He's quiet and loyal, a lover of Italian food and ice fishing, an extremely talented right winger, and one of the only people that I think loves hockey as much as I do. He has a slight Russian lilt when he talks and annoyingly perceptive light blue eyes that are currently narrowed at me in…skepticism.

*Here we go.*

He grunts and walks by me, headed to the kitchen to put the food down, I assume. I follow and go to untie one of the bags, but Niko pushes it away.

"Nope. Talk first. Then we can eat," he says.

I roll my eyes and walk over to the couch to sit. Niko follows me and leans against the side of the fireplace with his arms crossed. I don't love the power position he's aiming for here, but I can tell he's annoyed I've been keeping him in the dark about something.

I clear my throat. "About practice today—" I begin.

"Fuck practice. It's been weeks. Spit it out," Niko gripes.

I look at the corner of the room where I was picturing Ellie decorating a tree. I'm still staring at the made-up image when I catch movement in my periphery. Niko enters my line of sight and sits adjacent to me on the couch, slightly blocking my view of the tree corner.

I finally focus on him and nod my head behind him in the direction of my imaginary Ellie tree.

"I was picturing her decorating our Christmas tree in that corner before you got here," I say.

Niko looks to the corner and back to me. Back to the corner. He slowly faces me again with a furrowed brow before speaking. "Okay." He draws out the *y* as his brows lower farther over his eyes. "So you're in love? You're thirty-six, it's about time you settle down, no? When can I meet her? What's her name? Why have you been such a secretive little bitch about it?" His uncharacteristic, rapid-fire questions catch me off guard.

"I'm not in—" I cut myself off at the sudden realization that feels like a lie. "Shit."

I look at that corner spot again and remember the tight feeling in my chest at the image I came up with. And the helpless feeling from this morning. My earlier fantasizing about fucking *wallpaper* is making sense. I scrub my hands over my face. When I look back at Niko, I see him giving me a reserved smile.

"What's the problem, man?" he asks. "This is good, yeah?"

I roll the word around in my head. Seems accurate. Different than before though. This feels...bigger. Maybe it wasn't real in my relationships before? I cared about them a lot though. My mind is telling me it just wasn't *right* before.

I've only known Ellie a little while, I remind myself again. No need to get carried away, right?

But I do *know* her, my subconscious screams. Length of time be damned. It wasn't that long ago that I was talking to Ellie about it, actually.

I sigh and focus back on Niko and his questions. "Yeah, it's just...do you remember when I showed up late to the team meeting and then left morning skate quickly afterward? It was a few weeks ago," I tell him.

Niko studies my face with narrowed eyes. "Sure," he says slowly with a shrug.

"Well, this girl I've been seeing recently, I had just hung out with her for the first time the night before and I kind of didn't share that I played hockey. It was just nice being normal, you know. When she found out the next morning it was...a bit of a shit show, honestly. I messed it up." I wince at the memory. "But I hurried over after the skate to explain and

I think that went okay. Anyway, I convinced her to give me a shot. But I promised we could keep it secret so she wouldn't have to deal with…everything that comes with me."

I look around at my minimal memorabilia I have hung up around the room, the pictures with trophies and awards. A framed article. I used to love the idea of articles being written about me—about my job. But lately they just worry me. I look back at Niko, who's watching me with a careful expression.

"It's been good though. Great, actually. She's… You'll love her. She's so smart and funny," I tell him with a reflexive smile.

Niko grins back at me at that.

"I just know it eventually has to come out to the public if we keep seeing each other. And I really want to keep seeing her, obviously," I say as I look at the tree corner. "I don't know if she wants all of that though. We haven't talked about it since the beginning, but she basically turned me down until I offered up the idea of dating in secret. She referred to us as fuck buddies."

I laugh at that last part. *Confidential fuck buddies.*

"It was cute, but man, I hope that's not how she'll always think of us," I lament.

"So you don't know if you're on the same page? Or why she wants to keep things under wraps?" Niko asks, surprising me with his easy read on the situation.

"It feels like we are when we're together, but yeah I guess I don't know. And I'm worried she's going to call it quits if anything comes out. Or if I ask if we can be public."

Niko grimaces and nods before looking thoughtfully around the living room. "So you get on the same page and convince her it's not so bad, before some story breaks. It's not like we're fucking A-listers. Hockey fame is pretty tame. And you can teach her how to block it out, literally and mentally, like you've been trained to. How to stay private," he says, looking to me. He makes it sound like it's the most obvious thing in the world. Maybe it is. This fucker doesn't even do relationships and he's spewing decent advice. "You already do a good job of that."

I sigh and nod.

"You probably have time before anything comes out if you're being careful," he continues.

I wince again at that. I hope so. I *am* being super careful, and like Niko said, our level of fame is pretty tame. And we live in fucking Minnesota, not exactly a celeb hotspot.

"I'm sure it'll be all right, man."

I nod again even though I'm really not sure. I look over at the takeout bags on the counter and notice their logo for the first time. "So you *did* want Geno's, huh?"

I hear him mutter "Obviously" as he stands up and walks to the kitchen.

*Fucker.* I follow and take the sandwich he offers before sitting on one of my barstools.

We both eat in silence for a few minutes before Niko starts up with more questions. "So when can I meet her? What's her name? Is she old like you?" He snickers and I want to throat-punch him just a little. Apparently a three-year gap is grounds for a lifetime of "old" jokes.

"I'm not—whatever. Ellie's twenty-six. And I don't know when. She doesn't want to come to any games and I know she won't want to be seen with both of us in public," I say with a mouthful. "You never cared about meeting anyone before."

"And you never cared about fucking Christmas trees before," he grunts out between his own bites.

*Fair enough.*

"She got a last name?"

"Uh, Ford, I think? Why?"

Niko just hums as he picks up his sandwich again. We continue to eat quietly for a few minutes while I consider how Ellie would feel about meeting him. I'm not sure where it could happen other than her apartment if we are trying to stay low-key. Maybe I could have him come over with me after practice one day? I could bribe Ellie with takeout and ice cream...

"This her?"

I whip my head to Niko and see he's holding his phone out to me with a picture of a smiling Ellie on it.

"Where'd you get that?" I demand as I reach for it.

Niko raises his eyebrows at my tone and releases his phone to me. "Chill, man. I looked up her socials. God, you act so old sometimes," Niko says as he rolls his eyes and then picks up his sub again.

I study the picture up close. She looks a little younger, her freckles even more prominent than normal on her lightly sun-kissed face. The picture is dated July from two years ago. She's smiling and holding up a lobster roll. Always so fucking cute. I almost smile until I realize that fucker Josh probably took it.

I remember feeling so irrationally angry at someone I didn't even know when Ellie told me about him. Now I almost understand what he did, crazy as it sounds. I still hate the guy, obviously, but I'm guessing he was so into Ellie he didn't want to risk losing her over a decision he made before he met her.

Was lying wrong? Absolutely. Would I do almost anything to avoid losing Ellie though? Hell fucking yes. He just went about it all wrong.

I swipe out of the picture on Niko's phone and scroll through the rest of the images on her profile. There aren't many, but I enjoy seeing the ones of her with friends and family. I wonder if she's made more friends here. I know she hangs out with Dev and still talks to Zoey all the time, but I don't think I know of anyone else here yet. I make a mental note to ask her. I wish I could introduce her to some of the WAGs, but I guess that's out of the question for now.

I stop at a picture of Ellie with a middle-aged woman who looks remarkably like her. She's got the same freckles and eyes.

Her mom looks oddly familiar, but I can't really place it. Must be because I'm so accustomed to Ellie's features now.

Seeing her puts a pit in my stomach and halts my appetite. I push Niko's phone over to him and wrap up the remainder of my sandwich.

"She's pretty," Niko says, looking at the screen in front of him.

"Yeah."

*They both were.*

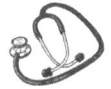

# CHAPTER TWENTY-FIVE

*ellie*

"Hey, sweetie."

"Hey, Dad. How are ya?"

It's Sunday morning, which means at eleven on the dot I can expect a call from Michael Ford. Ever since I moved, hearing his voice puts a lump in my throat. Leaving him was one of the hardest decisions I've had to make and I still sometimes wonder if it was the right one.

Most of the time though, I think we're both better off.

Even after multiple years, being around each other served as a harsh reminder of what we'd both lost. I know I'm the spitting image of my mom, and my dad is basically a different person with her gone.

I imagine looking at me cuts pretty deep—maybe the same way seeing him look so lost all the time puts a pit in my stomach. I don't know if I believe in soul mates, but I believe in love and partnership because of my parents. They just... went together. Two halves of a whole. Watching that get ripped apart was just another layer of grief.

"I'm doing pretty good. I've been asked to go speak at a university lecture this week, so that's been giving me something to look forward to. And be nervous about," he says through a laugh.

My dad is not one for public speaking, but he is one for helping others. I swallow the lump in my throat that's still lingering and work to lighten the mood in my own head. "I'm sure you'll do great. And if you don't, I doubt they'll be paying attention anyway," I tease, mimicking snoring noise.

"Very funny, Ellie," he chastises.

I chuckle at that. "I'm kiddingggg. I'm sure all the baby civil engineers will be riveted by you." I keep my laugh to myself this time.

"Well let's hope so," he says, missing my continued teasing.

"Have you gone to see the new *Star Wars* yet?" I ask him.

"Oh, not yet. I think I'll wait until I can stream it."

"What? Why? It's the first one in like five years, don't you want to go see it? You've seen them all in theaters, I thought," I ramble, confused. My dad loves *Star Wars*. Like loves with a capital L.

"Well, you know, I just don't feel like going by myself to the theater. It's not a big deal. At home I can eat while I'm watching and put subtitles on too, so it's really a win-win."

"But you could see it in IMAX, Dad! I bet Uncle Terry would go with you too. He loves those movies," I tell him.

"Terry seems like the type to talk during movies," he grumbles. "But anyway, I just used to go with your mom and I don't think I'm ready to go without her. It's really okay, sweetie. I'm excited to watch it at home in a couple months. Maybe we can even watch it together on one of your visits."

It takes me a moment to process what he just said. My dad doesn't want to go to the movies without my mom. My mom who has been gone for just over five years.

They used to go to the movies at least once a month, if not

more. It was their standard date night—dinner at the local dine-in theater. I always just assumed he was still going occasionally over the past few years.

I try to swallow that stubborn lump, but it's getting bigger and I'm starting to worry I won't be able to talk through it.

*My dad doesn't go to the movies anymore.*

I clear my throat in an attempt to get words through. "Yeah, that sounds nice, Dad. Hey, I actually have to run, but I want to hear about your talk this week, okay? Let me know how it goes," I rasp.

"Okay, sweetie, sounds good. Have a good day at work. Love you," he finishes.

"Love you too." I hang up the phone with a shaky finger and take a few breaths.

No one tells you that when one of your parents dies, you can lose the other one too.

I love my dad to pieces, but he's just…a shell of who he once was. It was so brutal to witness it in person that moving felt vital to me just *surviving*. But sometimes we have calls like this and I want to crawl home and hug him tight and take him to the goddamn movies.

Moving here is the most selfish, necessary thing I've ever done. I'm not sure if I'll ever forgive myself.

A NICE THING ABOUT MY JOB IS IT'S *LITERALLY* DANGEROUS TO let your mind drift. Staying focused is vital to keeping people safe and healthy and it means I can't dwell on the conversation with my dad from this morning. It also means I can't fantasize about seeing Matt tonight, if he decides to use his key after the game. I haven't seen him since he slept over last week and my bed has started to feel very…not full of Matt.

I don't like it.

"Hon?"

I glance up from the chart I'm working on to see Maggie leaning over the counter looking at me. She's the charge nurse and one of my favorites here at General—her gentle demeanor a painful but still welcome reminder of my mom. She's got graying blonde hair cut into a cute bob and laugh lines that speak of a good, long life. I give her a smile. "Hey, what's up?"

She doesn't smile back, instead giving me her work face. I set my pen down.

"Just got word we've got a VIP en route from the arena," she says.

"The hockey arena?"

Maggie nods. Something cold creeps down my spine, my back reflexively straightening. "A VIP?" I ask. I haven't heard that term used here before. "Like one of the players?"

"Yeah. They said EMS is about three minutes out."

There's a ringing in my ears growing louder as I try to stem my impending panic. I look down at my hands and squeeze them into fists to stop the tremors.

It's probably not even him. There are two teams there tonight, plenty of players. How many are on a team? Shit, I don't know anything about this stupid sport. He's only one guy though so the odds are pretty good, right? But I know he gets a lot of ice time…

Okay, I need to breathe. "Wait, don't they usually fix them up at the arena?" My voice cracks and I look up at Maggie. "I thought they have people for that," I say quickly, desperation slipping into my tone.

Maggie's brow pulls low and I catch her eyes studying my face with interest. "You know someone on the team, honey?" she asks quietly, leaning in toward me.

I debate for a half a second before thinking *screw it* and giving a jerky nod. Maggie isn't a gossip, and if this means she'll share more with me, I'll risk it.

Her face softens. She reaches over and puts a hand on one of mine. "I'm sure it's not him, Ellie, whoever he is. They have a lot of players there at the games. I'm sorry I don't have any other information." She seems to hesitate a moment before speaking again. "Are you gonna be okay working on this one with me? I can ask Darnell to switch over his patient to you if you'd prefer," she offers kindly.

I give myself a mental shake and put my big—professional —girl panties on. "Of course, I'll be fine. I'll meet you at the doors in just a minute," I let her know, doing my best to bury the panic in my voice.

She watches me for a moment before giving a quick nod and heading toward the ambulance entrance.

Okay. *Okay*. It's probably not Matt.

*But what if it is?*

The sheer panic I can't seem to shake makes the tremors in my hands intensify as I stand and grab some gloves. It takes two tries to pull them on and that's when I realize I need to calm the fuck down in order to do my job.

I close my eyes and take a deep breath, thinking of my triage routine rather than the what-ifs. Then I start running through the reasons a hockey player would need to be carted in via an ambulance to an emergency room. The *best* emergency room in the city. I remind myself it's also the closest and therefore most convenient. *Right*.

Okay, we've got loss of consciousness, wound that isn't

clotting, broken bone that needs to be reset ASAP, detrimental blood loss—

I'm jarred from my mental list as I hear the ambulance out front. I take a deep breath and hurry to reach the doors. Outside I'm met with the chaos of EMTs and staff from the hospital surrounding a gurney. I'm struggling to get a glimpse of the large body, but I do see black and gray. Those are Matt's team colors.

My heart might beat out of my chest.

The EMT voices sound far away, only bits of what they are relaying to the doctor coming through.

"Likely severe concussion...unconscious...unable to skate off the ice..."

I finally maneuver close enough to see the patient and promptly bend over and vomit on the ground.

# CHAPTER TWENTY-SIX

## *matt*

THE BUZZING ON THE LOCKER ROOM BENCH NEXT TO ME CATCHES my attention, my hands stopping their slow work of untying my laces. Ellie's working a shift tonight, so I know it's not her calling. It could be my mom worrying about Tyler, but I doubt they showed much of that on the broadcast. They *would* show Niko's fight defending him though.

Oh, must be my dad calling about exactly that. He's probably wanting to talk shit about the penalty Niko got after. Despite being a legit call, we all thought it was justified. Not even Coach was mad. I smile at the thought of passing off my overly chatty dad to him. But when I see who's actually calling, the smile slips from my face.

*Nate.*

It's rare for him to call when he knows I'm at the arena, especially on a game night. He usually just texts. And it's pretty rare for something at the bar to be urgent enough for me to be involved, but I'm not sure what else it could be. I pick it up hastily and slide my thumb to answer.

"Hey, man," I greet him quickly. "What's up?"

I hear some noise in the background, but it's a Sunday night so I'm guessing it's not too packed at the bar.

"Oh good, wasn't sure you'd answer. You gotta come get your girl, man."

The little alarms his words set off in my head are momentarily drowned out by a jolt of happiness. *My girl. Mine.*

Wait. Ellie, at the bar? The snap back to reality is so jarring it gives me whiplash.

I give Coach an apologetic look and awkwardly shuffle in my loose skates to the empty equipment room across the hall. "What? Ellie's at the bar? Is she okay?" I work to get my pads off with the hand that isn't holding the phone.

"Whoa, man, calm down. Sorry to freak you out. She's fine, yeah. She's just...uh...drunk," he finishes, the last word coming out quieter than the rest.

Ellie drunk? On a Sunday? I pull the phone away from my ear and look at the time. Ten twenty-four. Ellie's shift goes until three in the morning.

"She's supposed to be at work. Is she with someone? Did she say something happened with work?"

I pin the phone to my ear with my shoulder and finish getting my skates off.

"No." Nate clears his throat. "She's here alone. She didn't mention work, but she's in scrubs. Listen, I gotta go, but I'll keep an eye on her until you get here."

The phone disconnects and I grab my discarded pads and skates, sneaking back into the locker room to collect my things and throw them in my bag. I pull on some sweats and slides and try not to panic. Nate didn't say anything was *wrong*. He probably just wants me to make sure she gets home okay since she's alone. I just wish I knew why she was at the bar, drunk, instead of at work. While Ellie does consistently surprise me, this seems out of character. She loves her job and I know how seriously she takes it. She wouldn't just bail.

I grab my things and signal to Niko I'm heading out, pulling a baseball hat on to quietly make my exit. Hopefully our dominating win tonight has Coach in a good mood. I slip out the door and pick up my pace to get to my car.

Time to go get my girl.

*Is she asleep?*

I tear my gaze from the window and open the familiar door, looking to Nate in confusion. Ellie's head is resting on the hard—and probably sticky, *fuck*—bar surface, facing away from me at the far end of the room. I pull my cap low and make my way over to where she's seated. There are a handful of people here, so I'm hoping I can go unnoticed.

Nate is standing behind the bar across from Ellie, hands braced on the counter. A look of relief passes over his face when he sees me. As he leans down near Ellie's head, I watch his mouth move as he talks next to her ear. A little involuntary jealousy surfaces at the close contact. It's just *Nate*, I remind myself. I must still be keyed up from the game.

Nate's barely had time to say anything when Ellie's head shoots up off the bar and whips toward me.

A sense of calm washes over me as I scan her quickly and don't find anything too amiss. Then I take in her appearance slowly and can't help but smile. She's slightly disheveled, her ponytail loose and a few pieces falling around her face. Her cheeks are their signature pink. She's got a white long-sleeved shirt underneath her teal scrubs today and matching white sneakers.

And she's got a line on her cheek from where it was resting on the bar.

Adorable.

Ellie hiccups and slides off her stool, stumbling a little as she takes a few steps in my direction. She keeps moving until her forehead touches the top of my chest. She inhales deeply, maintaining her position against me.

"Canwegohome?"

It comes out slurred together, half muffled by my sweatshirt. I hear Nate chuckle and look up in time to see him leaving his position behind the bar to walk to some customers at the other end.

"Yeah, baby, we can go home," I tell her. I smile and kiss the top of her head, breathing in her comforting scent. Was that what she was doing to me before? Fuck, I definitely should've showered. "Do you want to walk or be carried?"

Carrying her will definitely draw more attention, but I'm also imagining the slow crawl we'll be doing if she wants to walk herself—I think she'd freeze. I'm also not going to say no to having her snuggled close to me. And I'd offer to drive, but walking will probably end up being faster and there may not even be a closer parking spot.

Ellie tilts her head back, letting her chin rest against my chest. Her pretty brown eyes are glassy and half-lidded, but focused steadily on me. Definitely drunk, but not completely fucked up. That's good.

"You're offering t'carry me?" she asks.

"I'd do anything for you, pretty girl," I tell her, swiping a thumb across her cheek.

Ellie drops her forehead back to my chest and exhales once more. I wrap my arms around her, holding her smaller frame against mine.

"Fudgenuts," she mumbles.

I laugh at her Ellie-ism, as I've come to know them, and kiss her head one more time. I've noticed she has a distinctly less-PG vocabulary in bed. I shake my head at the direction my thoughts are going and focus on Miss Disheveled here. "Is that a bad thing?"

"Mhmmm," she drags out.

*Huh.* I feel a small amount of unease at that, but I'm going to chalk it up to the liquor for now. "Let's walk out together and then I'll carry you when we're outside, okay? That will draw less attention," I tell her.

She picks her head up off my chest and nods. "Mmk."

I take a step over to her chair and grab her parka from where it hangs on the back, quickly putting it on her and zipping it all the way up to her chin. I drop a chaste kiss on her lips because I can't help myself. "Do you have a hat or earmuffs, baby?"

Ellie's eyes shift along the bar and then around the floor, finally meeting mine as she shrugs her shoulders. I hold in my laugh and reach over to search her pockets, finding success in her right one. I pull the earmuffs out and settle them around her head, making sure her ears are covered.

I step back to inspect my handiwork and feel satisfied she'll be warm enough for the short walk to her apartment. Clasping her hand in mine, I pull her through the small tables to the front of the bar. I turn and look for Nate, giving him a nod, both as a thanks and to let him know I'm leaving with Ellie. He gives a nod in return and starts putting some bottles away to begin closing the bar.

Ellie drags her feet as we step outside, the cold a striking contrast to where we're coming from. I wonder if it'll sober her up a bit or if she's too drunk to notice much.

"Brrrrrr," she says with a shiver.

I lean down to scoop her up, one arm going under her legs and the other behind her back. She puts her arms around my neck and somehow her fingers are already cool where they touch my skin. I hold her close to my chest and pay extra attention to where I'm walking so I don't slip on any ice. Precious cargo and all that.

"I like Nate," she sighs. It comes out borderline *dreamy* and I'm about to have some questions when she continues. "He gave me so many drinks. For freeeee," she sings.

I chuckle at her reasoning. "You know, given that I own The Bar with Nate, I kind of gave you the drinks for free too. Does that mean you like me?"

"Oooh, that's a good point. But isn't that your job already?"

I smile. "What exactly is my job, Ellie?"

"Well, let's not talk about your *job* job, but your *boyfriend* job definitely entails getting me drinks, right?"

I try to remind myself she's drunk and it doesn't count, but her use of the word *boyfriend* is giving me a high right now. "Yes, baby, it's my job to get you drinks. What else am I in charge of?"

"Hmm. This is good, us brainstorming like this. I like lists," she says.

I obviously wasn't expecting to dislike a drunk Ellie, but I also wasn't expecting to be this entertained. It's a good distraction from how fucking cold it is right now. Thank god I can see the door to her building a block up ahead.

"Let's put food first on the list. Food is my priority," she says seriously.

"Food, check. What's next?"

"Sex. The good kind."

"Is there a bad kind?"

"Well not with you yet, but I don't want you phoning it in."

I stifle my laugh and nod. "No 'phoning it in' sex, got it. What else?" I walk up the few steps to the building and lean Ellie against the door as I punch the code.

"How d'ya know the code?"

"You texted it to me after you gave me the key," I remind her. Although I might have seen her enter it and memorized it before then. But she doesn't need to know that. I push the door open and step inside.

"Oh right, duh. Ohmygod it's so much warmer in here." Ellie squirms out of my arms and I steady her so she doesn't fall.

As soon as she's out of my grasp she bolts up the stairs, leaving me in her metaphorical dust. I laugh at her surprising speed based on her current level of inebriation and file away that drunk Ellie might be a bit of a runner.

I trudge up the stairs, feeling the strain in my legs from the game and the walk home with Ellie in my arms. When I get to her apartment the door is ajar and the lights are on. And her scrubs are on the floor in a breadcrumb trail leading to her bathroom. I close and lock the door, take off my jacket and shoes, and make my way over to the bathroom. The shower is on and steam rises from above the curtain. I can hear Ellie humming. *How the hell did she get in here so fast?*

I sit on the closed toilet and peel the curtain back a few inches to check on her.

Ellie shrieks.

"Matt! What are you doing here? You almost gave me a heart attack."

"You saw me like two minutes ago, baby," I tell her on a smile. "But I'm sorry I scared you. Do you want me to head out?"

*Please don't say yes.*

"Will you sleep over if you stay?"

"I'd always prefer to sleep with you."

"Even in my small bed?"

"Even in your small bed," I confirm.

"Okay."

"Okay." *Phew*. "Ellie?"

"Hmm?"

"Can you tell me what happened with work today?"

Ellie looks down at her feet, pointing them in and out. "I got sick," she mumbles.

"You're sick?" I think of all the alcohol she's had and how that definitely isn't going to help if she's got something. She didn't seem sick though…

"No. I *got* sick," she says, as if that clarifies anything.

She got sick, she got sick… I feel like I'm deciphering a code. "I don't understand Ellie, sorry."

"I, ya know…" She gestures with her hand coming from out of her mouth.

*Oh.*

"You threw up? Was there something really…gross?" Is that bad to ask a nurse?

Ellie looks up from her feet finally and levels me with an insulted look. Okay, definitely not the right thing to ask.

"I do not get *grossed* out, thank you very much," she huffs.

I hold my hands up in surrender. Drunk Ellie is a little feisty. "I'm sorry, I just know there is plenty that would gross me out. What made you sick?"

She looks back down at her feet and I can see her face get redder than before. She's embarrassed? She's also drunk, so maybe I'm reading too much into this. But I am kind of getting desperate to figure out what happened today.

"I...I think maybe it was adrenaline. From stress, ya know?"

"Your job sounds incredibly stressful," I agree.

Ellie glances up and studies my face. It looks like she's deciding something. I keep my gaze steady on her and hope what she sees there is good enough for whatever it is she's pondering. Her throat bobs as she swallows. I feel like I'm on the edge of my seat.

"I thought it was you."

Ellie's eyes water and I feel a small crack in my chest. It takes me a moment to put it together. Jesus Christ. I fucking forgot about Tyler.

"They brought Tyler to your hospital," I surmise.

She nods and I hear a small sniff.

"I'm okay, baby. And they let us know that Tyler is too. He just got a bad concussion and will probably be out for a while to be safe. Maybe the rest of this season."

She nods and sniffs again.

My girl was worried about me being hurt. *Really* worried. That aforementioned crack is getting a little bigger.

I look at Ellie's soaked hair and wet body. She's standing under the water, presumably for the warmth, and there's something about her in this moment that looks so fragile. It almost reminds me of that day I met her at The Bar.

I think it's time for her to sleep off this alcohol. Hopefully she feels okay in the morning. Maybe I could bring her hangover-cure food before she heads to work? I could stop and pick it up after practice...

A gut-wrenching whimper stops my train of thought in its tracks. "Ellie?"

"My dad—" She hiccups. "Doesn't go—" Another hiccup.

"To the movies anymore." The last word is barely audible as Ellie starts sobbing in earnest.

My hands freeze midair where I was reaching for a towel. They hover now, trying to figure out what to do—how to help. Ellie crying like this might be the most heartbreaking thing I've ever experienced and I don't even know what she's talking about. "Your dad?"

"I don't wanna end up like that," she cries.

"Like what, baby?"

"Broken. He lost her and now he's broken."

That crack in my chest becomes a damn chasm as Ellie's body shakes with each sob. I panic and abandon the towel, stepping into the shower and hugging her to my chest *hard*. I don't know what to say to her or how to make this better. There's a part of me—a small, sick part—that feels a rush of warmth at what she might be implying here. But the bigger part of me—the one that doesn't want Ellie to be sad—knows I don't have the slightest clue how to talk to her about her dad.

My knee-jerk reaction is to say something like "that won't happen to you" or "he's not broken." But Ellie knows better than anyone that this *could* happen and she certainly knows her dad better than me. Maybe he really is broken. Losing someone like that is enough to break anyone.

I think of Ellie and how badly I don't want her to be feeling this way right now. How losing her would certainly break me. I'd crack my chest open the rest of the way and hand her my heart if I thought it would make a difference.

I think though, based on the way I feel right now, she might have already taken my heart. And I think she might have realized that I'm holding hers too.

I remember how I thought just a *part* of my heart was tied to hers. Like it wasn't fully in my control. But now it feels like she *owns* it. I want to relish that, to treasure this moment and how big it feels. To be vulnerable like this—knowing our hearts belong to one another. But based on her current state, I'm not sure Ellie wants someone else to own her heart.

I pull her tighter against my chest and rest my chin on her head. Her sobs are quieter now, soft shudders racking her body. I realize for the first time that I still have my clothes on. They're soaked, the weight of them more noticeable. What feels heavier though? Ellie's reluctant heart in my hands.

*I'm going to take really good care of this heart*, I vow. Help her through hard times and figure out how to talk to her about these difficult things. I'll keep it safe.

She's going to have to pry it from my hands if she wants it back.

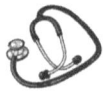

# CHAPTER TWENTY-SEVEN
## *ellie*

Sometimes when I think about my mom it feels like I can't breathe.

Like grief took a physical form and decided to hold me underwater, forcing its attention on me as if it's gone too long neglected. Forcing me to fight it. To struggle for my own breath.

And sometimes fighting is really, really hard. Too hard.

I haven't been able to fight it today—haven't even been able to get out of bed. I don't even know what time it is. Called out sick for the first time since moving here. Today is just about trying to breathe. Because I think that's all I can manage. How am I supposed to save anyone else when I feel like I'm drowning?

It sounds dramatic, I know that. But it feels worse.

I remember back in high school my best friend Savannah found out her dad had cancer. All of a sudden my problems seemed so small. Who cared about a physics exam grade when faced with the reality that your parents could get sick? It was a horribly sobering thought for a sixteen-year-old. Talk about a formative experience. Obviously the perception of your problems is relative, but that was a pivotal moment for me. It gave me perspective on how to look at life's big and small obstacles in a way that took some of the pressure off.

Off of being an all-A student, or off of losing my virginity in a *special* way, or just off of navigating big, real feelings like heartbreak or guilt.

But then it felt like my world tilted on its axis when my mom died. My entire barometer for how to view the world was shifted. Irreparably damaged. Instead of normal problems feeling small, they felt *irrelevant*. How could I care about anything else when my favorite person in the world was taken from me? Nothing mattered anymore. Because the biggest problem I could imagine facing had happened to me and that left me...empty. Aimless.

Time has helped with finding purpose again, but that emptiness just never fully goes away. Like something in my body is permanently missing.

Most days it's a dull ache in my bones. Just a gentle, unpleasant reminder I can't quite banish. Sometimes it spikes to a shock of pain if a particular memory comes up or if something catches me off guard. Like Matt bringing up his mom for the first time, or Maggie from work calling me "honey" like my mom used to.

Some days it's worse. Maybe more like a headache—not debilitating, but something that's impossible to ignore. It puts a bit of a grief filter on everything, making work a little harder and socializing impossible. The anniversary and pretty much all holidays are guaranteed headache days.

And then occasionally...occasionally it's hard to breathe. And on those days I take a pass on life and let the sadness consume me. It would be convenient if these days happened when I was off work or didn't have plans, but grief doesn't adhere to a schedule. It doesn't care about your plans. Grief's an attention whore and some days it's just all about her.

I can never really predict when these days will strike. It could have no impetus at all and catch me totally unaware—just an unexpected, really bad day from the moment I open my eyes. Other days it's something I probably should've seen coming. Like realizing I've fallen for someone special, someone who could be taken from me one day.

I bury the thought as deep as I possibly can.

No matter what the cause—obvious or not—these are the days of the Terrible and Depressing Thoughts. Like the Things My Mom Won't Be Around For or, my favorite, the Things I Won't Ever Experience Again. Just some light, easy topics to mull over.

Sometimes it's the smallest thing that will get stuck in my head on these days. A tiny thought that steals my breath and ability to even function.

*I'm never going to eat my mom's apple pie again.*

It's the thought that's been playing on a loop today, making this fight a losing battle. Every time it cycles through my mind it's like a fresh wave hits me and pulls me under again.

*It's just pie. It's just pie. It's just pie.*

I turn over and push my face into my pillow, pulling the covers up and over my head. I wish I could fall asleep and have some blissful ignorance for a bit. I'd even take as little as a few minutes. Because this full *awareness* is crushing me. Awareness that it's just pie, yeah, but I'll never have her pie again because she's gone. And she and her pie will never, ever be back.

And there are so. Many. Never-agains.

I'm never going to hear my mom's voice again. That one is uniquely crippling and one of my most common Terrible and Depressing Thoughts. She had such a nice voice. As an elementary school teacher she had that gentle, warm cadence locked in. It was so calming and just...lovely. And I loved hearing it slip when she'd use some creative non-curse word or on the rare occasions when she'd lose her temper. I still find myself using her silly, made-up curses. Sometimes I can almost hear them in her voice.

Some days it feels like I can't quite remember it though. Like it's on the edge of my mind but I can't bring it forward in full clarity. And I know one day it will be a distant memory—something I can only recall through a saved voicemail or video on my phone.

Grief can turn even the sanest into unstable hoarders. I have voicemails and videos, moth-eaten shirts and dumb birthday cards. Random movie ticket stubs and fortune cookie papers. When I come across something of my mom's or something that makes me think of her, I feel compelled to keep it, treasure it. There won't be any new memories with her or new knickknacks. No new voicemails or videos.

No new anything.

I'm never going to hear my mom's voice or eat her apple pie ever again. Isn't that the stupidest, most heartbreaking thing you've ever heard?

All because some people decided to get drunk and then drive. Consequences be damned.

I try to hold on to the anger that flashes at the thought, but it's fleeting and drastically overshadowed by the agony that is grief and her attention-whoring ways. It was easier at first, when things were still raw, to let the rage take over for periods of time. The anger was uncomplicated and simple. Distracting.

And I could really go for a distraction.

I roll onto my back and pull the covers away from my face to stare at the ceiling. I'm still not sure what time it is, but I don't think I care.

I don't think I care about anything right now.

ONE OF MY FAVORITE THINGS IN THE WORLD IS WHEN MY MOM plays with my hair. I think I have it logged as some core memory—something she started doing when I was so little I can't remember a time before. Sometimes she did it absentmindedly when I was watching TV with her. Other times I knew she did it to help me fall asleep faster, the gentle movement stronger than even any medication with "drowsiness" listed as a side effect. My clearest memories are when she did it to make me feel better though. Like when I had a fever that wouldn't go away for four days or when I cried after breaking up with Chase Griffin so I wouldn't go to college "tied down."

She hasn't combed her fingers through my hair in so long. I wonder why she's doing it now? Maybe I fell asleep on her lap and she's watching a show or reading a book? Whatever the reason, I fight to stay asleep so she doesn't stop.

Unfortunately, there's just something about trying to stay asleep that immediately triggers your brain to *wake up wake up wake up*. And my sudden awareness causes my breath to catch and a fresh set of tears to build behind my eyes. I peek them open as the tears slip out and see Matt's long legs, crossed at the ankles, extending out under me. He must be back from practice. I blink a few times to try to clear the tears, an involuntary sniff coming out louder than a bomb in the otherwise silent room. The hand in my hair stills.

"Ellie?"

I sniff again and then rearrange myself, rolling to face the other direction on Matt's thigh and look up at him. He doesn't have a hat today and his hair is unkempt on top. I'd call it bed head if I thought it had gotten that way from sleep. His gray T-shirt looks like it should be retired soon with its fading Bears logo and tiny hole near the collar. It's probably really soft. My fingers twitch thinking about touching it.

Matt's hand comes to my wet face, thumb catching the tears that steadily leak out. I focus on his eyes the best I can. They look sad.

"Hey, baby," he says gently.

"My mom used to do that..." I sniff. "With my hair." Matt's face crumples a bit at my words and his thumb stills. "I'm having a bit of a bad day. Called out of work a little ago."

Matt's eyes move around my face and he nods slowly. "I'm happy sitting here with you, but I can leave if that would be easier," he says as he grabs my hand and brings it to his mouth for a soft kiss.

I don't feel any different—any less sad—but there's something to be said for not being alone.

"You can stay."

Matt exhales and kisses my hand again before setting it back down. "Is there anything I can do?" he says.

I hear a desperation in his voice I haven't before. I wish there was something *I* could do to make *him* feel better, but I don't think I'm capable. I shake my head and scoot forward, burying my face in that gray shirt that smells like Matt. I knew it would be this soft. I make a mental note to steal it.

He hesitantly puts his hand in my hair, probably unsure if he should continue something that caused tears only a few moments ago. I hum against his stomach and let the memories flood my mind, accepting the simultaneous torture and bliss.

# CHAPTER TWENTY-EIGHT

## *matt*

I'M TRYING TO PICK WHICH SUITS TO TAKE ON THIS TRIP, BUT ALL I can think about is how long ten fucking days is going to feel. Occasionally a string of away games line up perfectly so that it makes more sense to just stay on the road instead of coming back home in between any. So now I'll be gone for a week and a half at arguably the worst possible time.

Ellie reassured me when I left this morning that she was feeling better. She said she was planning to go to work and would make sure to text me the name of a podcast she heard about before my flight, in case I wanted to listen. Something about sci-fi movie reviews, I think. My heart swells at her thoughtfulness and then thumps so heavily I feel sick. My sweet, sunshine-y girl was so sad yesterday she couldn't get out of bed.

When I came back over after practice to drop off some hangover food before her shift started, I thought she was just oversleeping. Then I heard her delicate sniff and nearly dropped the takeout bags in my hands. She didn't even hear me open the door.

The memory of her tearstained face and vacant eyes is

going to haunt me every moment of this damn trip. I'm not sure if being there was helpful, but the idea of not being there if she goes through that again is just...unthinkable. I had to semi-force her to eat and drink.

Does one bad day mean she's more likely to have another one soon? Or does it kind of reset? Did something trigger it? Are there even rules around this kind of thing? The questions are never-ending.

I feel so far out of my depth it's almost laughable, except nothing about this is remotely funny. I'm trying to think of what I can do while I'm gone to not feel so damn useless. And to not worry myself sick.

We're also over halfway through March and closing in on playoffs, which means every match-up is getting more crucial. Not having my head in the game isn't really an option.

My phone buzzes, dragging my attention away from the suits in front of me. Looks like Ellie sent me that podcast. She says Zoey recommended it.

Suddenly an idea comes to me. Two ideas, actually.

I grab two suits at random and throw them in a garment bag. I know I have to leave in a few minutes to make the team flight, but I now have some calls to make and need to download a different type of podcast. The sci-fi one will have to wait.

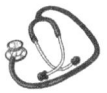

# CHAPTER TWENTY-NINE
## *ellie*

"I've decided to forgive you, on one condition."

I narrow my eyes. "I wasn't aware I was in need of forgiveness."

"Yes, we'll get to that. So this condition is simple."

I raise my eyebrows and brace myself. Zoey's idea of simple is not usually the same as mine. The last time she declared our itinerary for the group vacation *simple*, we barely had enough time to eat between activities. "All right, hit me."

"Take me to The Bar."

"That's it?" I raise my eyebrows. The simplicity of the request has me suspicious.

"That's it."

"Okayyyy..." I say, still perplexed. "Now?" It's just after eight and Zoey got in a few hours ago. From a flight and subsequent car service Matt set up. My insides go all melty thinking about him and everything he did to orchestrate this surprise. *For me*. All I've been able to do was text him a massive thank-you so far and a selfie of me smooching Zoey's face. I think my excitement was palpable.

She was only able to get two days off and I work Sunday, so

we really only have the rest of tonight and then Friday and Saturday to hang. I plan to make the most of it.

Matt booked her return flight for Sunday morning. He's the main topic we haven't gotten to yet, and I have a feeling Zoey is trying to figure out how to ask me about him. I mean as far as she knows, my *fuck buddy* freaking *flew her out here*. She's got to have questions.

It's been a while since we've really caught up and all she knew up to this point was I was casually seeing someone. *Sleeping* with someone. By now she knows who he is and probably that it's more than casual sex, based on everything he did to get her here. I've been struggling with that fact myself, so I haven't wanted to bring it up then or now.

"Yeah, let's do it! If you're up for it?" she asks hopefully.

I'm still not sure why she wants to go to Matt's bar, but it's walking distance and it'd be nice to see Nate, if he's there. Maybe I can apologize for last Sunday.

"Let me just change out of my sweats," I tell her, hopping off the bed we've been lazing around on to search for some jeans. I grab a pair and drop my sweatpants to pull them on. "I can't believe you flew in a cute outfit. I always go in, like, the most comfortable thing I can find. I usually look like a hot mess. Minus the hot."

Zoey looks at her own jeans and shrugs. "The flight's only a few hours and I thought I should look less like a plebe in first class. Though I totally fucked that up anyway." She sighs.

I pause buttoning my pants and look at her, already grinning. "What did you do?"

Zoey rolls her lips together, hesitating. "They handed me what I thought was like a mint or something. In my defense, they didn't say *anything* and they used tongs, so I figured it was edible. I didn't realize what it actually was until I tried to bite it."

*Oh no.* "What was it?"

"A fucking warm towelette," Zoey cackles. "I wanted to melt into the floor when I realized."

We both laugh so hard we end up in tears.

"Ellie, good to see you again." Nate taps the bar with his knuckles and slides a napkin in front of me. "And you must be Zoey?" He slides one to her as well and flashes a crooked smile. *What a flirt.* He must have talked to Matt. "What can I get you ladies?"

"Ooh, how about—"

"If the question involves tequila, the answer is no," Nate interrupts with a straight face. I stare at him with an open mouth. "Matt already thinks I gave you too much." He puts his hands up.

"I was going to say 'how about *something fun*,'" I huff. "And apologize for Sunday." It comes out as a grumble. Maybe if he hadn't started that way, the apology would've been nicer.

He waves off my half-assed apology. "Are you asking me to make you a girly cocktail?"

"In case you haven't noticed, we are girls. I was thinking a sour or something bubbly maybe?" I flutter my lashes dramatically and place my hands together in prayer position.

"How about a cider?"

"Ooh, yum. I'm in." I clap my hands and Nate's mouth twitches.

"Cider for you too, Zoey?" He pivots slightly to look at her. I glance over only to see her giving us a big, cheesy grin.

"I'll just take a sauvignon blanc, please. Thanks."

"You got it," Nate confirms, leaving to go grab our drinks on the other side of the bar.

"So this is Matt's bestie?"

"Yeah, they grew up together," I tell her.

"He seems nice."

"I don't know him that well, but yeah, he is. So how was Chandler's baby shower? I feel bad I couldn't make it." Am I avoiding the Matt conversation? *Maybe*. But I also want to know.

"Nah, don't feel bad. We all missed you, but honestly you lucked out. Not only did they make us play 'guess the poop,' but Josh asked about you like seven times. Dude needs to take a hint."

I ignore her Josh comment. He's also reached out to me a handful of times, but I'm just not interested in reconnecting in any way. "Guess the poop?"

"It was melted candy bars in diapers, Ellie. *Diapers*."

She shudders and it makes me laugh. I missed her so much. Moving away from friends sucks.

"Promise me you won't make me play that game when you have kids."

"I promise," I say, looping my pinky with hers and then letting go. "All right, now that I've met your condition, are you going to tell me what you've forgiven me for?"

Zoey raises a single eyebrow at me. "I think you know, Ellie-bellie," she sings.

*Fudge*.

Nate reappears with our drinks and sets them down. "I'm so going to call you that now." He winks and I roll my eyes as he leaves, looking back at Zoey.

"Well, go on," I direct. "Ask me what you want." I knew this was coming, and I know she isn't really one to pry, but I'm still nervous for some reason.

Zoey takes a sip of her wine before talking. "Fine. Why didn't you tell me your *fuck buddy*"—she uses air quotes with her non-drink hand—"was a famous hockey player? And when were you going to tell me he wasn't just a fuck buddy?"

It's busy for a Thursday, so I glance around to see if anyone is overhearing us. It's not exactly the best place for an important conversation, but I don't want to blow her off. Zoey's not smiling, so I know she's not just joking around with me. And I know her well enough to know she's not *mad*. But as I look at the question in her eyes and remember how she used the word *forgive*, I realize it's almost worse. Zoey's hurt I didn't tell her.

"I'm sorry," I start. I sigh and take a glug of my cider. "I... don't have a good excuse. It's not that I didn't tell *just* you, you know? I haven't told *anyone*. Dev only knows because she ran into him at my apartment one night. And despite her efforts, I haven't given her any details, really. I guess I'm feeling...I don't know. Something that's keeping me from wanting to talk about it." I pause. "And you know how I feel about hockey, so that's been..." My nose scrunches as I trail off.

"Oh, Ellie. I didn't think about that. Shit, I'm sorry." Zoey squeezes my hand that's resting on the bar and I know I'm forgiven. She's quiet as she threads our fingers together. "It's okay to not want to talk about it, I just want to be there for you. I want to know about your life," she says. "It's really weird being this far apart, and being in the dark on this just made it such a stark change from before. I was worried I was losing you a bit."

"No. No, never." I squeeze our hands together tighter. "If I was going to tell anyone, it would be you." I look Zoey in the eyes and think of all of our conversations over the years about boys and feelings and…so much more. "I don't know what I'm doing," I admit.

"With Matt?"

I nod and drink more. "Like *sex*?" Zoey mouths the second word.

"No, that's all…good. Better than good," I say as my cheeks turn scarlet, I'm sure.

Zoey's brow draws down as she studies me. "Okay, we'll circle back to that later. Is it about being more than fuck buddies?"

Why she chooses to mouth the word *sex* but can say *fuck buddies* at full volume confounds me, but luckily no one seems to be paying us any attention over here at the far end of the bar.

I shrug, unsure how to talk about this. "I just haven't felt this way before," I finally come up with.

"Oh, Ellie-bellie," Zoey sighs sadly. "What about Josh? You guys were in love, right?"

It's funny how Josh feels like an afterthought now. Like my time with him was years ago instead of months. Is it possible that the time away from that relationship is why it feels less… strong? I remember feeling love for Josh, but not this all-consuming intensity. My gut tells me it's because I wasn't *in* love with him. Like maybe I subconsciously kept him at arm's length to avoid this mess. Maybe my subconscious knew he wasn't worth it. I'm not sure how I feel about that. "I thought we were," I murmur.

Zoey's answering smile is so big I have to rethink what I said. "What?"

She hums. "Eleanor Anderson. Ellie Anderson. Oh yeah," she says. "Has a nice ring to it, like royalty or something."

I swallow at the implication and drop my head. I'm transported back to the other night when I had a little breakdown.

"Hey." Zoey's soft voice is closer now. I look up at her. "That was a stupid joke. I'm just excited. This is the real deal, I feel like. It's good, right? You deserve more than what you had with Josh, whether it was real love or not."

I feel a sting behind my eyes and my throat gets thick. This is why I didn't want to have *this* conversation. Movement behind the bar catches my eye and I see Nate cleaning a glass, eyes on me. He looks concerned so I give him a small smile in reassurance. He waits a beat before dipping his head and turning back to another customer. I face Zoey and realize she watched that whole interaction.

I clear my throat. "What if he leaves me?"

Zoey's face scrunches up. "Ellie, I'm pretty sure he's obsessed with you. He's not going to leave—" Zoey must put something together in her mind. "Oh."

She takes a sip of her wine and then sets it on the bar. She seems to be thinking something over. A few moments later she swivels to face me fully, her knees hitting the side of my leg.

She grabs both of my hands. "Ellie."

I look at her hands holding mine and feel that unique brand of solidarity only your friends can give you. Zoey's always been there for me and knows me just about as well as anyone could. "I'm scared." It comes out barely above a whisper as I sit staring at our hands.

"I know. Love is scary. You know that better than anyone. But what would life be like without it? The life you had with Josh, is that what you want? Looking back and thinking *maybe* it was love? Some halfhearted relationship?" She squeezes my hands again and I look at her. "Love you're scared to lose is love worth fighting for, even if you're fighting yourself. You deserve to be with someone who fights for that love *with* you. Someone who knows what they're up against and keeps going anyway." She gives me a look. "Someone who loves you so hard they worry about leaving you after a really bad day, and flies your best friend in for backup."

I think back to Monday, how after he realized what was going on, Matt never left my bed until I did except to get me food. "I think he's listening to a grief podcast for me," I tell her. "I saw the title on his phone when he sent me a screenshot of this plant watering app he's so geeked over."

Zoey laughs lightly at that. "As he should," she says with authority and a soft smile. "Has he told you yet?"

"That he's listening to that podcast?"

"That he's in love with you."

I shake my head and then cringe. "I had a drunken breakdown the other day where I basically told him I didn't want to be in love. Probably bummed him out."

"Nah, I bet it was the most endearing, non-confession of love he's ever gotten." Zoey nudges my leg with her knee. "I know it's not feeling like a good thing right now, but I'm really, really happy for you, Els." She looks over at Nate, who notices and starts heading our way. "And I'm so glad you've got people looking out for you here," she whispers close to me before he reaches us.

"Everything okay?" Nate asks as he leans on the bar.

"Perfect. We were just getting hungry and I was wondering if you had a recommendation?" Zoey asks him.

I didn't know *we* were getting hungry, but I guess I could always eat.

Nate starts asking questions about what type of food and I let them know I'm going to the bathroom. By the time I'm headed back to my seat it looks like they are talking about something way more serious than takeout. Nate looks...sad? I look to Zoey as I get closer and she's got her teacher face on. *Oh boy.*

She stops talking as I get to my seat. "What's she lecturing you about?" I ask Nate.

He looks at me. There's a distinct edge of sympathy clouding his face now. I narrow my eyes. Nate clears his throat and does his best to wipe the expression away. "Ah, just that we should really serve food at the bar." He tries to smile but it doesn't look right.

I doubt that's what they were talking about, but I nod.

"You ready to go? He said there's a good burger place around the corner, walking distance," Zoey says.

"Yeah, sure." I drink the remainder of my cider and ask Nate for the check. He waves that off and collects our empty glasses.

Zoey loops her arm through mine as we walk out of The Bar.

"So what did you say to Nate?"

She gives me an innocent smile. "Just gave him a quick talk."

"A talk."

"Mhm."

"Zoeyyy," I whine. "Please tell me you didn't scare off one of my newest friends here. He may not even call us friends yet. Not to mention he's Matt's bestie."

"Hey, it's not like I could lecture Matt! He bought me a first-class flight to come visit you. I just wanted to be sure I got the message across."

I cringe. "What message?"

"The same message every best friend has the right to give. Hurt my BFF and I'll kill you."

"Zoey! I'm not dating Nate! Isn't that message for boyfriends?"

"I know. I told him to pass it along to Matt."

*Great.* "Then why'd he look at me like—" *Goddammit.* "Did you tell him about my mom?"

Zoey looks sheepish now. "I just wanted him to understand the gravity of my message."

I sigh and tighten my arm around hers. What are best friends for if not to threaten the guy you're dating through their friends?

Wait. I stop walking. "Is that why you wanted to go to The Bar?"

"To my credit, we got a free drink out of it too."

"You're ridiculous," I mutter.

"I have never pretended not to be."

I smile and drag her forward. "Let's go eat, you maniac."

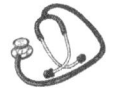

# CHAPTER THIRTY

*ellie*

I tiptoe out of my room, leaving a sleeping Zoey in my bed. It's just after eleven and I have something I want to do before I fall asleep. I checked and it's not a game day, so I'm hopeful he's still awake and free.

I curl up on the couch and pull a blanket up under my chin, tapping Matt's contact on my phone. He picks up on the second ring.

"Hi, baby." The low timbre of Matt's voice puts little butterflies in my stomach.

I'm never going to get sick of that sound. The excitement and comfort I feel hearing him is such a heady combination. "Hi," I say, just above a whisper.

"Why are you being so quiet?"

"Zoey's asleep in my bed. I snuck out to the couch to call you."

Matt sighs. "I'm jealous of your friend."

"I can't believe you flew her out for me. I don't know what to say." I swallow. "Thank you."

"It was nothing," he says dismissively. "I'm just glad my

agent found her number for me and she was able to come. It was a good surprise?"

"It's definitely not nothing, but yes, the best surprise."

"Good. I, uh, wanted to ask you about something actually."

I settle back into the couch farther, content to close my eyes. "I'm all ears."

"I talked to my parents earlier today and they're planning to come visit for a week or two, maybe more." Matt pauses, either hesitating or waiting for me, I'm not sure. I hear him clear his throat. "Would you like to meet them while they're here?"

I feel my lips pull up. Was he nervous to ask me? "I'd love to. When are they coming?"

Matt exhales before he speaks again. "They get in next Friday, the day after I get back. I was thinking maybe we could all have dinner at my place?"

I internally cry at the idea of having to get myself there, but I know I'm due for a drive to make sure I don't fully break down whenever I get in the car next. My therapist in Boston recommended I try driving once a month, if possible. It's been just a little bit longer than that. Okay, a lot. I stifle a sigh. At least it means finally seeing Matt's place and the people who raised him. "That sounds great. Are they just visiting for fun?"

"Kind of. They'll probably go to our home games while they're here, maybe the closer away ones too. They are definitely going to try to convince you to go to one with them, so I apologize in advance."

I wince, but that sounds like a problem for future Ellie. No need to panic now. "I'm excited to meet them. Do you talk on the phone with them a lot?"

"I try to call every week."

Ugh, that's so cute. "My dad calls me every Sunday," I tell him. I'm not sure what compelled me to.

"Yeah? Michael, right? What does he like to talk about?"

"Yep, that's him. Oh, you know, normal dad stuff. Work, things he sees on the news, TV shows and whatnot."

"Sounds like my dad. You miss him?"

"All the time."

Matt's quiet for a few moments. "Maybe I could meet him if he comes to visit?"

I swallow the sudden emotion in my throat. "He's a bit of a homebody, but maybe you could come with me to Boston next time I visit him."

Another pause and then, "I'd like that very much."

I smile and hold the phone tighter. "He's a big sci-fi guy, so you'll have plenty to talk about."

"Ah, finally someone who will appreciate my little alien movies."

"Yeah, well, we can't all be *E.T.* fanatics."

Matt barks out a laugh. I yawn and open my eyes to look at the time on my phone. I should probably go to bed. Knowing Zoey, she'll be up at some ungodly hour. I tell that to Matt.

"Ellie?"

"Yeah?"

The line is quiet for a while.

"I just...miss you. Dream of me, okay?"

"Bossy," I jokingly tut, knowing that happens every night anyway.

# CHAPTER THIRTY-ONE

## *matt*

"Looks like she's here."

My mom's voice is carefully neutral, but I can hear the barely contained excitement just beneath the surface. I wasn't sure how to talk to my parents about Ellie, with us being *confidential* and all that, so I waited as long as possible to bring her up on one of our weekly calls. And even though I gave a disclaimer about things being casual, I can tell my mom knows something is different. She hasn't pressed me much for more details, but I can tell she wants to.

And now as I watch her imitate an overexcited dog at the window by the door, I begin to wonder if she'll be able to be cool during this dinner with Ellie. Leave it to her to use the "g" word—girlfriend. Or worse, something about the future. I mentally prepare to run interference to make sure she doesn't freak Ellie out.

"Is she okay? She's just sitting there," my mom says lightly, mild concern clouding her face as she looks back at me in the foyer.

"I'm sure she's fine, Mom. But if she sees you in the window like a damn golden retriever, she might not be."

My mom huffs and lets the curtain close before retreating to the living room. I peek out the same drape my mom just left and notice what she did—Ellie sitting in her car. I haven't seen her in over a week and, despite my admonishing, it could easily be me doing exactly what my mom was. In fact, what I'd really like to do is walk out there and yank her out of the car for a hug and *maybe* a little more. It took everything in me not to let myself into her place after we got home last night, but it was almost two in the morning and I didn't want to wake her up.

I'm about to force myself to turn away and let her have her moment when I notice her hands are still gripping the wheel. *Huh.* I watch her for another minute, waiting to see if she moves. She doesn't.

*To give her space or go see if she's okay...* I hem and haw for a moment, then remember one of the things I heard on the grief podcast. It's easier for someone to turn down help than it is to ask for it. *Right.* That makes up my mind and I swing open the front door to walk over to her. I'm keenly aware she still isn't moving as I get closer. Ellie's car is an older-model sedan, the navy color making it nondescript. It looks to be in good shape, but I'm not much of a car guy.

I slow my approach to the driver's side door, careful not to surprise her. Up close now I can see Ellie's hands are gripping the steering wheel so tightly her knuckles are white. She's utterly still too, staring at seemingly nothing in front of her. A prickle of unease spurs me to gently tap the window. I feel my heart lurch when Ellie startles and turns watery eyes on me.

She seems to snap out of whatever place she was in and releases her hands suddenly, almost like she didn't realize what they were doing. Using the back of one, she swipes under her eye.

I pull open her door and drop down to my haunches in an attempt to get closer to eye level. "Hi, pretty girl." I keep my voice low.

"Hey, sorry," she starts, clearing her throat. "Am I late?" Ellie turns and reaches for her phone in the center console to check the time, I assume. Or maybe to hide her face.

"You're not late. Are you okay?"

She flexes her hands, curling them into fists and releasing them before facing me again. She doesn't make eye contact though. "Yeah, I'm fine. I just, um, haven't driven in a while."

I think of those tiny fists gripping the wheel and something heavy settles in my stomach.

I knew Ellie didn't drive much, but like an absolute piece of shit I didn't really think about that when I invited her to have dinner with my parents. I was so nervous to ask her and excited about doing something more official, something a normal couple would do, that it never crossed my mind she'd have to use her car to get here. The fact that she walks in below-freezing temps to get to work, how she orders her groceries in and refuses to go out with Dev unless it's walking distance... It's all slamming into me at once. How could I forget?

*God dammit.* Ellie was scared. And it's my fault.

We could've met her for dinner downtown. Or if she didn't want to be in public, we could've done takeout at her place. My parents wouldn't mind the small space—they would've had dinner in the damn car in order to meet her.

I hang my head, the guilt pulling at me like a physical weight. "Fuck, Ellie. I'm so sorry." I pick it back up and wait for her to look at me. When she does I slide my hand under her jaw, my thumb resting on her face. I gently swipe it back and forth. "I wasn't thinking about that when I made this plan."

She reaches up and holds my arm in place, leaning into my hand. "It's really okay. I need to drive occasionally to make the process more bearable. I just waited too long this time so it was a little rough." She closes her eyes. "I missed you," she breathes.

"I guarantee not as much as I missed you." I lean forward and press a kiss to her lips, relishing the soft hum she lets out at the contact. I pull back to look at her. Those honey eyes blink open and it takes a lot of willpower not to remove her from the car and crush her to my chest. "Would it help if I drove you home later? Or is that worse?" Despite what she said, I feel a desperate need to make this better. To make up for what I carelessly made her do.

Ellie's nose wrinkles. "Worse, sorry. Being a passenger is… just worse. But it's really fine. This is good practice."

I barely contain my groan as I think about her driving home in the dark tonight, scared and holding the wheel like she was earlier. Maybe I could convince her to stay here tonight? I file that idea away to broach later.

"Are you still up for this? I could send my parents out for a nice dinner somewhere and we could just relax."

"No way, I'm excited to meet them. Let me just—" Ellie reaches for her bag on the passenger seat, my hand falling away from her face. She pulls a smaller bag out of her purse and unzips it to hunt for something.

I wait patiently as she touches up her makeup in the car mirror, content to watch her do her thing.

She grabs her jacket and turns to me when she's done. "How's that?"

The makeup is highlighting her flushed cheeks and long lashes. Those always edible-looking lips. I'm struck speechless by how much I love this face. Not just her delicate features, but the way her warm brown eyes look at me with unmistakable affection. Or the subtle uptick to her mouth reminding me how strong she is even in times when it might be difficult. I swallow down the emotion crawling up my throat and stick to the simple truth. "Perfect."

"Okay, phew. I'm a little nervous," she admits, that curve turning into a bigger smile. "Do you think they're going to like me?"

The idea of anyone not liking Ellie is unthinkable. And my parents? Well, I have a feeling they're going to want to pack her up in their suitcase and take her back to upstate New York with them. I kiss her once quickly and then again because I want to.

"Yes, of course," I tell her.

What I want to say though? *They're going to love you almost as much as I do.*

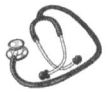

# CHAPTER THIRTY-TWO
## *ellie*

I'M STILL SHAKY FROM THE DRIVE, BUT HAVING MY HAND FIRMLY in Matt's grasp is bringing me some much-needed comfort. It's also giving me the chance to ogle his massive house as he brings me to the front door. I knew it would be big, but wowee. I would do one of those impressed whistles if I knew how.

The redbrick exterior has ivy crawling up and around the windows and their black shutters. A matching black front door is centered, giving the house a symmetrical look that screams *classic*. The big brass knocker and matching lampposts add to the traditional look and feel. It looks old, but in a way that says *old money* rather than *outdated*.

I guess I should've known it would be big and beautiful— he *is* kind of rich. I had forgotten that over the past several weeks. Matt doesn't really do anything that makes you think he has money. Not that this house is ostentatious, but I guess I wasn't expecting it to be so...perfect. Like those houses on the fronts of magazines, the ones you can only dream about owning one day. It also looks more like a house you'd see in New England over Minnesota—a realization triggering homesickness so suddenly it makes my knees weak.

I wish I could snap a picture and send it to my mom. She loved those damn magazines.

Matt squeezes my hand as we reach the door and looks to me with a smile. And like some kind of tailor-made cure, my homesickness fades as suddenly as it came on. "Ready?"

I do my best to swallow the nerves and give him a nod.

The first thing I see when we go inside is Matt's mom. I know people always compare men to their dads, but Matt is the spitting image of her. The dark hair, the forest-green eyes, the straight nose...it's so clear where he gets his beautiful face from. And his mom's hair might be heavily threaded with gray now, but I've also noticed a few more of those coming in Matt's hair too. Not that I'd tell him.

"You must be Ellie," she says, walking over. She envelops me in a hug so warm it makes my eyes sting. No one hugs like a mom. "Oh gosh, aren't you just the cutest thing," she sighs. "Come sit!"

Shirley moves toward the L-shaped couch in the living room and settles on the side against the floor-to-ceiling windows. *Wow*.

"Matt has told us so much about you, but he did not mention those freckles. My goodness, you must get a lot of attention."

My face gets hot and I try to refrain from covering my cheeks with my hands.

Matt groans and gives me an apologetic look. "Should I go put that in the kitchen?"

I look down at the polka dot plant I brought, its pretty pink leaves tempting me to keep it for myself. I'd probably kill it though. I'm a little bit more of a fake-plant lady. It was tricky getting someone from the shopping app to get the right one, but they did a good job picking. Matt has sent me a few pictures of his plants over the past month like a proud plant dad and I wanted to get him one he didn't have yet. I reluctantly hold it out. "The instructions say to make sure it doesn't get too soggy."

"Not too soggy, got it." Matt grins at my instructions and takes the plant from me. He turns back to his mom, who's been waiting patiently on the couch a few feet away from us, big smile firmly in place. "Mom, do you want to take Ellie on a quick tour while I set this in the kitchen and find Dad? I'm sure he's down by the water even though it's freezing," he grumbles fondly.

"Oh! Of course. Here, let me take your jacket first. Then we can go look around," she says. Despite it nearly being April, I'm still in my heavy parka thanks to the never-ending winter here.

Matt gives me a wink and then disappears, off to the kitchen, I'm guessing. Shirley returns without my jacket and leads me in the opposite direction.

"I keep telling him to decorate, but he never listens. Try not to hold it against him," she says conspiratorially, giving me a wink just like her son did moments ago.

I laugh at what she said and the obvious similarity between them. If she's anything like Matt, I think we'll get along great.

"So how long are you guys in town? Are you doing anything specific while you're here?" I use the cloth napkins Matt set out to wipe my mouth. He made lasagna and now he's officially on the hook for cooking sometimes because *yum*.

"Oh, just going to the games mostly. We're probably

staying until he breaks the record, so our timeline is up in the air. We'll wait to book a return flight until after," Peter, Matt's dad, tells me. He's got lighter gray hair and a rounder face, his eyes a light blue. It seems like all Matt got from him was the tall stature and deep voice.

I think about what he said. "Record?" I look from him to Matt, whose cheeks are getting pink.

"You didn't tell her?" Shirley chimes in.

Peter looks up from his food to Shirley and then Matt.

"It's not a big deal," Matt says, waving his hand dismissively. I hear his dad cough. "They come to town for most milestones," he says to me.

"That's so nice," I say, a little distracted. Record? Milestone? Matt hasn't mentioned anything, but then again, he's definitely picked up on my distaste for hockey and probably wouldn't volunteer that kind of information. Or maybe he's just being humble? Either way, the thought makes me sad. I should try harder to ask him about his job—*his passion*. I need to do better. I clear my throat. "What's the milestone?"

Matt finishes chewing with his eyes on me, a contemplative look on his face. "A thousand assists," he says casually.

A thousand sounds big, but I don't really know anything about hockey statistics. "Wow, that's cool," I say, hoping it doesn't sound too dumb.

Matt gives me such a sweet smile I'm convinced I failed.

"Very cool," Shirley affirms with a nod.

I glance around the table and see that all of them have matching grins. It feels like I'm missing a joke.

"So you said you come to town for these milestones? Does, um, Connor ever come?" I ask his parents, hoping I didn't stutter on Matt's brother's name too much. He's mentioned him a few times, but mostly in passing.

"Oh, yes. We all love to come to the games. Peter and I missed a few in the middle of his career because we were traveling, but we don't want to miss anything now. Connor couldn't come this time because of some work deadlines, I think," she finishes, then turns to Matt and points at him. "He said you're not allowed to retire before he makes it out for another record."

Matt pushes his chair back and gives his mom a noticeably tight smile before getting up from the table and grabbing everyone's plates.

I smile at Shirley and then stand up to do the same, following him into the kitchen and setting the dishes down on the counter near the sink. "Everything okay?" I keep my voice low and turn to face him.

Matt puts his hands on the counter on either side of me, caging me in. He leans forward and drops a quick kiss to my mouth. "Could I convince you to stay here tonight?"

I ignore his nonanswer and file my curiosity away for later. "Sure."

"That was easy," he whispers against my mouth before he kisses me again.

"I aim to please."

He pulls away and grabs my hand, leading me back to the table. His parents are collecting the rest of the dishes.

"We're going to head to the guest suite downstairs, Matt. It was a long day of flights and I'm beat," Shirley says, stopping before leaving the room. "We'll see you soon, Ellie? Maybe you can come to a game with us?"

"Yeah, sure. It was great meeting you," I tell her sincerely. I feel bad, but I'll figure out how to get out of the game thing later, if it comes up again.

Shirley smiles brightly back at me and then looks at Matt. "Night, Matty."

"Night, Mom. Dad, remember to adjust the thermostat if you guys get warm down there," he calls to their retreating backs. He turns to me. "Want to see my room?" He waggles his eyebrows at me.

I laugh and trail him down the hall, so giddy over seeing his bed for the first time, you'd think I was back in high school.

# CHAPTER THIRTY-THREE

## *matt*

"Holy crap, it's huge."

"Oh, how I've longed to hear those words."

"Hilarious," Ellie deadpans. "Is this custom?" She walks around the bed slowly.

*My* bed. There's something about having a custom bed that seems...over-the-top? I know Ellie isn't one to judge, but I'm still hesitating to give her confirmation.

"Maybe," I finally spit out.

She jumps onto it, rolling from one end to the other. "So much room for activities." Ellie's denim-clad ass wiggles suggestively and I have to stifle a groan. I've been thinking about that ass for nearly two weeks.

I walk over and grab her ankles, dragging her closer. Ellie squeals as I flip her over and release my grip. I put a knee on the mattress between her legs and rest on my forearms, caging her in. Up close like this I can smell her shampoo. I run my nose along hers and hover above her mouth. "Did you just quote *Step Brothers* to me?"

Ellie nods, a goofy grin on her pretty face. I push my knee up until my leg grinds against the apex of her thighs. Her smile drops and her mouth opens slightly. I take advantage, pulling her pouty bottom lip with my teeth.

I release and then, "Do you think this is the type of activity they had in mind?"

Her lips curve again and she shakes her head. "I don't think it was that kind of movie."

I laugh. "I think you're right." I lean down and capture Ellie's mouth with mine—something I've been desperate to do since the moment I saw her today. She kisses me back, pulling me closer with her hands in my hair. I sigh at the contentment that washes over me. Everything with Ellie just feels...right. I don't think I felt like things were back to normal after my trip until I laid eyes on her freckled face and held her small hand in mine. And this? This feels like being home finally.

I'm so in love with this girl it feels like more effort not to say it than it would be to just blurt it out. Like it's constantly on the tip of my tongue and I have to check myself before I talk. It's borderline painful. I almost slipped when she called me to thank me for Zoey's surprise visit.

I know I could just tell her, but after her drunken confession I'm not sure when or even *if* she'd want to hear it. And I don't want it to be a point of stress for her. I want her to be excited—to maybe even want to say it back.

One day at a time, I tell myself. Who knows, maybe the moment will feel right tomorrow or a week from now. I just have to be patient.

Ellie pulls away and studies my face as she catches her breath. "Something on your mind?"

*You. Always you.* "Just missed you." I peck her lips quickly. "And this."

Ellie's smiling, but her eyes are searching for something. "What happened at the dinner table?"

*Ah*. I'm not really sure why I haven't talked to Ellie about this. I guess I'm embarrassed it's causing me this much grief. It feels so melodramatic. And yet, it *is* how I feel and I want to share everything with her. She just has a way of putting things in perspective that can make my problems feel less…big. Not on purpose. And it's not even a bad thing. In fact, the more I think about it, maybe making this problem feel small is exactly what I need. I don't know why I didn't think of that before.

"My retirement is just a bit of a sore topic, I guess."

Ellie lowers her eyebrows, that adorable little wrinkle between them making an appearance. "Why? You're not ready to? Is someone making you?" Her voice takes on an angry edge with that last question.

It makes me smile and gives my chest that tight feeling I'm getting accustomed to. "Nah, it's mostly up to me. I'm just having trouble deciding when." I pause and study her face. "And what to do after." I tuck my arm under her shoulder and roll until she's on top of me. Her hair falls around her face. So damn beautiful.

"How come? The possibilities are endless. You're only thirty-six."

"I think that's the first time you've used my age to call me young."

She smiles and uses a delicate finger to trace my nose. My cheeks. The scar on my chin.

"I don't really know who I am without hockey," I confess quietly.

I try not to dwell on that thought often, let alone admit it out loud. This is the first time I've said it to anyone, actually.

*I promise you're safe with me.* Her lighthearted comment from that first night plays on a near-constant loop in my head like some soothing proverb. I don't think she—or I, truthfully—realized how much I'd cling to those words.

Ellie pauses her tracing and studies my eyes for a while. A few moments pass before she speaks in a quiet voice.

"You know, I was starstruck by you before I knew you were a star. Obviously, you know I thought you were good-looking, but it was so much more that gave me butterflies. You were just...captivating. So genuine and *so* kind. From the very beginning I always felt like you gave me your full attention. Like you didn't want to be anywhere but there in that moment with me. I know hockey is a big part of your life, but it's never been a big part of what makes you special to me."

Those pretty eyes stay steady on mine.

"You're just Matt. Matt who likes vanilla ice cream and alien movies. Matt who ran in the freezing cold to apologize to his one-night stand for something that normally wouldn't really require one quite so sincere. Matt who calls his parents weekly and who never lets a house plant die. Matt who works hard to put others first even with a job that demands otherwise. Matt who listens to a podcast on grief to help his..."

"Girlfriend," I supply, my voice thick. "How'd you know that?"

She gently places her hands on the sides of my jaw, running her thumbs back and forth over the thicker stubble I let grow while on the road.

"You sent me a screenshot of that plant app and it was at the top of your screen, old man." Ellie sticks her tongue out at me. She stops moving her thumbs and holds my face steady, studying my eyes. "I never considered anything about my life lucky until you, Matt. And that has nothing to do with your job or your name."

I feel my throat move on a heavy swallow as I reach a hand up to hold one of hers in place. What did I do to deserve her?

"I'm no expert, but being done playing doesn't have to mean being done with hockey, right? Your passion won't just go away when your job changes, Matt. If you want it to be a part of your life, it will be." She kisses me quickly and leans back to watch me again.

"How do you do that?" I rasp. I know the gravel in my voice is betraying the emotion I'm feeling right now, but I don't care.

"Do what?"

"You just... I just feel like I can *breathe* when you're with me. Like the weight of the world is suddenly so much *less*." I squeeze her hand under mine. "I've never felt that before."

"Isn't that what partners do? Share the weight?"

Chills break out over my skin. I'm transported back to the first night I met Ellie. When I asked about her relationship endgame and she told me she was looking for a real *partner*. I give her a jerky nod. "Partners," I repeat.

I swallow the words I so desperately want to say and roll us back over, pinning her hands above her head. If I can't tell her how much I love her, I'm going to show her.

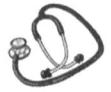

# CHAPTER THIRTY-FOUR
## *ellie*

Matt's body hovers over mine with enough weight that I feel every delicious inch of him. His hands are gripping mine tightly above my head and his mouth is trailing lazy kisses around the sweet spot under my ear. He drags his mouth so close to my lips that I part them for him, but the kiss I'm craving never comes.

I open my eyes and find him gazing at me with an unreadable expression. I want to touch his face, but his hands are still squeezing mine.

"You're so beautiful."

There's something about the way he says it that makes my heart rate pick up.

"Every time I look at you, I find something else to obsess over." Matt touches his nose to my cheek and then presses a soft kiss there. "I love these freckles." A kiss to both of my eyelids. "Your honey eyes." He makes his way over to my earlobe, his teeth nipping the edge. "These cute, biteable ears."

Matt lets go of my hands and sits back, grabbing the hem of my sweater and gently tugging it. I prop myself up so he can pull it off and then lie back down as he sets it aside. He takes off his own sweater in that hot-as-fuck guy way, pulling it from behind his shoulders over his head, tossing it somewhere behind us. He resumes lying over me, his face now just above my collarbone.

He kisses my scar three times, each at a slightly different spot. "Hearing you talk about what could have happened if that glass hit somewhere else made me love this too."

I swallow and bring one of my hands to the side of his head, gently caressing the hair cut shorter there.

Matt slides down and blows out a breath as he stares at my bra. It's a simple bandeau style, the material thin and soft. He drags his nose across one nipple and then makes his way over to the other to do this same. They tighten and pucker through the fabric, the light touch sending zings of pleasure down low. "You know how I feel about these."

He continues his path down my body, stopping to kiss my belly button and the soft swell of my stomach underneath. I support myself with my arms so I can admire the view.

He drops his forehead heavily on my stomach, breathing in through his nose. The sensation of his exhale on my skin sends goose bumps across my body. Matt looks up and gives me a lazy smile. His eyes are heavy-lidded. "I *love* that." He traces the pebbled flesh until they disappear.

Matt pops the button on my jeans and drags the zipper down, sitting up to peel them off my legs. I lift my hips to make it easier. He looks from my simple underwear to my face. I think he's asking permission. Why that sends my heart racing even more, I couldn't tell you. I give him a jerky nod and watch as he slowly hooks his fingers in the waistband and slides them down, careful to unhook them from around my feet. He sets them with my discarded sweater and pants.

Following suit, he gets up and removes his own jeans and briefs and leaves them on the floor.

Matt picks up my foot and drags his nose along the instep. "I love your tiny feet and watching you in those ridiculous boots I always worry you'll trip in."

He kisses a random freckle on my ankle and then works his way back onto the bed and up my legs, stopping at my thigh.

"I love when your legs shake after we have sex." He nips the skin there and then moves higher, stopping and settling in with his hands holding me just above my hips.

I don't think I could look away from him if I tried. My heart beats painfully against my chest as I watch him dip his head. I feel his tongue slide up my center followed by a slight rumble as he groans.

"I fucking love the way you taste."

I know I'm dripping wet at this point, so caught up in his kisses and words I can't think straight. Matt and I have had a lot of sex, but there's something so different about this time. I'm afraid to put a name to it.

What Matt is doing feels borderline religious. He's *worshiping* me. And while my mind is in shambles trying to make sense of it, my body is humming with his thorough attention.

Matt swirls his tongue around my clit, flicking it and then dipping back down, nudging my legs farther apart for better access. Warmth spreads through me like a shot of liquor.

His hands leave my waist and grip under my pliant legs to move them over his shoulders. Satisfied with our new position, he lightly blows on my sensitive flesh before repeating the same motion as before. A swirl around my clit, a flick, followed by a lick down and back up my center.

Repeat.

Repeat.

Repeat.

*Fuck.*

That warmth turns into fire, my body melting into him. I can barely hold myself up. Large hands move back to my waist and slip up along my ribcage until his thumbs touch the underside of my bra. They skim under the edge and it's like my mind goes blank. I finally drop my head back to the bed, unable to keep myself propped up any longer.

Those skilled fingers push my bra up and tweak my nipples, sending another jolt of arousal right to where his tongue is still working. Matt trails one hand down, dragging his fingers over me until it disappears. Then I feel one slide into me just under where his tongue works. He adds a second finger and *oh shit*. I'm going to come.

I want to tell Matt, but I think I lost the ability to talk sometime between his casual declarations and his mouth between my legs. He curls his fingers, hitting *that* spot, and I'm lost to a release so strong I feel like I'm floating.

"I will never get enough of your perfect pussy gripping my fingers when you come."

I'm vaguely aware of Matt talking and now crawling up my body. He mimics our earlier position, gripping my hands and dragging them above my head. His mouth claims mine in a drugging kiss before he pulls back.

I open hazy eyes to him looking at my mouth with that expression he's been wearing lately. One I'm scared to decipher.

"I love everything about your mouth."

Another kiss.

"I love these lips around my cock."

Kiss.

"I love how I never know what's going to come out of them—what you're going to say."

Kiss.

"I love the way my heart stutters in my chest when they pull into a smile."

Kiss.

Matt releases one of my hands and reaches down to fit himself against me. He hooks my legs over him, nudging forward just slightly. *Oh god.* He reclaims my hand, his grip harder than before. Pressing his hips forward, he pushes into me torturously slowly.

"I love the way you fit me so perfectly." His voice is gravel as he fills me all the way.

I think I sigh. *This.* I want this for the rest of my life. It's perfect. He's perfect. *Shit.*

Matt pulls out and slowly pushes in again. Kisses me. "I love how you feel."

Another kiss. Another drag in and out. My legs start to shake.

"I love how you *make me* feel."

My heart beats so loudly I'm surprised he can't hear it. I'm scared. This feels like so much more than sex.

"I love that you're mine."

My breath hitches and Matt dips his tongue in my mouth, swallowing the little gasp. His hips thrust forward and pull back.

He touches his nose to mine and looks at me. "You're mine, right?"

All I can do is nod. Something spills from my eye and Matt wipes it away with his cheek. He rests his forehead against mine, letting our breath tangle.

His hips thrust forward again. "So perfect."

Again.

"All mine."

They're barely whispered words, but I can hear them. It's *all* I hear. *His*. I'm his. I don't know when it happened, but I'm so undeniably his that it feels like my heart beats *for* him.

I grip his hands harder above our heads and press my mouth up to his as I shatter, another tear trailing down my face.

# CHAPTER THIRTY-FIVE
## *matt*

I have the uncharacteristic urge to whistle as I lace my skates. *Fucking whistle.*

We may not have exchanged those three little words last night, but I did drop the g-word and she didn't balk. Progress.

And not that I thought it would go any differently, but my parents *love* her. I mean, who wouldn't? My mom's already asking when I'm bringing her home to New York to visit. And that idea doesn't even freak me out like it used to before Ellie. I want her to be familiar with every part of my life.

Because Ellie unequivocally makes my life better. Like my own personal rose-colored glasses. I've never felt this sense of rightness. As though something clicked into place and my life is suddenly more *complete*. The feelings I had for previous girlfriends just…pale in comparison. It's like my world has shifted and instead of only hockey and family, there's now *her* right in the damn center. And she somehow takes away some of the doom and gloom that comes with thoughts of life after hockey.

I still feel lost when I think about it, sure, but I know Ellie will be there to help me figure it out. Because that's what partners do, she said. *Partners*. The word still gives me chills.

Thinking about last night gives me chills too. Holy fuck. I did not know sex could be like that. So deeply personal and intimate. Special. I probably sound like a sap, but I didn't put much thought into the phrase "making love" before, and now it seems like the only thing you could call what we did.

Man, this high I'm riding right now rivals my biggest wins. And as a two-time Cup winner, that's really saying something. The screaming, proud fans. That heavy, coveted trophy lifted in the air. The utter joy and sense of accomplishment. I can *feel* the emotions that went with those wins and this might be better. Bigger. Do other people feel this when they fall in love? I'm doubtful.

Even though Ellie left this morning before my parents were up, I have a feeling they know she stayed over. They asked if she was coming to the game tonight. I lied and said she was busy, but I am hoping maybe I'll be able to convince her to come to one soon. I know my mom would love having someone other than my dad to talk with and she'd probably even explain the game to Ellie. Maybe a game next week when she's off work?

I finish lacing my skate—I avoid whistling—and take my hat off to put in my bag before we head down the tunnel for warm-ups. The light from my phone catches my attention, so I grab it to check the notification before heading out.

There are a fuck-ton of them, all within the last hour. Texts, some missed calls... The one that catches my attention first is from my brother. This many notifications isn't unheard of for me, but it's not quite typical either. I decide to check Connor's quickly before I have to head to the ice, knowing it's probably a good luck text or maybe something about Ellie if he's talked to Mom today.

It turns out to be neither of those things.

I skip over his texts to the headline of the link he's sent.

### **FULL CIRCLE LOVE STORY?**
***Matt Anderson's new girl and how his rival almost KILLED HER!***

I'm not often in trashy tabloids like this one—I might be famous in the hockey world, but I'm not *that* famous outside it. And usually if I am in one, it's based on something flimsy or straight-up untrue. I know how they make their money and I do my best to ignore it. Sometimes the articles even give me a laugh. The ridiculous clickbait titles are nearly comedic.

But "new girl" has the hair on the back of my neck standing up. I click on the link and scroll down through an ad, freezing at the images they have there. They're distinctly low quality, but the pictures are clear enough.

It's me at The Bar with Ellie.

One picture shows us hugging and another shows me putting on her earmuffs. I remember that night with crystal clarity. I guess in my relief at finding her okay, I forgot to really think about someone capturing the rare PDA moment. I faintly think about how pissed Nate's going to be that someone was able to get pictures of me in The Bar without him noticing.

My thumb shakes as I go to scroll farther, a small pit forming in my stomach.

*The elusive Matt Anderson is off the market, folks! An onlooker caught an intimate moment between him and his new girl, Eleanor Ford, at a local bar. Can anyone say CUTE?! We love a smitten man so much we might be willing to let go of our dreams of landing the hockey hottie ourselves...*

*And it appears Miss Eleanor Ford is one worthy lady of the star's affection! She and her mother were involved in a deadly DUI car crash caused by none other than one of Anderson's on-ice opponents, Bryan McCormic, after a post-win celebration.*

*Eleanor sustained serious injuries and her mother was KILLED in the accident where McCormic lost control of his vehicle while under the influence. McCormic and his passenger, Christian Hallafax, were only minorly injured.*

*The good news is we spy Boston on the Bears' calendar next week and we CAN'T WAIT to watch the fallout when the opponents meet on the ice! Talk about a worthy FIGHT! Karma is calling...*

*One thing is for sure—this makes for one hell of a full-circle love story!*

I stop scrolling and reread the second paragraph. As the words sink in, that pit in my stomach turns into something much, much worse.

Sick, twisted puzzle pieces begin to fit into place and I desperately grasp at the fading ignorance I was unknowingly harboring.

*No, no, no.* Memories slam into me with a force that nearly knocks me off these damn skates.

Ellie's reaction to finding out I played hockey.

The way she responded when I asked if her ex had played.

Her gentle refusals to go to a game.

Her quiet confession about where her scar came from.

*The odd familiarity of her mom's face on Niko's phone.*

Now I know that it was because I'd seen it before. Because this story made waves in my world until the league promptly buried it and everyone just...moved on.

Including me.

The shame and disgust I feel is crippling. I'm jolted from my self-loathing as the notifications on my phone become so constant it's as if I am getting back-to-back calls. And if I'm getting this much attention...

*Ellie.* Fuck.

Her social media isn't private, and with that trash tabloid doxing her...

This is what she was afraid of. It has to be.

I exit out of the browser and pull up her contact, hitting the call button as fast as I can. *Straight to voicemail.* Either her phone is off or she declined it.

"You ready?"

I look over at Niko by the door and snap back to reality. Half the team's already down the tunnel to start our pregame warm-up. *I'm out of time.*

Niko's brow draws low and he looks at my phone. "What's wrong?"

I shoot a Hail Mary text to Nate and debate tucking the phone somewhere in my uniform. With the constant buzzing I decide against it and set it in my locker, sending a quick plea to the universe that Nate checks it and does what I ask.

I grab my helmet and stick and walk over to Niko, unable

to shake this avalanche of emotions I'm buried under. Shock, guilt, sadness, *panic*. How am I going to play through this?

I look at Niko and clock the unease all over his face. Guess he sees it on mine too. I clear my throat and give him the headline that barely scratches the surface of "what's wrong."

"I found out why Ellie doesn't like hockey."

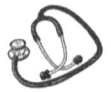

# CHAPTER THIRTY-SIX
## *ellie*

I HEAR KNOCKING AT THE DOOR, BUT MY EYES ARE GLUED TO THE device on my coffee table. I've been staring for so long I've lost track of time. *It won't stop.*

I'm surprised it hasn't died yet, given how long it's been buzzing and perpetually lit up. Just an endless barrage of notifications. Calls, texts, social media alerts... Every time the screen goes bright I hit the button to make it stop. But then it just starts again.

*It won't stop. It won't stop. It won't stop.*

"Hey, Ellie. I know. Here, I'm going to take this and deal with it, okay?"

I said that out loud? I'm startled from the tunnel vision I have on my phone when it gets grabbed by a large hand. I follow the motion and watch Nate pocket it before he sits on the coffee table facing me. How did he get in my apartment?

"You okay?"

I look at his pocket with my phone and shrug.

"Would it be all right if I hung out here for a bit?"

I shrug again.

"I'm going to deal with your phone and order some food, okay? Maybe we can put a show on?"

I nod this time and watch numbly as he grabs the remote and puts some sitcom on. He moves and sits on the other side of the couch, visible in my periphery. He must know by now.

*Everybody is going to know.*

People are going to want to talk to me about it. They are going to have questions. I bet the media is going to have a field day. Back when the accident happened, we got contacted by a lot of local and national news channels about doing interviews. Being crushed by grief is one thing. But everyone wanting to talk about it was like having alcohol poured in an open wound. I didn't want to go over the worst day of my life again and again. I didn't want to talk about the famous players who killed her.

The league certainly didn't do any interviews. They released one statement and that was it. One measly apology, on behalf of them and those two assholes.

Don't even get me started on the legal ramifications. Thirty days in jail and a license suspension. *Thirty days.*

I don't know what I wanted from the league or the judicial system, but it wasn't that.

I don't want to deal with any of this again. The attention. The *feelings*.

And now, with Matt, it's just going to be even bigger. I wonder what he's thinking.

I realize for the first time he might find this situation hypocritical. I got upset when he didn't tell me about being a hockey player. And now he's probably finding out I never told him the full story about my accident. About my mom. About the drunk hockey players. His *colleagues*.

The customary rage that accompanies thoughts of them

flares, my hands balling into fists where they rest on my thighs. What if Matt knows them? What if he's *friends* with them? Oh god, the thought makes me vaguely ill.

"Ellie?"

I turn to look at Nate. He's looking at my lap. At my lack of response he glances up, sympathy plastered all over his face.

"Chinese okay?"

I nod and face forward again, bringing my legs up onto the couch. I pull them close to my chest and lay my head on my knees.

I should've known this was coming. I wonder how it got out? Maybe I would know if I checked any of the hundreds of notifications on my phone, but I don't think I'm up for that. I knew it was a risk being with Matt, but I thought we were pretty careful about not being seen in public. And I knew that wasn't going to be realistic forever, but I didn't think this was going to be a long-term thing at first and then... Well, then I guess I'd been living in blissful ignorance. *Falling in love*, my brain shouts. Was it worth it?

I close my eyes and try to think about something else. *Anything* else.

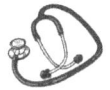

# CHAPTER THIRTY-SEVEN
## *ellie*

"How is she? Is she asleep? Did she eat?"

"She's been like that almost the whole time, man. I wasn't sure if she was asleep, so I didn't want to wake her up when the food got here."

"Did she let you in when you knocked?"

"Nah, but it was unlocked so I let myself in after there was no response."

A sigh. "I guess that ended up being a good thing. What did you do with her phone?"

"Here." A pause. "I just made her socials private and put it on DND for now."

"Thanks." Some shuffling and a patting noise. "I owe you."

"You know you don't. I hope she's okay. She seems kind of...numb? I don't know. You staying here tonight?"

It's a few moments before, "I'm not sure. Hopefully."

"Even if it's the couch, I think it would be a good idea. I'll check in with you tomorrow."

The hushed voices stop and then the door opens and closes quietly. Soft footsteps make their way closer before the couch dips next to me. A few moments of nothing and then a light touch to my head. A kiss?

The TV turns off and then the warmth next to me disappears. I hear those same soft footsteps moving around my apartment and the flicks of light switches being flipped. The door locks. More footsteps, closer now. An arm slides under my legs and another behind my back before I'm lifted and nestled against a solid chest.

Matt carries me through my small apartment and gently settles me on my bed. I blink my eyes open. He's pulling his shirt off, pausing when it's hanging off his arms in front of him.

"Hey," he breathes. "Can I stay here?"

I scoot backward to make room for him in front of me. He drops his shirt and slides in, adjusting the comforter over both of us. One of his hands cups my face. I take a deep breath, leaning into that warm, familiar touch.

"I'm sorry this happened." His voice is low. Pained.

My shoulders lift. "I knew it would eventually, I guess." I swallow and debate if I want the answer to the question that's recently been swirling in my mind. Curiosity gets the best of me. "How'd it come out?"

Matt winces. "I should've been more careful, Ellie." He sighs heavily and swipes a thumb along my cheek. "Someone got a picture of us at The Bar when I picked you up a couple weeks ago. It was some trashy tabloid that ran it first."

Makes sense. I guess sad, drunk me let my guard down. I'm pretty sure I face-planted on his chest when he walked over to me. Not exactly subtle.

"Ellie, I'm so sor—"

"You don't need to be sorry, Matt. You didn't do anything wrong. I should've thought it through. I knew the risks when we started seeing each other." *You didn't.* I want to add it, but I'm still so worried he might be thinking I'm a hypocrite.

Matt shakes his head. "This is my fault." His face contorts into some expression caught between sadness and panic. "The Bar, the pictures, the article... None of this would've happened if it wasn't for me and my job. I knew it was important to you that things stayed secret and I should've been more careful. I should've taken more precautions." His hand falls from my face and he scrubs both of his over his own, turning from his side to his back. "Ellie, I play hockey with those bastards. Multiple times a year. I've played all-star tournaments with him, for fuck's sake. And now you have to deal with all of this, because of *me*." His breathing has changed, coming out in pants.

"Matt," I say, trying to break him out of whatever this is.

"I remember the accident now and how it was so tragic, but we all knew nothing was going to happen. I didn't *do* anything, Ellie, I—"

"Matt!"

"I was just complacent and you were, oh god, you were probably still in the hospital," he rasps. "You don't deserve this. Me."

I climb onto him and pull his hands away from his face, holding them near my legs. His panic is so out of character I almost don't recognize him.

"Baby, stop," I say softly. "Please."

His chest rises and falls rapidly under me. "I need you to know that I'm not friends with those guys and I don't agree with how—"

"I know," I cut him off, louder than before. Despite my earlier musings, I think I knew deep down Matt wouldn't associate with people like them even if he had to play with them. And I know he doesn't drink and drive. "I know you, Matt. I definitely lumped all hockey players into a shit bucket after the accident, but that wasn't fair and you proved me wrong anyway."

I let go of his hands and place my palms against his chest. It's still moving faster than normal, but it's slowing and he's finally looking at me, so I keep going.

"I...I'm scared, okay? They wrote so many stories last time. There were so many requests for interviews," I whisper, my face scrunching up at the thought. "Of course I don't want to deal with that again. Don't want to think about it. About *them*." I blow out a breath. "But I don't place any blame on you, okay? You didn't know me then and you didn't know about the situation until now. I should've told you about this before. I'm sorry I didn't."

A breath rattles out of him as he brings his hands on top of mine. "Fuck, *please* don't apologize to me. For that or anything. I'm screwing this all up." He groans and closes his eyes, taking a few quick breaths. "I was supposed to be comforting you, not the other way around." He blinks those evergreen eyes open, keeping them steady on me. "I'm sorry for freaking out. I'm just so...*terrified* of losing you." He swallows. "Of being the cause of your pain. I wouldn't blame you if you didn't want to be with me."

I look down at our hands. Would not being in this situation be easier? Yes. But the idea of leaving Matt is so painful it makes my breath catch at the thought. Which is a terrifying reminder of something I'm still too chickenshit to deal with.

Matt's voice brings my gaze back to his. "I understand this is...complicated. My life makes it complicated." He sounds so utterly dejected that I have the urge to hug him. He squeezes his hands over mine and I catch his Adam's apple bobbing in his throat. "No matter what you decide, I'll help with the fallout from this, I promise."

Thinking about the *fallout* makes me want to barf, but I focus on what's important right now. "You're my...my boyfriend, right? My partner?"

Matt gives an eager, jerky nod.

"Good. That's good," I say on a relieved exhale. "Because I could really use a partner to get through this, okay? I had my dad last time, but we were both still in such deep grief it was just really overwhelming. He wasn't really a support then, you know? Not that I blame him. But it was a lonely experience, on top of everything else."

Matt brings his hands up and cups my face. "I'm always going to be here for you, Ellie. Always. No matter what."

I lean down and press a kiss to his lips, eager to soak up the comfort I get from being close to him. "Thank you," I whisper, kissing him again and then pulling back to sit up like I was before.

"I, um, actually talked to one of the Bears' PR people after the game."

My eyebrows shoot up. "Oh?"

"Her name's Sloane. She's up in management now, but she's been doing PR for the team for a while, maybe six or seven years. I just... This feels so out of my control and I've never used a publicist before. So I explained the situation and she asked if she could help. Like, professionally. Kind of like a publicist for you, so she can take care of a lot of this." Matt's eyes are bouncing around my face in that way that lets me know he's paying attention to my reaction. "If you're up for it, of course."

"Oh." I didn't think something like that existed for me. Or rather, was affordable for me. I guess it isn't, probably, but

Matt's job is making it possible. "What would she do exactly?"

"Everything. Anything. She said she'd want to get you a new phone number to start. She'd like access to your socials to scrub anything that got in before Nate made them private. And she'll handle all those interview requests. She has some suggestions for other things too, like what to tell friends and family and whatnot, but I told her I'd need to talk to you first. If you want to work with her, we can meet as soon as tomorrow morning."

I bite my lip and mull it over. I'm pretty sure tomorrow is Easter. This all sounds like more than just a favor. And expensive. "That seems like a lot of work. I'd want to pay her for her time, but I don't know if I could afford—"

"I already told her I'd cover any hourly rate for her help, but she wasn't interested."

*Oh. Okay.* There's really no reason not to do it then, right? A thought does occur to me—is this going to be my life with Matt? Someone else in charge of so many things?

But then another thought—does it matter? It's things I don't want to deal with anyway, so it shouldn't. And a publicist is something I probably *would* have used before if I had the means to.

I remember last night Matt mentioned how the weight of the world felt like *less* now, being with me. I can't help but feel the same. *Was it worth it?* I can't believe I asked that question earlier. Can't believe I had an inkling of doubt about the decision to be with Matt. I feel guilty I was even capable of that thought. I'm going to blame the bitch I call grief for that momentary lapse in judgment and shelve this under *things to never mention or think again.*

I rearrange myself so I'm lying on top of Matt, my body

pressed to his. He asked me last night if I was his, but does he know he's mine too? I think of his earlier panic and realize maybe not.

"Okay. Let's call her tomorrow," I murmur, too exhausted to think about dealing more with this right now.

I snuggle in close, kissing the side of his neck and thinking of ways to prove to him just how much he means to me.

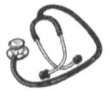

# CHAPTER THIRTY-EIGHT
## *ellie*

THE BEARS' ASSISTANT DIRECTOR OF COMMUNICATIONS MIGHT BE the most attractive woman I've ever seen in real life. The type of person you have to force yourself *not* to stare at. I feel a twinge of insecurity that she works with Matt, but she's got an obscene engagement ring on her finger and has hardly paid him any attention during our meeting anyway.

And she's *all* business. Aside from offering me a sincere apology about what I've gone through, she's operated with a level of efficiency and focus that points to her being extremely good at her job. She asked to come to my apartment when we called her early this morning so that she could "take care" of my phone. On Easter.

So for the past hour she's been sitting in my tiny living room in a perfectly fitted white long-sleeved shirt and high-waisted brown flare slacks, the picture of sophistication and style. Even her dark hair is in a sleek, perfect ponytail. Flyaways? She's never heard of them. Clothing wrinkles? Not on her watch. A swell of gratitude washes over me for my job that has a uniform and does not require any level of tailored hairstyles or makeup. I would never be able to dress cute every day for work, let alone do my hair and put on more than mascara.

"You said you work at General?"

Sloane looks up from where she's been sitting in the leather armchair, her pale hazel eyes zeroed in on me. Next to her olive skin tone, it's hard not to marvel at the combination. I wonder what her parents look like.

I give her a nod. "I work in the emergency department."

She frowns ever so slightly at that. I'm not sure I would've caught it if I wasn't so locked in on her inhumanly perfect face. Matt is beautiful beyond compare, but part of his beauty is his little imperfections that add to the conventional good looks he's got going on. Sloane doesn't have a single one that I can tell. I'm tempted to ask if she's had work done, but (a) that's rude as fuck and (b) I think she'd tell me no anyway.

"Is that bad?"

She looks surprised. "No, of course not. Security tends to be a little tougher in ER settings, but a hospital is generally still very safe."

Matt tenses next to me. "Ellie's job is important to her. She moved away from home for it."

I'm hit with a pang of guilt. That is why I moved *here*, but I guess I haven't talked to Matt about why I applied for a job that would get me out of Boston. I think my shame has kept that one bottled up.

"Ellie is perfectly fine to keep her job, Matt." Sloane focuses back on me with a patient smile. "Security is not my area of expertise, which is why I was just clarifying your work location. I'll touch base with my security contact, but I wouldn't expect it to be an issue. If you ever feel worried about something, or if anyone asks you personal questions there, don't hesitate to alert the security on-site. It might be best to let your supervisors know the situation now so they are aware."

"I can tell my charge nurse, Maggie," I confirm.

"Good. Have you talked to any friends or family yet?"

"Not yet," I tell her. "Matt mentioned last night you had ideas, and I wasn't really ready to deal with it anyway. But I probably need to talk to my dad today and I'll see a couple of coworkers-slash-friends at work later who might have seen the stories."

"Yeah, that would probably be best. And I bet they're worried about you." She gives me what I'm sure is a practiced empathetic look. "I have a few guidelines for things to talk to them about, but everything I tell you is advice and it's really up to you how you want to handle things. Unlike Matt, you don't report to my employer, so there are no obligations here, okay?"

Matt huffs and I give Sloane a smile. "Got it. And I know I already said it, but thank you again. This is incredibly kind of you. I'm sure you're already really busy."

"I'm happy to do it, truly," she says. "And I like staying busy." *Preach*. She smiles and then reaches over to her fancy bag to pull out a piece of paper. "This is my standard spiel I give anyone coming into some level of scrutiny. I went ahead and listed myself as your publicist for the sake of simplicity. Why don't you take a look while I step out and call my security guy?"

I thank her again and grab the paper, aware of Matt's hand giving my thigh a gentle squeeze. I know he's still feeling so bad and I'm sure this isn't really helping, even though it's all going to make things easier in the long run. I'm not exactly feeling peachy myself, but with Matt next to me I feel like it's all going to be okay. I give his hand a quick squeeze back and then read the information Sloane gave me. There are four main guidelines listed for speaking with friends and family.

### MEDIA REQUESTS
EVERY REQUEST (JOURNALISTS, PODCASTERS, NEWS OUTLETS, BLOGGERS, REPORTERS), NO MATTER HOW SMALL, CAN BE SENT TO MY PUBLICIST, SLOANE KENNEDY. IT'S BEST NOT TO ANSWER WITH ANYTHING OTHER THAN SLOANE'S CONTACT INFORMATION, WHICH I WILL SEND TO YOU. "NO COMMENT" IS ALSO PERFECTLY FINE.

### QUOTES
PLEASE DON'T SPEAK TO THE MEDIA ON MY BEHALF. EVEN HARMLESS OR CASUAL COMMENTS CAN GET QUOTED AND/OR TAKEN OUT OF CONTEXT.

### PRIVACY
PLEASE ASK ME FIRST BEFORE POSTING ANYTHING ON SOCIAL MEDIA ABOUT OR WITH ME. THIS IS ESPECIALLY IMPORTANT REGARDING MY LOCATION IN ORDER TO PROTECT MY PRIVACY.

### RUMORS
IF YOU SEE SOMETHING ABOUT ME ONLINE OR ELSEWHERE THAT SURPRISES YOU, PLEASE TALK TO ME DIRECTLY AND REFRAIN FROM ANY PUBLIC REACTION. NOT EVERYTHING YOU SEE WILL BE ACCURATE.

The paper includes some more information, including

Sloane's contact details, a backup contact, and a slew of companies that offer personal security. *I hope I never need that.*

Matt clears his throat, dragging my attention away from the organized list in front of me. "Seem okay?"

His poorly veiled anxiety tugs at my already tight chest. I do my best to reassure him. "Yeah, it all seems doable. Having her spell it all out makes it less daunting. Do you think...do you think people are going to get contacted?" I think of my dad getting bombarded again and swallow. So much for reassuring him.

"I don't think so, no. We can ask Sloane what she thinks though, okay?"

Matt's just pulling away from kissing my forehead when she walks back into my apartment and gracefully sits in the chair angled toward us on the couch.

"Did you have any questions after reading through?" She looks at me expectantly, her expression just as warm as before.

"Um, I guess I just wonder if you think they'll get contacted a lot. Mostly my dad," I ask, my voice probably quieter than before.

"To be honest, Ellie, I really don't think so. Hockey isn't big news in the grand scheme of things. And as long as nothing else happens, this will die down really fast. I'd guess your dad will get a handful of requests for quotes, all within the next week or two, and then I'd be surprised if he gets contacted after that."

I release the breath I was holding and sag against Matt. *Phew*. "Thank you. That makes me feel a lot better."

"It'll all be okay, promise. Now, I just chatted with Craig, my security guy, and he's not worried about General. He said their security is excellent even with it being so busy, since it's a well-funded hospital. So other than what I mentioned, there really isn't anything to do. If that changes and you ever feel unsafe, you just let me know, okay?"

"I can do that."

"Great. He did ask about your apartment building and recommended some extra security precautions here after I gave him some basic information. Just an additional automatic deadbolt on your door up here and then a video surveillance system we'll get cleared with the building manager. It will go outside your door and the building door. You'll be able to check it from an app. He said he'll get it installed tomorrow before you go to work. Try to remember to always lock your door, all right? The type of deadbolt we install will automatically lock when you close the door, but it's always good to check."

I make a mental reminder to put a sticky note on the door so I don't forget to lock it. Sloane grabs a box out of her bag and puts it on the table, quickly tugging at her sleeves that had started to move up her arm. Is she cold? It doesn't feel cold, but I make a second mental reminder to check my thermostat.

"This is the new phone we talked about. I wrote the new number on the box. If you ever start getting bombarded again because of a leak, we can just change the number. I already put my contact information in there for you." She slides it closer to me.

Getting "bombarded" nearly sent me—and Matt, honestly—into a tailspin, so I really hope that doesn't happen again. I find his hand and thread our fingers together, silently asking for a precious Matt hand-squeeze. He doesn't disappoint.

Sloane's eyes flick to our joined hands and then she focuses back on me. "Ellie, remember you can reach out to me at any time, for any reason. It's impossible to annoy me. Nothing is too small, okay?"

"I really appreciate that. Thank you." I try to inject as much sincerity as humanly possible into my words.

"Like I said, I'm happy to do it." She pulls the zipper closed on her bag and then gives me her full attention again. "Is there anything else you want to talk through? Any other questions?" Her hands are clasped in front of her and that iceberg of a diamond is sparkling at me.

Matt kisses my hand before releasing it to grab the phone from the coffee table. He heads to the kitchen, presumably to plug it in where he knows I keep a charger.

I look back to Sloane and shake my head. "I think everything makes sense." I nod my head toward her hands. "Your ring is really stunning."

Sloane looks down at the jewelry and pushes it around her finger with a thumb. "It's certainly hard to miss." It comes out quietly, something clouding her tone that puts me on edge. I try to hide my surprise at her response. She looks away from her ring and back to me. "You call or text me if you need anything at all, okay?" This comes out at normal volume. I nod and then she grabs her bag and stands, making her way over to the door. "I'll text tomorrow to check on the security system, Ellie. Bye, Matt," she calls over her shoulder as she leaves.

Matt says his goodbyes and brings my new phone over to me on the couch. His large hand gently cups my face and I lean into him, a subtle wave of comfort washing over me.

His voice is soft when he speaks. "Turns out it was fully charged. Ready to get this over with?"

Ready to tell my dad about my hockey-playing boyfriend

and the possible shit he's going to deal with again because of it? Definitely not.

I must hesitate longer than I intend to, because Matt swipes a thumb along my cheek and gently tilts my head to him.

"I'll be right here."

I focus on my favorite evergreen eyes and swallow the last bit of nerves, giving him a nod. "Let's do this."

# CHAPTER THIRTY-NINE

## *matt*

IT'S OFFICIALLY BEEN A WEEK SINCE THAT DAMN ARTICLE CAME out and things are good...*ish*.

Good because Ellie seems to be doing well, and working with Sloane has solved a lot of problems. Hardly any media requests have gotten to me or Ellie directly and the articles have been limited. I've also been doing my best to make sure Ellie doesn't see them when I'm able.

The conversations with friends and her dad also went better than she expected, I think. And from what she's said, they didn't ask her too many questions. Her dad was worried for her, but overall seemed supportive. I was petrified that me being a hockey player would mean he'd hate me sight unseen. Thankfully he was mostly just happy Ellie was happy. *Happy with me.* Fuck, I don't know how I got so lucky. Especially after how horribly I handled the night the story broke. I still want to punch myself over that.

Ellie, on the other hand, is handling it like a champ. I can tell she's still affected by the shit she does see, but all things considered, she's doing great. And that's really all that I can ask for. Happy Ellie equals happy Matt. Something her dad and I have in common.

*Ish* because now I know the whole story, and every day I seem to get more angry. While Ellie gets better, I'm getting worse.

I also know our schedule like the back of my hand and I've been dreading tonight for the past six days because we've got a home game.

Against Boston.

And I'm considering accepting a fine for voluntarily skipping a game for the first time in my career.

How the fuck am I supposed to face this literal piece of human garbage and not actually kill him? I can't believe I have to share the ice with someone like that. Can't believe he gets to even be *on* the ice. He should be rotting in prison, not playing fucking professional hockey.

Do I wish I felt this strongly before I knew it was Ellie and her mom in that accident? Yes. But I can't change the past and this is my reality now. And the thing is, I know this is going to be a big issue. We aren't in the same conference, but we play Boston multiple times a season and it won't exactly go unnoticed if I consistently miss those games. Especially now that everyone would make the connection.

I also don't think anyone has ever put it in their contract that they won't play a specific team—seasoned player or not, that's just insane and no team would allow it.

Now, am I likely to get cut for not playing? Probably not. But it's not exactly a good example to set, and Coach would undoubtedly be disappointed. My team too, probably. They're obviously aware of the situation now—several guys on the team have checked in with me and even asked about Ellie now that they're aware of her. And I know they've got my back, generally speaking. But like myself, these guys take hockey—the passion they're lucky enough to get paid for—really seriously. And opting not to play for personal reasons other than family emergencies or illness and injury is just...not done.

You come to work whether you feel up to it or not. Hockey is a team sport, and to leave them hanging in this situation would be selfish. Playoffs start in two weeks and we can only afford to lose one more game if we want to secure our spot. Every matchup is high stakes and a first line center sitting out is unheard of at this stage. Unheard of at all, really.

So while I'm sure no one would outwardly say anything to their captain, they'd definitely be surprised and maybe even angry on some level. I can't be sure, but I don't want to risk it. I don't want to let them down. *The name on the front of the jersey is more important than the one on the back*—it's a saying we're all familiar with and most players agree, me included. The name on the front of my jersey is Minnesota Bears.

But what if I play and my own feelings get in the way and they're let down anyway? What if I can't play like I normally do, too distracted by this all-consuming rage? So much of hockey is about keeping a level head, despite what people assume. We may practice plays and try to imagine every scenario, but the game is fast-paced and requires the ability to think on your feet.

I imagine how I'll feel if I don't play *and* we lose and know I have my answer.

I just hope if we lose *because* of how I play, I can live with that too.

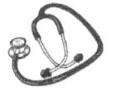

# CHAPTER FORTY

*ellie*

*Today 9:17PM*

**DEV**

You watching?

**ELLIE**

I'm going to need you to be more specific

**DEV**

You kill me

**ELLIE**

??

**DEV**

Your boyfriend

**ELLIE**

he's not here

**DEV**

Oh my god ELLIE

I was asking if you were watching your boyfriend's hockey game lol

But I am going to go ahead and guess no

> ELLIE
>
> OH
>
> you guess correctly 🙂

DEV

You may want to tune in...

> ELLIE
>
> and pause my true crime doc? meh

DEV

Idk...game's been pretty interesting tonight

> ELLIE
>
> you can't see me but I'm rolling my eyes at your vague-ness
>
> lucky for you, I think someone's at my door so I'm letting it go. enjoy the game 🙃

# CHAPTER FORTY-ONE

## *matt*

*I fucked up.*

I've been standing outside Ellie's door for seven minutes trying to figure out how to play this. I don't want to lie to her, obviously. But I know she's going to ask questions when she sees my face.

And notices I'm here an hour earlier than normal.

Sloane warned me not to get baited into anything or stir up any drama. She said it was unlikely anyone would try something, given the serious nature of the situation. But she also knew I was too close to it all to keep a level head. And she was fucking right. *God dammit*. I really hope this doesn't cause more issues for Ellie.

I'm honestly still so worked up I'm not even sure I should be here. Maybe I should go to my house...

The door swings open and my heart stutters in my chest in that now familiar way at the sight of Ellie in her big sweatshirt and fuzzy socks, smiling at me.

She's just...adorable and cozy and *mine*. Some of the tension thaws just from looking at her.

"Hey! I got a notification on the security app and then I

saw you standing there on the feed and figured maybe your key wasn't working or something so I just decided to open the door, but sorry if you were having a moment or whatever." Ellie looks down at her watch. "Also, you're early!"

I smile at her rambling and then wince as my lip stings from the pull. Ellie's face falls and I watch her zero in on the cut that's probably bleeding now.

"What happened?" She reaches a hand up to my face and softly touches her thumb to the side of the cut. "Is this what Dev was talking about? Don't they normally fix you up and tell you to 'get back out there'?"

This is why I was standing here, not using my key. I should've considered the damn camera though.

I know I could tell her something vague to avoid the details, but I promised I wouldn't lie to her after that first night, technically or otherwise. And giving selective truths feels almost as bad.

"I got ejected so I decided to just come here early," I say as I grab her hand from my face and kiss her palm, threading our fingers.

I lead her back inside and shut and lock the door behind us, dropping my bag and taking off my shoes. Sliding my keys onto the counter, I flip my hat around before dragging her over to the couch and onto my lap. I set my hands on her waist only to have them fall as Ellie hops up and runs to the bathroom.

"What did Dev say?" I ask loud enough that she can hear me from there.

She's back a moment later, resettling on my lap with a wiggle that makes me stifle a groan. She presses a gauze pad to my lip and then focuses on my eyes. "That I might want to tune in to the game. Why'd you get ejected? Does it have something to do with your lip? Are you hurt anywhere else?"

I put my hands back on her waist and close my eyes. I know this conversation is going to suck, but having Ellie here with me is doing wonders for my mood. The rage has quieted and I'm just...happy to be holding her. I bask in that for a moment, fully aware this next part might not feel as good.

I open my eyes and look back and forth between hers. Ellie's smart—she's going to ask the right questions. "I'll probably have a bruise on my ribs tomorrow, but I'm not hurt anywhere else," I tell her with a slow shake of my head.

Her posture relaxes a little at that. "And the rest of my questions?"

I give her waist a quick squeeze and sigh. "I got ejected for slashing."

Ellie looks back down at my lip before refocusing on me. "Slashing." Not a question. She narrows her eyes. "You hit someone with your stick?"

I hide my surprise at her quick interpretation of the term and nod.

"On purpose?"

I hesitate and then nod again.

"You hit him and they made you leave? Why is your lip split?"

See? Right questions. I know I could just give her a play-by-play, but part of me is still hoping she'll drop it and we won't have to have the rest of this conversation. I made my bed...

"He wanted to fight afterward." I withhold a wince. "So did I," I tell her truthfully.

Ellie straightens at that. "You never fight." Another non-question. She traces my two scars, one after the other, brow slightly furrowed. "Why'd you want to fight?"

This is the hard part.

I started a fight with Bryan McCormic at tonight's game because he makes me sick and I *kind of* want to murder him. Because I can't look at his face without seeing the guy who killed Ellie's mom. Because he's the reason my girl can't get out of bed some days. Because Ellie's mom isn't the one who should be fucking gone.

And because he deserves it and so. Much. Worse.

But I don't want to talk to Ellie about how violent Bryan makes *me* feel. "It was a long time coming," I answer simply.

Ellie's eyes squint again and she gives me a slow nod, probably assuming this is some rival. In a way, he is. Boston is one of our longest rivalries to date, and we have both been on our respective teams for the past several years.

"Who were you playing?"

I've really come to enjoy Ellie's indifference to my team and job, but right now I wish she already knew the answer to this question. *Dammit.* I really hope she isn't mad, or worse, sad.

"Boston," I tell her carefully, watching her face.

I watch her mouth silently repeat the word before her mind makes the connection and her body goes inhumanly still on top of mine. I grip her waist a little tighter and try to anticipate any reaction. She gets to feel however she wants, I remind myself. I made this a little bit about me and I'll face whatever consequences I need to.

Ellie moves to get up so I release my hands from her and try not to frown at the direction this could be going. *Fuck.* I would literally do anything not to upset her. Too little, too late,

I tell myself. But honestly? I can't bring myself to say I regret hurting that fucker.

She gets to her feet and goes to her room, surprisingly not shutting the door behind her. Okay, that's a good sign, right? I hear her rummaging around, but can't tell what she's doing from here. I'm about to get up to follow her when she reappears and starts making her way back to me. She's got her laptop secured against her chest by her arms in the shape of an X.

Ellie sits next to me on the couch and crosses her legs before she sets her laptop on them. She opens it and pulls up an internet browser. *What is she doing?* I watch her navigate to Google as a sinking feeling takes hold. She searches my name and today's date and hits enter. *Ah, shit.* There's already multiple pages with video clips of the fight. I cringe and brace myself to watch what happened from the viewers' perspective.

From Ellie's perspective.

She clicks the one with the most views and straightens her spine as it starts. It's not hard to see why I got ejected—game misconducts like that aren't tolerated for a reason, even when they aren't fully on purpose. Someone could get seriously hurt.

Unfortunately for me it's plainly obvious I didn't *accidentally* thrash him in the chest with my stick. It's also clear after the gloves were dropped that I wanted to pummel the shit out of him. *And I did*. I don't feel any satisfaction though. I'm mad at myself for being a cliché. And he should be behind bars, in my mind, not available for a beating while playing at a professional hockey game. I feel the rage coming back and close my eyes to breathe through it. I open them when Ellie squeezes the hand resting on my leg.

I look over at her to see her eyes on mine.

"It looks like you were trying to kill him," she says quietly.

I continue to look at her and decide not to reply.

"Are you in trouble? Beyond getting ejected or whatever?"

"Probably. I'm sure I'll find out soon," I answer with a shrug way more casual than I feel. I'm actually one hundred percent expecting a call about a suspension or fine, which is going to sting with so few games left to qualify for the playoffs. Thankfully it looked like we were going to win tonight by the time I left, but if I miss a game and we lose, it's going to be difficult to not blame myself. I still can't quite bring myself to regret what I did though, even now. "I'm sorry if this means more stories come out, Ellie."

She ignores my apology. "Has that ever happened before?"

I exhale and shake my head, dropping a quick kiss to the top of her head. She always smells so good. So comforting. I pull back and look to her face again.

Ellie seems to be thinking something over. She opens her mouth to talk and then closes it. It's not often I see her unsure of what to say.

"Did it make you feel better? Hitting him?"

Her hesitant voice strikes something deep inside me. Did it make me feel better? Honestly, I don't know. I don't think anything could actually make it better.

"Ellie." I let out a breath. "I'm sorry I made this about me. It was like I didn't have control over myself in that moment. I just saw red." I pause and link my fingers with her hand that's still loosely holding mine. "Nothing is going to make it better. He just deserved it. So much worse, really."

She nods and squeezes our linked fingers. I think about what she asked and realize she might not be asking that question for my sake. She might be asking it for *hers*.

There's something so heartbreaking about the idea of Ellie

taking her anger out with those tiny fists. I'd hold his hands behind his back and kick him to his knees for her if I thought hitting him would make her feel better.

Right now though, I need to answer her question. I try to choose my words carefully, thinking about how each one will come across. "It felt like...I needed to. Like I was in a position to punish him in a setting that wouldn't land me in jail. I used my job as an excuse, Ellie. But it didn't feel good and I don't feel better, no."

Ellie has been facing forward, but now looks at me.

"I think if *you* hurt him, you might feel better for a second, baby, and then you'd get in trouble and he wouldn't and you'd realize everything is still...the same," I tell her.

Ellie's lip quivers and I think I feel my heart crack under my ribs. She faces forward, looking at the TV with nothing on it. "You're right," she whispers on a subtle nod.

I pull her hand farther over and squeeze it between both of mine. Bringing our joined hands up to my chest, I press them over my heart where it still feels like there's physical pain.

Ellie turns and I watch her throat bob as she looks at our hands and then up at my face. "Thanks for hitting him," she says. "But no more getting in trouble for me."

I don't think I'm capable of promising that, so I lean forward to kiss her in answer, knowing I'd commit actual crimes for this girl.

Ellie pulls away and looks to the cut on my lip. "Did they have you ice it to help with the swelling?"

I shake my head, refraining from laughing out loud. I know they don't give a fuck about a swollen lip, but I don't really want Ellie to think the medical team isn't up to her standards. I remember that night she thought I was hurt and feel myself sober. I drop Ellie's hand and pick her up, settling her on my lap so she's straddling me again.

"They do a good job treating injuries that need it," I tell her. She looks at my lip with narrowed eyes. "Would you want to come see?"

Ellie glances up at that. "See what?"

"The medical equipment and staff at the arena. I think even you, Miss Nurse, might approve." I give her a wink.

"Would your teammates be there?"

"Depends. We could go to the practice arena, but that would be a drive. The arena downtown has pretty good facilities though and we could go on a day with no game. It's possible there'd be someone there though. They're all good guys, Ellie, promise. They'll always be real respectful around loved ones," I assure her.

She smiles at that. *Progress*. "Okay, I'll make sure it gets the Ellie stamp of approval."

I pull her tight against me, burying my head in the crook of her neck. I press a kiss there and inhale slowly, savoring my favorite scent in the world—eau de parfum à la Ellie.

"Are you smelling me?" she murmurs from a similar position as me.

I nod against her neck and swear I can feel her smile.

"What do I smell like?"

*Home.*

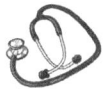

# CHAPTER FORTY-TWO
## *ellie*

I GRAB MY STOMACH AS I MAKE MY WAY TO THE SECTION LISTED on my ticket. Somehow my aversion to hockey has translated into physical discomfort. I thought maybe the walk to the arena would make it go away, but the pain seems to have only gotten worse. I'm also sweating despite the nearly freezing temperature I just spent fifteen minutes in.

I thought about not coming, but decided I can suck it up for one game. I've commenced Project Show Matt How Much He Means To Me, and attending a game was first on the list. *I can do this*. I also feel a little guilty that he was suspended for a game, since the fight was kind of about me. So this feels like a way to make up for that.

I'm walking around the arena looking for the correct section number, trying to focus on this task and not where I am. Thankfully the layout is familiar since I was here a few days ago for that tour Matt promised me. The memory still makes my cheeks burn.

Matt had pulled me to a set of double doors, telling me it was the last stop before we could leave to go get tacos. I was pumped. The tour had been fun, and the medical facilities definitely passed my test, but I was starving and anything hockey-related still wasn't really my cup of tea. Other than Matt. So leaving sounded awesome.

"Here we are," he says.

Locker room *is listed on the signage off to the side of the doors. I wonder if girls are allowed in there or if that's just a high school thing? As we walk through them, I'm hit with the very distinct smell of male sweat.* Stale *male sweat. And holy moly, that shit is strong. I try to subtly breathe through my mouth, but the stench makes its way past that and my stomach gives a sickening roll. Is the smell always this bad or is it particularly awful today?*

"...and Niko sits—"

*I know Matt's trying to tell me all the things, but as we walk farther into the room, I'm hit with the sickening realization that I'm going to puke. I slap a hand over my mouth and look around for a bathroom sign.*

"Baby?" Matt asks.

*I turn wide eyes to him, willing him to understand how dire this is.*

"What's wrong?" Matt looks me up and down, searching for the problem.

"Mers the bthfrm?" *My eyes water and I dart toward what looks like a trash can in the corner of the room. Hopefully.*

*I empty my stomach in a very ladylike manner (read: I puked my guts out) and thank the universe it's just Matt and me.*

Matt didn't believe me, but I was totally fine after we left.

I don't know how they spend so much time in there and *not* get sick. All I know is you couldn't pay me to go back. I wonder if it's the memory that's making me feel sick now? This feels different though. Less *nausea* and more *pain*. Ugh, I really hope he didn't tell his parents about that. I'd prefer not to be known as the girl who can't handle a men's locker room.

As a nurse, that would be the height of embarrassment. I can handle bad smells. Usually.

I see the number of the section matching my ticket up ahead and bolster myself for what's to come. *It's just a hockey game*, I remind myself. And Matt's here. Not really in reach, but here nonetheless. I take solace in that fact and continue to the open concrete doorway leading to my seat.

Matt told me his parents like to sit high up in the lower bowl because it has the best view. They offered to switch to the club level for my first game, but I insisted we follow their normal routine.

I hold my breath as I leave the hallway and step into the stands. I take in the large rink, the sea of black and gray jerseys, and the surprisingly cold temperature. I suck in the crisp air, finding it oddly refreshing. I can see why Matt likes it so much.

Glancing down at the row letters, I follow them until I see mine—row P. It's got a few rows behind it, but most of them are in front, leading to the ice. As I scan it looking for his parents, I notice something else.

There are a lot of people with *Anderson* on their back. A *lot* more than any other jersey I'm seeing.

I knew he was popular, but it's hitting me just how many fans Matt has. I glance around at the crowds filling the arena and can see his number *everywhere*. I suddenly feel like I would have blended in better wearing his jersey instead of my jeans and sweatshirt. I think of all the time I spent rifling through my drawers, leaving my room looking like it was freaking robbed, and make a mental note to just buy a stupid jersey.

"Ellie!"

I look back to my left and see Matt's parents and Nate

standing and waving in the middle of the row. Their obvious enthusiasm sends a jolt of warmth through me. I slide over to them and give quick hugs to his parents before sitting next to Shirley. Peter is next to her and Nate is on his other side. He gives me a wink before he sits back down.

"It means a lot," Shirley leans over to say closer to my ear, "that you came." She squeezes my hand.

I have a feeling Matt warned them not to bring up the article, which I'm grateful for. I squeeze her hand back. "Do you think he's going to get his thousandth?"

"Well, he's one away. And I have a feeling he's going to want to show off tonight." She winks at me. "So I think the odds are good, but you never really know. This is a tough team and the Bears need to beat them to stay in contention for a wild-card spot. It's a good game to be here for, either way. High stakes usually means good hockey."

I looked it up the other week after I met his parents and they mentioned why they were in town. Only fourteen players have gotten a thousand assists. Ever. And from my perspective there's something so fitting about Matt hitting this specific milestone. Mr. Selfless. I know he'd say it's just him playing smart so they can win however possible, but I can see through him. Setting up *other* people to score that much still takes some level of altruism.

And I remember Matt telling me they needed to win tonight to have a shot at the playoffs, which I know he cares about a lot.

I'm jolted out of those thoughts as the arena goes dark and a loud countdown takes over the Jumbotron. Music blasts through the speakers and an announcer introduces the away team, followed by the Bears.

I press a hand to my aching stomach and brace myself for my first ever hockey game.

I've really been trying to focus on the game, but the pain in my stomach has gotten so much worse. I know now it's more than nerves. Food poisoning, maybe? I really hope it isn't appendicitis. I still feel sweaty, which should be impossible with how cold it is in here.

I try to catalogue my symptoms—a self-triage, if you will—but I keep getting distracted by the noises of the arena and sweet Shirley explaining the game to me. No one on either team has scored yet in the first period. I don't have any frame of reference for if that's normal or not, but things seem tense.

She's describing the latest penalty to me when she stops midsentence. "Are you all right, Ellie?"

I try to smile in reassurance, but the pain has gone from moderate to something far more extreme. And as soon as I go to speak I feel a wave of dizziness take over. *Shit.* I need to go home and lie down until this passes. Or maybe I should head to the hospital to make sure it's not my appendix? Walking is out of the question, which means calling an Uber. Or maybe Dev could come get me? Neither is ideal, but at this point I just need to get out of here.

"I'm actually not feeling great. I'm going to go to the bathroom real quick to splash some water on my face," I tell her. I have her number now so I can text her why I had to leave afterward.

"How about I go with you? You look a little green." Concern is etched on Shirley's face. I grab my jacket and push off the armrest to stand up. I want to tell her not to worry, but my mouth is suddenly so dry I can't speak. I can't even swallow.

I finally straighten and orient myself to exit the row. My vision tunnels and I stagger one step forward. I move to take another step, but I never feel my foot land. I hear my name behind me, sounding oddly far away.

And then everything goes dark.

# CHAPTER FORTY-THREE

## *matt*

I'M SKATING IN AIMLESS CIRCLES AS THE REFS REVIEW A PENALTY when commotion in the stands catches my eye. As a player, they teach you to tune it out—the fans, the noise, anything other than the game, really. Staying focused at all times is important, not just when the puck is live but between plays too. And normally that doesn't pose a problem for me. Especially at a game as important as this one.

But the commotion taking place is in the section my mom, dad, and Nate are in. The one Ellie is in. It's taken a lot of effort not to continually check in since it's her first game, but now my eyes are glued to all the fans standing, desperate to see what's going on.

I can see arena staff are making their way over. *Shit*, that's usually not good. Movement on the bench draws my attention and I turn quickly to see Ed, our head of medical, listening to his radio and moving behind the bench to get to Coach. They converse with a clipboard in front of them and then Coach looks out at the ice, searching for something. His eyes land on mine and stop. They flick to the scoreboard and then back to Ed.

A sinking feeling takes hold in my gut.

Ed says something into the radio and starts to make his way down the bench to the tunnel. I frantically look back at the stands where *more* staff have gathered. I finally see Nate amidst the chaos and he looks uncharacteristically panicked. I can see my mom and dad next to him now, but they're crouched down? I don't see Ellie.

My heart beats painfully fast in my chest as I feel the blood drain from my face. A cold dread sweeps my senses and some foreign feeling pushes its way past the rest. *Fear.*

I find myself racing to the boards and hopping over them to the bench without making a conscious decision to do so.

"Matt—" Coach Dan yells, but I'm already halfway down the tunnel.

I hear a chorus of my name being called from behind me as I force myself to pick up the pace. *She's fine.* She has to be fine. Maybe she just got overwhelmed? I shouldn't have pushed for her to come. I was so excited to have her here I didn't think about how hard it might be for her.

Why would they call Ed though? And why was there so much commotion? Did she fall? Faint?

The questions start piling up, my mind frantic for some explanation. I finish my awkward skate-run to the locker room and grab my phone to dial my dad. Thankfully he picks up on the first ring.

"What happened?" I rasp as I rip off my jersey and my pads.

"I don't know, Matty. She stood up and passed out. Your mom says she looked sick and was holding her stomach. They're putting her on a stretcher because she's still unconscious. They're going to take her to General, they said."

*Unconscious.* I suck in a breath. General is where Ellie

works. That's good, it's close. Untying and shucking my skates as fast as possible, I throw it all to the side, assuming someone will move it later and I can owe them one. "Did she hurt herself when she fell? Did she wake up at all? Can Mom go with her? I don't want her being alone."

"The people next to us caught her. I don't think she woke up though, bud. And yeah, of course. She's following them now. Are you going to drive or do you want Nate to? We're parked in a visitor lot."

"I'm driving." My car's closer.

"Okay, I'll head to the player entrance to come with you. Nate's going to grab his car and meet us at the hospital."

I grunt and drop the phone from my shoulder to put my sneakers on. As I grab my bag and my hoodie, one of our assistant coaches, Hunter, appears next to me.

"Headed to the hospital," I force out quickly before he can ask questions. I don't stay long enough to see his reaction, but I do hear him telling me to text him if I need anything as I race out of the room to get to my car.

Thankfully my dad is already at the door so he holds it open and follows me to my car parked close by. I unlock it and slide in. When I go to turn it on, my hand shakes so badly I can't get the key to line up right. I take a deep breath and close my eyes, leaning my head against the seat back. I need to be calm enough to drive the three minutes to the hospital.

"I'm sure she's fine, Matt. She doesn't have any medical conditions, right?"

"No," I say on reflex. "I don't think so, I mean." *Fuck*. I would know if she did, right? You should definitely know if the person you're in love with has a medical condition.

I feel a sharp pain pierce my chest at the realization I haven't even told her that yet. *Oh god*, please let her be okay.

I'll fucking shout it from the rooftops if she is. Screw waiting for the right moment. *What a stupid fucking idea, Matt.*

My dad doesn't say anything while I internally spiral, but he reaches over and grips my forearm in a comforting gesture. It feels like there are tight bands wrapped around my chest, making it hard to breathe and hard to *think*. I can't even process reasons she could've collapsed. Ellie would know—she'd be able to make a list and rank them by likelihood. She's so smart. And kind. And, Jesus, she's already been through so much. More than anyone should. I *need* her to be okay.

"Can you call Mom? See if they have any update?"

"Sure thing."

I take a deep breath and open my eyes, starting the car successfully this time. *She's fine. She's fine. She's fine.* I repeat it in my head until we get there, willing it to be true.

"I'll park. Go ahead and I'll find you," my dad tells me.

I leave the car running and rush out to get into the emergency room. My mom didn't end up having any information other than telling us they made it to the hospital and took Ellie "back." She wasn't allowed to go with her.

I stop in front of the desk and watch a scene play out I've seen what feels like millions of times. The nurse's eyes get wide as she opens her mouth. Her Bears lanyard gives her away before anything that will come out of her mouth. I'm just starting to cut her off when a matronly blonde nurse appears behind her.

"Here for Ellie?" she asks.

I could hug her. I nod frantically about eight times. Her

sad smile sends a fresh wave of fear through me as she waves me to the side of the desk down a hallway.

"I'm going to put you in a private room until a doctor can come talk to you. We've got the game on in the general waiting room and the commotion has already caused a little stir," she says.

She leads me into a small room with a few chairs and a two-person table with a vase of fake flowers. I text my mom the number I saw outside the room so she can find me.

"No TV in here, sorry," the nurse needlessly apologizes.

Unless the TV can tell me what's going on with Ellie, I don't give a fuck. "Is she okay?" I ask for the first time, terror plain as day in my voice.

The nurse—I'll get her name eventually—pats me on the arms. "I'm not sure, hon. I'll have a doctor in as soon as I can, okay? Why don't you take a seat." She gestures to the chairs along the wall of the compact room.

I ignore her and begin pacing, wondering who I could call to get more information. I have to know *someone* with connections at this hospital. Other than Ellie. *Ellie Ellie Ellie*. I've never known panic like this. I just need to see her.

"Do you know if she's... If she's—" I take a deep breath and close my eyes, trying to slow my breathing so I can get the words out. "Do you know if she's, like, in a room or bed or, just...do you know where she is?" My jumbled thoughts can't quite seem to organize themselves as the alarms in my head continue to flash and blare.

The nurse, who I'm guessing is in her fifties, gives me a look of such motherly sympathy I wonder if I sound worse than I think. "I don't think I introduced myself before. I work with Ellie here in the ED. I'm Maggie. Love that girl to death. I'm not really supposed to share medical information with you, okay? Because I'm not her doctor. But I know she's getting triaged right now. They need to find out why she collapsed and why she's in and out of consciousness," she finishes. "Did she mention feeling sick to you or anything else earlier?"

I think back over the last few days. I don't think she mentioned feeling sick? Then I remember the locker room incident.

"She threw up a couple of days ago. Wednesday, I think?" I tell her quickly. "But she felt fine after that. She thought maybe it was triggered from a bad smell."

Maggie's brow is furrowed. "Okay," she says slowly. "I'll make sure I let them know, all right? I'm going to go check in. I'll try to have someone come talk to you as soon as possible." She gives me a quick, mild smile before she leaves, closing the door quietly behind her.

I drop in one of the chairs and put my head in my hands. *She's going to be fine. It's probably nothing serious.*

No matter how much I repeat it, I can't seem to make myself feel any better.

# CHAPTER FORTY-FOUR

## *matt*

It's been one hour and twenty-four minutes since Maggie returned to tell us Ellie was being taken back for surgery. No other information, no doctor, no nothing. Just *surgery*. It feels like the world shrank to that one word.

My parents are sitting quietly at the two-person table and Nate's in one of the chairs against the wall. They're all probably tired of me pacing the tiny room. I can't stop though. Every time I try to sit I feel like I am going to puke. Ellie is having surgery. And I don't know what for. What I *do* know is even the simplest of surgeries has risks and that is why I feel sick to my stomach. What if something happens to her? The thought is so horrific I can't even entertain it. She has to be fine.

My phone has been blowing up, but the only thing I'm interested in on there is the time. I'm sure people are wondering what's going on. I just can't think about anything other than Ellie.

"You should probably call her dad, Matty," my mom says quietly.

*Shit*. Shit. I definitely don't even have his number. Maybe the hospital would have it as an emergency contact for her? Or maybe I could call Zo—

The door clicks open and my head whips in that direction. A middle-aged woman in scrubs and a white coat steps inside. She's got a clipboard. Hopefully she has a fucking update or I might lose my shit.

"Are you Eleanor's family?"

"Yes," I nearly shout.

My parents and Nate stand up. "We'll go grab coffee. We have our phones, okay?" My mom's voice is low, but I can hear the stress there.

I nod without taking my eyes off the doctor. I feel Nate hesitating, but he follows them out the door. I'm so anxious for the doctor to start talking that I don't want to waste the time to tell them they could stay.

She watches them leave with a perplexed look on her face and then flips a page on the clipboard. She looks back to me. "Mr. Ford?"

*Mr. Ford?* Ah, Ellie's last name. She thinks I'm her husband? "Matt," I tell her. My impatience makes my voice come out harsher than I intended. Correcting her fully would take too much time and, also, I quite like the idea of people thinking we're married. Belonging to Ellie. Ellie belonging to me. The frisson of pleasure at that idea is abruptly snuffed out with the doctor's next words.

"Do you want to have a seat?" She gestures to the chairs along the wall. My heart stops beating in my chest. I shake my head.

"Okay," she says with that same mild smile Maggie gave me. Do they teach that to medical professionals? "I'm Dr. Sultana. I'm one of the OB-GYN physicians taking care of Eleanor."

"Ellie," I mutter reflexively. I rack my brain for what OB-GYN means. Don't they deliver babies?

"Ellie," she confirms with a nod. "When Ellie arrived she was in critical condition because her blood pressure was quite low and she was showing signs of internal bleeding."

I try to suck in a breath while she keeps talking, but it feels like there isn't enough air in this room.

"The emergency doctors ran some quick tests including an ultrasound and some blood work, and discovered she had a ruptured ectopic pregnancy. This means a fertilized egg had implanted outside of the uterus—in her case, in one of her fallopian tubes—and the tube burst, which is what caused the internal bleeding."

I walk a few steps over to the chairs on numb legs and drop into one. *Pregnancy. Internal bleeding.* I feel my breath coming fast, like I still can't get enough oxygen. The doctor walks over and sits on a chair near mine. "She was pregnant?"

"She likely didn't know because she had an IUD. Unfortunately, IUDs can increase the risk of an ectopic pregnancy, though the risk is very low. Now, because this was a life-threatening condition, we had to move quickly and get her into surgery to stop the bleeding. We performed what's called a unilateral salpingectomy, which means we removed the ruptured fallopian tube. It was necessary in order to get the bleeding under control and to prevent further complications. The other tube and her uterus were not affected."

*Life-threatening.*

"Is she—" I start. I try twice to clear the lump in my throat. No luck. "Is she going to be okay?" I don't recognize my own voice.

"She's stable now, which is great. We expect her to make a full recovery. And as soon as she's moved to a room, you can go see her. It should be another fifteen to twenty minutes until they move her over. Can I get you some water?"

I shake my head again.

She hesitates. "All right. I'm going to have Maggie come get you when Ellie is in her room. She works with her and will be monitoring her through the night. Once Ellie's awake, I'll come talk to her and share everything I just told you. She might be a little groggy and confused at first, since she was in and out of consciousness before the surgery."

I nod to let her know I understand. It takes a minute, but then I hear her get up and the door click shut behind her.

*Stable. Full recovery.* I try to focus on those two things, but my mind is determined to focus on everything else.

Ellie was pregnant. I wait for the panic that normally accompanies that idea, but all I feel is sadness. She *was* pregnant. And it almost killed her. My body shudders at that thought. Is *she* going to be sad? They said her other tube is okay, so she should still be able to have babies, right? If she wants to? She's never explicitly said, but based on how things went with her ex, I assume she wanted kids then at least. Would she want kids with me? *I hope so.*

The foreign thought takes me by surprise. And then a knock at the door brings me back to reality. First I'm going to make sure Ellie is okay with my own eyes. Then we can deal with everything else.

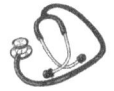

# CHAPTER FORTY-FIVE
## *ellie*

I WAKE UP TO THE RHYTHMIC *BEEP BEEP BEEP* OF MONITORS AND the familiar hum of the air circulator I only associate with hospitals. Did I fall asleep at work?

My eyelids feel heavy, almost like they're stuck together. I flex my fingers and gently scratch the fabric under them. Definitely not my sheets. And something is stuck to my wrist—an IV? There's a gentle, warm pressure around my ankle and it's the only comforting thing I can focus on. Ugh, why is my brain so foggy?

I finally peel my eyes open a sliver and try to blink away the blur. I survey the room the best I can. I'm definitely in the hospital and I'm definitely a patient. What happened? I don't remember coming here. I try to dig through my brain for my most recent memory.

*Hockey*. Right. I was in pain at the game. Did I get a ride to the hospital after all? Shit, I bet it was my appendix if I'm here.

I hear a monitor reflect my newly elevated heart rate and turn to look at it. My gaze catches on a large, slumped figure next to me. I blink a few more times to dispel the fuzziness and some of my anxiety melts away at the sight.

Matt's head is resting next to my thigh, facing away from me. His hand is under the blanket near my feet. Ah, the gentle pressure on my ankle makes sense now. I stretch my fingers until they graze his soft hair, lightly touching the back of his scalp.

His head leaves its position so suddenly my fingers are frozen in midair.

Matt's face is full of relief and something else. He leans forward and gently cups my face, planting soft kisses on my lips, eyes, cheeks, chin, hair. He's saying something, but I can't quite hear it. I strain my ears as he goes to kiss my temple and I finally make out his words.

"You're okay. You're okay. You're okay," he continues to mumble.

Involuntary tears collect at the corner of my eyes with Matt's feather-like touches. I squeeze them tight. He pulls away and I feel his thumbs swipe under my eyes. I peel them back open to look at him.

"Hi, baby," he breathes. "You scared the shit out of me. Please don't do it again." Matt sniffs and I notice the watery rim of his eyes.

"Sorry," I croak-whisper. I sound awful, jeez. My mouth feels like sandpaper.

"I forgive you." Matt gently offers me a sip of water from a cup I didn't notice before returning it to the bedside table. He gives me a wobbly smile and brings one of my hands to his face. He holds it with both of his in front of his mouth.

I try to swallow, but it still feels like sand is lodged there. "What happened?" I ask him. He opens his mouth, but then the door opens softly and a doctor walks in. I don't fully recognize her, but she looks familiar. I think her name starts with an S? Maggie is behind her, and the sight brings me relief.

"Hi, Ellie," the doctor says. "I don't think we've worked together yet. I'm Dr. Farah Sultana from the OB-GYN department. How are you feeling?"

Everyone hears it as my heart rate picks up. *OB-GYN?*

I glance to Matt, eyes wide with panic, but he's still looking at me with that same expression as before. I turn back to the doctor. "Fuzzy," I finally come up with.

She gives me a warm smile. "That's normal. And hopefully I can help clear everything up for you."

As I listen to Dr. Sultana relay the last four hours of my life, all I can do is stare at her. I feel Matt's eyes on me, but I can't bring myself to look at him. I was pregnant?

And now...now I'm not. And I'm down a fallopian tube. Okay. I want to process all of this, but one feeling is stronger than all the rest.

*I want my mom.*

It's a knee-jerk reaction I haven't quite been able to knock. When the nice doctor asks if I have any questions, I can only shake my head. My eyes sting and I do my best to blink through it as she and Maggie leave the room with promises to check back in shortly. My hand is still in Matt's, against his lips. I look up at the ceiling and close my eyes.

*It'll pass. It'll pass. It'll pass.*

A few tears leak out the corner of my eyes and I squeeze them tighter. Matt makes a strangled noise next to me. "I'm okay," I try to reassure him, but it sounds hoarse and shaky. "Just...over...whelmed." My breath hitches in between syllables. *Dammit.*

When I turn my head to Matt and open my eyes I'm met with a blurry, pained expression on his face. I use the hand not in Matt's to swipe at my eyes, careful of the IV port in my arm.

"This is a lot to process," I whisper. "I didn't even know I was—" An edge of panic creeps in. I remember Matt's history.

"I know, baby," he rushes to say. He nods and then kisses my hand again, keeping it tight against him.

He looks calm. Too calm. "Aren't you...freaked out?"

Matt's still looking at me. I don't think he's taken his eyes off me since I touched his hair. "I was plenty freaked out before you woke up," he answers.

"What about the...the..." I can't seem to say it. It doesn't feel real.

"The pregnancy?"

I nod. Matt searches my face for a moment and then drops his forehead to the hand he's holding in his.

I hear him exhale before he picks his head up to look at me. "You know that I'm in love with you, right?"

If it wasn't for the monitor next to me, I'd think my heart stopped for a moment. I guess I was pretty sure he was, but there's nothing like hearing it come out of his mouth. *Matt* is in love with *me*. All I'm capable of is a small dip of my head in stunned acknowledgment.

"Then you should know the only thing I was freaked out by was not knowing if you were okay. That's all that mattered to me, all right? We can figure everything else out."

My heart thumps heavily in my chest. "I...I'm in love with you too."

Matt's answering smile takes my breath away. "I know you are."

He releases my hand and braces himself on the bed to lean forward and kiss me. It's a soft touch of his lips to mine.

He pulls back just enough to look at me. "I'm sorry if this overwhelms you more. I had been trying to wait for a good time, but I needed you to know." He swipes a finger along my cheek and then sits back down on the chair next to the bed.

"How long have you been waiting?"

He shrugs noncommittally. "A while."

I smile at that as I try to adjust myself in the bed to sit up a little straighter. The tug of pain low in my abdomen makes me wince and I freeze. Matt immediately stands up, but I wave him off. "I'm fine, just going to use the remote to sit the bed up more instead."

He hesitates and then sits back down. "Maybe we should call the nurse?"

"Matt, I am a nurse."

"You're a patient right now though," he argues gently.

"I'll ask for more pain meds next time they check on me, okay?"

He doesn't seem satisfied with that answer, but eventually he nods then clears his throat and rests his hand on my leg. "Do you want to talk about—"

"Not yet," I interrupt. He squeezes my leg and nods. "Where are your parents and Nate? Do they, um, know what happened?"

"I sent them back to the house. Nate's dropping them off. They all wanted to check in on you, but it's late so they'll come tomorrow during visiting hours." Matt rubs his thumb back and forth where his hand still rests. "I gave them the overview, yeah. I hope that's okay. They were really worried about you."

"Yeah, it's okay. A little awkward, but..." I finish with a shrug.

Matt scratches the back of his neck. "There's, ah, someone else who's going to be visiting you tomorrow too." He looks nervous. "I probably should've checked with you first, but I was freaking out, and I didn't want him to be in the dark and—"

"My dad's coming?"

He nods. "His flight gets in tomorrow morning pretty early."

"You called my dad for me? And he's coming?"

"I didn't want him to find out some other way and I thought you might want him here. Sorry, baby, I just made a panicked judgment call." That thumb makes another swipe. "My mom was the one who brought it up," he adds. "I wasn't thinking all that clearly." His shoulder lifts. "I reached out to Zoey to get his number, so she'll be calling you to check in, I'm sure. I asked her to wait until tomorrow."

It's pretty common for patients to be emotional after surgery. Sometimes it's linked to medications, and other times we don't really know specifically *why* it's happening, just that it appears to be normal. I think I'll blame this persistent desire to cry on that and not the fact that my boyfriend is a walking green flag. Who loves me. And now I get to see my dad for the first time in over six months.

"That was really thoughtful of you. Thank you," I choke out. My eyes catch on the clock on the wall as I try to keep the tears at bay with some strategic room scanning. "You're welcome to stay at my place tonight, since it's so close. You've got to be tired."

As if the universe heard me, the door opens and Maggie strolls in carrying some sheets, a blanket, and extra pillows.

"Hey, honey," she says to me. She drops the bedding on the couch against the wall and turns back to us. "The bedding you asked for." She nods at Matt. "You might find it lacking," Maggie jokes with a wink, then shifts her focus to me. "You ready for some pain meds, Ellie?"

"She's my favorite nurse," Matt declares to me. "Other than you, of course."

I roll my eyes and watch Maggie administer the medication in my IV, trying not to get emotional again thinking about Matt sleeping on that teeny, tiny couch.

*Walking green flag, indeed.*

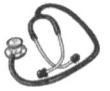

# CHAPTER FORTY-SIX
## *ellie*

"Well, this sucks, huh?"

I choke on my own laugh, squeezing my dad's hand. He's smiling, but I can see the sadness that just never quite leaves his eyes. It might even be a little deeper than usual right now. He asked me a few questions about what happened, the surgery, and how I was feeling, but he's mostly just been *here*. That quiet support that's so familiar and sturdy. I can tell it was a long night for him. Probably worrying about me and processing the news in his own way.

"It does suck," I agree. "Would've preferred your first visit to be under vastly different circumstances. Or I guess second."

My dad helped me move here last year by driving my car and most of my stuff over, allowing me to fly instead. He knew how hard that long of a drive would have been for him. At least he got to fly this time. Thanks to Matt.

Matt left the hospital for the first time about an hour ago after Dev promised she'd check on me every twenty minutes. It had been about fifteen hours since I was admitted. He proclaimed he had an errand to run and would be returning with lunch and his parents in a bit. I'm not sure if the errand is real or if it was a ruse to give me and my dad some alone time at the hospital since he got in this morning.

I can tell Matt's anxious about leaving me alone. He made Nate bring him clothes this morning instead of driving the five minutes to my apartment himself. I cringed a little thinking about Nate seeing my disaster of a room, but I guess it's handy Matt had some spare clothes there instead of sending Nate all the way to his house.

I told Matt he's being ridiculous and I'll be fine for an hour alone, but I secretly kind of love it. Being alone is overrated.

*I wonder if my dad feels that way.* The thought is like a kick to the stomach. When Mom died, he was lonely. But then I left him and now he's *alone*.

My dad and I don't have hard, emotional conversations. He's a superb father—endlessly patient and understanding, kind and supportive, just the right amount of silly. But even our deepest conversations have a surface-level feel to them. Like maybe neither one of us knows how to break beneath that layer to the nitty gritty. We had Mom for those harder conversations. But not anymore. At least I have Zoey and Dev. And Matt. I wonder who my dad can talk to, if anyone.

It's the thought that urges me to speak.

"I'm sorry I left Boston," I start, my voice surprisingly level.

My dad turns his head from the window to me. His brow is furrowed and he looks...surprised. "Why would you be sorry about that, sweetie?"

I swallow. "I...I left you."

He blows out a breath. "Ellie, no." His head shakes back and forth. "All I want is for you to be happy. Your job is making sure that happens, not worrying about keeping your dad company."

"But you're alone now," I murmur. "It was selfish of me to apply in the first place."

"Is that what you've been thinking? That you were being selfish?"

I nod and study my hands in my lap.

My dad sighs and is quiet for a bit. When he talks, his voice is low. "You know, I read this book a couple years ago. About grieving. I went in with a bad attitude—the whole 'this is going to be a load of shit' type attitude. But it taught me something important."

I pick my head up and focus on him.

"Everybody grieves differently, right? I knew that in theory, but I didn't really think about what it meant. Specifically for you and me. But then some things started to make sense."

He clears his throat.

"I'd want to look through pictures of your mom and you'd politely tell me you had something else you had to do. Or you'd want to try a new restaurant and I'd decline in favor of takeout from a regular spot. And when I was reading, I realized why all of that was happening."

He pauses and smiles.

"Seeing and thinking about your mom is comforting for me. I like reliving memories and remembering my favorite things about her. But for you, forcing those kinds of things was painful. I didn't understand that until I was reading the stupid book."

My dad sighs again and he sounds so, so tired.

"Maybe my way drags out grieving even longer. But the book helped me realize that there isn't a right way to grieve, and the best thing I could do for you was to let you grieve how you needed to." He grabs one of my hands and squeezes it. "Being in Boston was hard for you. *Being around me* was hard for you. I know that, sweetie. I was so happy for you when you told me about this job. I knew it would be so good for you." He uses his other hand to pat the one he's holding. "I think grieving can make us feel selfish as we try to navigate a very changed life. But choosing to be happy is not selfish, okay? Your happiness brings me peace, Ellie, and that's all I can ask for in this life."

"I want you to be happy too though," I get out with a sniff.

"I'm as happy as I can be, Els. I promise."

"What about the movies?"

His brow draws down again. "The movies?"

"You said you don't go anymore. But you used to go all the time and I thought you liked doing things that remind you of Mom."

My dad chuckles at that. "You're right. But I don't exactly like getting choked up at a public showing of *Star Wars* because the seat next to me is empty." I must not look convinced because he sighs and continues. "Tell you what. I'll take your uncle Terry to see one sometime soon, all right? See how it feels to go again. Even if he talks during the whole damn thing."

"Fine," I huff. And then softer, "Thank you."

"Now, do you want to tell me more about this boyfriend of yours?" he asks. "He sure seems pretty taken with you."

*Taken with you.* The phrasing almost makes me smile. I debate how to ask my dad the question that's been weighing on me a lot lately. "Matt's...amazing. I don't know how I got so lucky." I swallow and look at my hands, hesitating. "Do you ever wish you'd never met Mom?" My dad scoffs and I look up.

He's reared back a bit, looking borderline affronted. "Why would you ask me that?"

"Because...because she died, Dad. You loved her and now your life is...is—"

"Ellie," he interrupts. His face is patient. Understanding. "I would do it all over again. Even knowing how her story ends. Your mom was the best thing that ever happened to me until you came along. And I promise you, there hasn't been a single moment since your mom died that I wished I hadn't met her. I loved our life—the crazy adventures, the mundane days at home. It was all so special to me because of how much I loved being with her. And then you joined us and everything just got better."

He chucks my chin and shakes his head.

"I know I'm different with her gone and I'm sorry about that, sweetie. But I would still tell people I've had the richest life in the whole world because I got to love and be loved by you and your mom."

*Well, shit.* I wipe at my face and ignore the pain in my body as I lean forward, wrapping my dad in a hug. "I love you too."

He squeezes me tightly and I hear a gruff sniff. "It's worth it, Ellie, I promise."

# CHAPTER FORTY-SEVEN

## *matt*

I COULD WALK THESE HALLWAYS WITH MY EYES CLOSED. IT'S NOT the first time I've thought that. This arena has been a second home of sorts, somewhere I've spent a significant portion of my life. But walking in today I was hit with the alien thought of *I shouldn't be here.* No, I want to be at the hospital, holding Ellie's hand, making sure she feels okay and doesn't need anything. Telling her I love her again. *Again.* Finally.

So today it doesn't feel like a home. It feels like going to *work*. I mean, that's what it is, right? My job is "professional hockey player." Sometimes I lose sight of that.

I know we have the day off, but I've decided it's time for a chat with Coach. And I wanted to give Ellie some time alone with her dad now that he's here. That was not what I imagined my first meeting with Michael to be like, but knowing Ellie has family here is helping me feel less anxious about leaving her for a couple of hours. Ellie's apartment isn't big enough, so I convinced him to stay at my house and got him a rental car. I'm hoping I can also convince Ellie to be at my house while she recovers this week.

I stop in front of Dan's door, noting it's cracked before I knock and push it open.

Dan startles for a moment, placing a hand over his chest. "Matt, I wasn't expecting you. How's...Ellie, is it? Is everything okay?"

I've been working alongside Daniel Miller for fifteen years and we've maintained something akin to a friendship. Or as close as you can get, given our coach-athlete dynamic. I made sure to text him an update late last night after Ellie had fallen back asleep.

"She's going to be okay. She's in recovery now. Getting discharged in the next couple of days."

"That's great. I know everyone was worried, myself included."

"Thanks, yeah, the whole team's been reaching out." There's a beat of awkward silence as I'm sure Dan is trying to figure out why I'm here. I glance at the chairs in front of his desk and move forward to sit down.

Looking around his office, I take in the awards and pictures. The stupid locker room trophies from over the years. The countless memorabilia from various stars he's played and worked with. I'm focused on his desk when I get stuck on a framed family photo of him and his wife and their two kids. I swallow hard, thinking of yesterday, and pull my gaze away from the picture to Dan. He glances at the frame I had been studying and then back to me, his expression thoughtful.

"I'm sorry about the game. And playoffs," I finally offer. Losing last night meant we were officially knocked out of playoff contention. We have a couple games left, but our season is effectively over.

Dan scoffs. "Matt, you know very well you're not to blame

for us not making the playoffs. And no one is upset you left the game, especially now that they know why."

I shrug, hearing him but not fully able to let go of the guilt. It didn't really hit me until late last night. I thought I would also feel sad, or maybe even a little mad. But other than the low level of guilt for letting my team down, all I was really feeling was overwhelming relief Ellie was okay and comfortably asleep in front of me.

It was the first time in my life hockey felt unimportant. I've been sitting with that realization all last night and this morning.

"Is there anything I can do for you, Matt? You didn't need to come here to apologize, I hope you know that."

I clear my throat and nod. "Yeah, I, uh, wanted to talk to you about next season."

"Oh, sure. I actually wanted to ask how you felt about the new kid, Miles, pairing up with Drew on D? I think they could mesh really well."

"Um, yeah, I think that could work. Drew will love having a stronger skater next to him," I say. I hesitate, finding this a little harder to verbalize than I thought. "I actually wanted to talk about something else." Another pause. "I'm not sure if I'll be here next season."

Dan's mouth parts. "What? Is this about your contract? You know they'll work with you on whatever terms you want, Matt."

"No. No, I know." I swallow. "I'm not sure if I, um, want to come back."

I think Dan could be knocked over with a feather right now. To be fair, I could never have imagined those words coming out of my mouth either.

"Your stats have been going up the last three seasons

though. You're one away from a thousand assists! Which you could get before the season is over, but still. You're playing better than ever, Matt. We could have a decent shot at the playoffs next year," Dan rambles. For someone normally very composed, it's both funny and endearing seeing this side of him.

"I know. I know all those things. It's not a decision I would make lightly, I promise. And I'm not sure yet, anyway. But I wanted to keep you up to date on how I'm feeling. We've been in this together for a long time."

That seems to give him pause. He smiles, but it's twinged with sadness. "We have."

The uncharacteristic emotion in his voice gives me a wave of gratitude. I've been lucky to work with this guy for so long.

"Is there anything I can do? Say?"

I shake my head and lean forward, rubbing my hands over my face. "Thirty years I've lived and breathed hockey. Hard to believe it's been that long. The past few years I've started to wonder what I would do after my career was over. How would I love something as much as hockey? It's been my entire life. Nothing has ever compared." *Until now.* The words aren't spoken, but I think Dan can see where I'm going.

He nods seriously. "You're not alone in that. It's the pro athlete's curse."

*Pro athlete.* Another title of the job I've had for eighteen years. And another welcome reminder that while it is my career, it's not my whole life. A feeling that's becoming more and more clear—more *okay*.

I look back at the picture framed on his desk. His wife and kids. They're at the beach in this picture, all wearing white shirts and khaki pants, smiling big. It's cheesy and cute.

*I want that.*

Just maybe not on the beach. Fuck sand.

Sometime between yesterday and this moment, it's become so obvious. I don't know when I changed my mind and I don't care. All I know is that I'm sure now.

My eyes flick to Dan and he's sporting that sad smile again. His gaze moves to the picture. "It's the best thing in the world," he says softly. He understands.

I nod in hopeful agreement. "I think it will be."

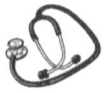

# CHAPTER FORTY-EIGHT
## *ellie*

After a thirty-minute car ride and a slow hobble up to Matt's front door, I'm beginning to wonder if getting discharged today was worth it. I could've sucked it up and stayed for another day or two, but no, I just had to beg Maggie nonstop to work her magic and spring me. Turned out being a patient again was more triggering than I thought.

And because Matt left the hospital early to make sure everything was "set up" for me at his house, I had to deal with my sweet dad awkwardly trying to figure out how to help me in and out of the car. I should've taken Dev up on her offer to help after she stopped by this morning to check in.

I lean against the front door for a beat before walking inside. I think his parents will probably be in there and I am fresh out of socializing energy. *Any* energy, my body shouts at me.

"You okay, sweetie?" My dad pauses with my bag in his hand.

"Dandy," I pant.

He shifts toward me and then stops. "Should I have Matt come out?"

"Nah." I wave my hand at him and push off the door. "I just need to sit once we get inside."

My dad nods and uses the key Matt gave him to unlock the door. I almost forgot he's been staying here the past two nights. He might be more familiar with this house than I am, considering I've only been here once. Surprisingly, the thought makes me bristle a touch.

As he pushes open the door I'm bombarded with two things. First is the heavenly smell of fresh baked apple pie. Second is the absolute gut-punch feeling when my brain realizes it won't be my mom's. I've avoided apple pie for five years because of that.

My already weak knees are saved from hitting the deck when Matt appears out of nowhere and slides an arm around me.

He kisses my head. "Let's get you to the couch."

After my dad seems satisfied Matt's got me, he lets us know he's taking a work call and then disappears down the hall. Matt half leads, half carries me over to the living room and carefully gets me settled.

Crouched in front of me, he gives me a quick kiss and then pulls the ottoman closer before sitting on it. "Drive go okay?"

*Blegh*. "It was fine," I say with a tight smile. "Where are your parents? Are you baking?" I sniff the air to indicate why I asked.

Matt gives a mild grimace at my first response. "Sorry, baby." A quick squeeze of my knee. "They're grabbing some groceries to make dinner tonight. And I baked, yes." His cheeks tint pink. "Well, tried."

I'm almost afraid to ask, my heart not ready to tell Matt I haven't been able to eat apple pie since my mom died. Because it's not *hers*. And he's obviously nervous about his efforts.

"You're good at everything, I'm sure whatever you made is great." I swallow thickly. "So what did you bake?"

Matt hesitates, looking to the kitchen and then at me. He watches my face for a moment before talking. "I hope this was okay. I asked your dad for the recipe," he says quietly.

I freeze.

"You, uh, mentioned missing your mom's apple pie a while back." Matt winces. "*Mentioned* is probably a bit strong. It took me a while to figure out what you were saying, and then...well, then I just knew I wanted to find a way for you to have her pie again." He sighs and grabs my hand. "I should've asked, and maybe it won't be the same, but after this whole ordeal I just wanted you to have something comforting. Something of your mom's."

*Something of my mom's.* "You baked my mom's apple pie?" There's a wobble to my voice I can't control.

Matt nods. "I made a practice one first. This one is better though, I think—I just pulled it out of the oven before you walked in."

Love is such a small word for something so big. Because these feelings I have for Matt? They feel like they're overflowing. Like they're pushing against my chest so hard I want to rub my hand there to fight the pressure. He baked my mom's apple pie for me.

Another little thing that feels so, so big.

"Can I...can I have a hug?"

Matt drops to his knees in front of me, leaning forward and wrapping me up in those strong arms.

I wind my own above his shoulders and hold him tight to me. "I love you." It's just a whisper—soft words spoken right next to his ear. The first time I've said those three words and been so scared, so happy, so *sure*. "So much."

His arms band around me, squeezing tighter. "I love you too, pretty girl."

# CHAPTER FORTY-NINE

*matt*

Ellie's lying in my bed, propped up on some pillows, reading a book. She's supposed to take it easy this week and I've been insistent she follows the doctor's orders since she came to my house two days ago. The season ended with our last game yesterday, but even before that it was a pretty relaxed schedule with us being out of contention for playoffs. And with Ellie staying here and her dad back in Boston now, that means a lot of uninterrupted time with my girl.

That is, aside from the visits from Nate and Dev and frequent calls from Zoey, which I don't mind because Ellie seems to appreciate the company. She even got to meet Niko finally when he popped over last night after our game to celebrate my thousandth assist.

I've been wanting to talk to her about something, but I also wanted to make sure she'd had enough time to process what she went through and what it might mean for the future. The doctor made it clear the procedure she had shouldn't affect fertility, but it was obviously scary and traumatic and I wouldn't blame her if it shaped the way she felt about it all. I also remember how she distinctly wasn't ready to talk about it when we were still in the hospital.

I push away from the doorway I was propped against and head toward the bed. Ellie glances up at the movement, a smile stretching across her face. My favorite thing in the world.

"Hey, I didn't hear you get back."

"I think when you read, you tune out the world," I joke. I was purposefully quiet coming in from a workout, but I've witnessed it enough to know she really does get that engrossed in her books.

"It's called focus," she says, sticking her tongue out at me and setting her book down next to her.

I smile and climb on the bed to lie down, turning so I'm on my side facing her. "I wanted to talk to you about something."

Ellie raises her eyebrows. "Oh?"

"Remember when we first really talked, you asked if I had done the whole 'do you want kids' talk with exes?"

Her cheeks tinge pink. "Of course."

I swipe my thumb over one and revel in how she leans into my touch. "I thought maybe we could have that conversation. If you're up for it."

"Oh," Ellie says hesitantly. "Sure."

"It doesn't have to be now, if you'd rather not talk about it yet."

"Now's fine."

I nod in reply. Then debate how to start for about five seconds before threading our fingers and giving her hand a squeeze. "We were going to have a baby."

Ellie searches my face, those beautiful eyes looking for any clues about how I'm feeling on the topic, I'd guess. "Yeah," she finally lets out slowly.

I clear my throat. "How are you feeling about that?"

She shrugs, adding surprising casualness to what I expected to be a hard topic. "I guess...I feel like everyone expects me to be more upset about it all. But I didn't really find out about it until it was no longer...happening. At first I was shocked and emotional over the event of it all. And losing a tube is freaky. But now it feels kind of abstract? Almost like it happened to someone else." Ellie finishes quietly and I see her throat move on a swallow. "Maybe that's an odd way to feel."

"I think you get to feel any way you want, baby. But for what it's worth, I don't think it's odd. It makes sense to me."

Ellie gives my hand a squeeze back. "How are you, um, feeling about it?"

I watch fondly as her blush deepens and think carefully about what words I want to use. "It wasn't really until after I saw you with my own eyes and knew you were okay that I even took any time to process it all. Then I was a little sad about the pregnancy. Just knowing what could have been."

Ellie's eyebrows rise in what I assume is surprise and I want to kick myself for letting her doubt how I was feeling about this for even a few days. Time for the question that's been weighing on me. *Why am I so nervous?*

"Do you want to have kids?"

"I..." She hesitates and I feel like my life is teetering on some ledge, just an answer away from falling in one determining direction. "I've always wanted kids, yeah."

"Wanted—you still do?" I clarify.

She nods and a breath I didn't realize was stuck in my chest rushes out.

"But I remember what you said before, and obviously this was a surprise and I've thought about it—"

"Ellie," I interrupt softly. "Ask me."

Those honey eyes freeze on mine for a beat. "Do you want kids?"

"With you, yes."

"Oh," she breathes. "Really?"

I lean in and kiss her. "Yes," I murmur against her lips. I kiss her again and then lean back into my previous position.

Ellie's mouth curves up. "When do you want kids?"

I shrug. "Whenever you do, baby."

"What if I wanted them now?"

"Then I'd let Coach and our GM know I was retiring to start a family."

Her smile drops. "What? That would make you want to retire?"

I dip my head. "Very much so."

"But why? Lots of hockey players have kids before they retire, right?" she asks.

"Sure, but I want to make it—them—my priority. I've been fantasizing about being a stay-at-home dad the past few days and I have to say I'm getting quite attached to the idea. I don't want to miss anything. I don't want to be at an away game when they take their first steps or say their first words. I don't want to leave my pregnant wife at home to go play a half-assed game where all I can think about is missing the chance to feel kicks or bring you whatever it is you're craving at the time."

Ellie grabs my other hand and squeezes it, both firmly in her grasp. "You've thought a lot about this, huh?"

"Pretty much twenty-four seven the past few days," I admit.

Ellie's gaze flicks between my eyes, going back and forth. "You love hockey," she says softly.

I shrug again. "I do." Then squeeze her hands back. "I love you more."

Her eyes water and for once I don't feel any pain from it,

just that tightness in my chest I'm used to. I think these are happy tears. I maneuver our joint hands to wipe away one that trickles down her cheek.

Ellie sniffs. "Wife, huh?"

My smile spreads reflexively. "Caught that, did you? Was hoping to work on some subliminal messaging over the next few months to ease you into the idea."

"That's smart," she says on a nod, and my heart rate picks up. "What if I don't want to have kids for a couple more years?"

"Then maybe I play for another year or two, until we're sure. I figured we could take it season by season and make a decision together."

"Together," she repeats.

"We're a team, right?"

Another tear slips down her face and I release her hand to swipe it away. She nods a few times and leans forward toward me. I meet her in the middle, fitting my mouth to hers.

I asked Ellie that first night together what her endgame was. I didn't realize how badly I wanted to figure out *my own*. I was so wrapped up in hockey that I couldn't separate what came after, only that it would be some consolation prize in comparison. Something to stay busy and keep my mind off dwelling on the "good old days."

I know now how stupid that sounds. Because my endgame is Ellie—our life together. And those good old days? I have a feeling they're just getting started.

# EPILOGUE

*about two and a half years later*

### ELLIE

"I'm calling it."

"But this was your idea."

"I know," he huffs.

There's something about a grumbling Matt that just makes me want to laugh. I curl my lips around my teeth to keep them from stretching wide.

My foot wobbles again and Matt curses. "We should've gotten you hockey skates," he says quietly as he tightens his grip on my hands, pulling me toward the exit. His eyes dart from my face to my stomach and then back.

It's mostly cute how worried he is, but this was his idea, as I already pointed out. And I don't think the type of skates would make a difference.

"But these are so prettyyy." I drag out the word and attempt to point my toe out to the side. The action makes me falter again and Matt stops his backward skating to scoop me up until he's got me, bridal style. The figure skates *are* pretty and they looked way cuter than the bulky ones Matt showed me online. I kick them out to admire them in the air. Guess I won't be using them. "I think you're overreacting, you know," I tell him. I didn't even care about learning to skate, but Matt was the one who wanted to go tonight and teach me.

"I'm not used to thinking about the ice as such a fall risk."

"Are you serious?" I laugh. "It's freaking *ice*! It's like the definition of slippery."

He grunts in response as we get through the rink exit and he brings us over to a bench. The outdoor rink is lit up with string lights and garlands draped in red bows, painting a dreamy holiday picture. Of course Matt found one walking distance from our apartment and paid to have it closed to the public for a night. Because he continues to be perfect.

"Well the people I skate with normally aren't so..." Matt hesitates. "Wobbly. No offense."

*Almost* perfect. At least he looks sheepish.

"Thanks," I mutter as he gently sets me down next to him. I bend over to untie the mostly unused skates, but Matt grabs my hand to stop me. He gets off the bench and kneels in front of me to take them off himself. "Matt, I'm not even pregnant. This is ridiculous. I can untie my own skates. And it would've even been okay if I fell."

"You might be though, and I'm not risking it."

We're in our second month of trying to get pregnant, but Matt is treating every day since the first day we tried as though I already am. And despite my reassurances—backed with medical evidence, mind you—he can't seem to shake the habit. My period isn't even due for another few days.

"Even if I was, I'd be barely four weeks along. That's the size of a poppy seed, babe. A poppy seed. And that's a big *if* anyway. I don't want you getting your hopes up too much."

Matt stops loosening my skates and looks up at me, an

indulgent smile on his handsome face. "I promise my hopes are in check." He leans in to give me a chaste kiss before finishing removing my skates and slipping my sneakers on. After he's got his off and all of our stuff in the bag, he shoulders it and we head back to our apartment.

Pretty much the entire summer after the story broke a couple years ago, Matt lived out of my apartment. It took him two months of that to ask me how I felt about getting a bigger place together. It took another month to find the perfect spot. And it was on the day we said goodbye to my apartment—which had been fully emptied by then—that Matt proposed. My little apartment was filled with so many candles when we walked in that I was worried the sprinklers would go off. He even flew my dad and Zoey in for the surprise celebration that night at The Bar. I still can't think about that day without getting choked up. It was just...the best day. I think the wedding has been the only day that's topped it.

Our new place is much bigger than my one-bedroom, but still just as charming. And still walking-distance from the hospital, thank god. It's part of what took us so long to find it.

Matt said we could sell his house over on the lake since I don't want to commit to a commute yet, but I wanted to keep it for visitors and his younger teammates. And maybe for the future.

I also decided to see a new therapist after we got engaged, which has been going pretty well. We've made a *little* progress on driving with some forced practice, and a lot of progress on everything else. She even encouraged me to try and make friends with some other players' wives (I still can't believe I'm a WAG, albeit now a retired one—if that's a thing) and go to an occasional game. Which meant I was able to attend some of

Matt's last big milestones and his final game with some support. It was important to me to be there for that.

I still have bad days, of course. Days where I can't get out of bed. Our wedding was bittersweet in that way— it was hard getting up, knowing my mom wouldn't be celebrating with us. The day was so full of joy and sadness at the same time. She should've been there. I wanted her with me more than anything.

But I find myself happy above all else most days. Because of my job, my life, my friends and family.

*My Matt.*

And I can't ask for much more than that.

I grip his hand tighter and let him lead me home.

## MATT

I may have lied to Ellie at the rink earlier today.

My hopes are not in check. In fact, they are so far out of check it's probably unhealthy. But it's been over *two years* since our first conversation about kids. Two years where the idea of a family with Ellie grew from a tiny seed (ha) to something much bigger and wholly consuming. Not even my final season of hockey this past year could fully distract me.

And now all this damn poppy seed talk has me brainstorming as we eat dinner at our apartment, about ways to ask her to take a test tonight.

I don't even think she thought about it, but she said I was too rough while having fun with her tits last night. Tits I am very well acquainted with and would never dream of being too rough with. I'm one hundred percent sure I was actually more gentle than normal. Because of the aforementioned hopes and all that.

So I think we should just *check*. If I can convince her without making it obvious I lied about being chill.

*Ice cream.*

A little light bulb goes on in my head. Ice cream is always the answer.

I set my fork on my plate and look at Ellie. "How about ice cream and a movie tonight? You can pick the movie." I waggle my eyebrows in a silly attempt to sweeten the offer-slash-ruse.

"Sure! I think we're out of ice cream though." *Exactly.* "Are you opposed to a crime doc? There is a new one I've been meaning to check out."

"Just because I don't understand the obsession doesn't mean I'd get in the way of it," I joke with my hands up before standing and bringing our plates to the sink. "I'll run to the store to grab the ice cream." I kiss her on the head and then get my jacket and slip on my boots. Thankfully there's a store only a few minutes down the block.

When I get back I find Ellie in the bedroom putting on her pajamas. Her perfect fucking tits are out and I have to swallow a groan.

Time to stay focused. "I saw something cool at the store," I start.

"Oh?" She puts on a large T-shirt that's both a blessing and disappointment. It's got a big smiley face in the center that brings me back to one of our first dates at her apartment. My chest gets tight and I almost forget the script I practiced on the walk home.

"They have these packs of pregnancy tests that, like, come in bulk. They're strips instead of those bigger ones. That way you can test whenever you want without feeling like it's a waste, you know?"

Ellie raises her eyebrows and grins. "And you just happened to be in the aisle with HCG tests?"

"HCG?"

"Human chorionic gonadotropin, technically. It's what pregnancy tests are measuring."

Ah. *Shit.* I try to think of what else I saw in that part of the store.

"I was getting...lube." I feel my face heat at the lie. I didn't think this through.

"I see. Where is it?"

"I...um...didn't like the options," I offer.

"Of course," she snickers. "But yes, I'm familiar. We use something like those strips at the hospital."

My half-assed plan is rapidly unraveling. Why didn't I think of that? I scratch my neck and pass her the package of tests, keeping my eyes on them. "Well now you have some here. To use whenever you want."

"Whenever I want," Ellie repeats. "Matt." I look up as she comes and stands directly in front of me, her head tilted up to mine.

I'm never going to get over how much I love this girl and her beautiful face. Her freckles and honey-brown eyes. Her nearly ever-present flush. Somehow I got lucky enough to make this amazing person my *wife*.

*My* wife.

My wife who's giving me such a patient look I know I'm totally busted.

"If you want me to take a test, you have to promise me it won't ruin your night if it's negative. It's really early and it's only been two months of trying. It can take a while, and we don't know if my fertility was affected with that procedure."

I cross my fingers behind my back like a ten-year-old and give her a quick peck. "I promise…" *…not to make it obvious I'm bummed.* I make another internal promise to quit lying.

When I lean back I see her eyes squinting at me. I'm afraid this perfect person of mine can read me like a book.

"I don't believe you, but I'll do it anyway." She spins away and heads for the bathroom.

And like a loyal dog, I follow along behind her.

Ellie pauses and turns, a single eyebrow raised, stopping me in my tracks. "Are you planning to watch me pee in a cup?"

*Am I not supposed to?* The way she's asking makes me think I'm not. She must see the confusion on my face because she sighs and then grabs my hand, turning back toward the bathroom. Ellie drags me inside and shuts the door. She releases my hand and moves to the medicine cabinet, setting the pack of tests down on the counter. As she grabs a disposable cup, she turns to me. "Face the door."

I open my mouth to object and then think better of it. At least she let me in here. I angle my body away from the toilet.

"Do you want to open one of those tests while you wait?"

I blindly reach to the counter next to me, feeling around until I touch the bag. Man, I really hope we don't have to use all of these. There must be a hundred. I remove one and open the packet, revealing a narrow test strip.

When I hear the toilet flush and lid close, I turn around and hold it up for Ellie to see. "It's so small."

She laughs and sets the cup on the counter before grabbing the test from me. "Yep, you don't really need much to detect HCG." I watch as she dips the tip in and holds it for a few seconds. Then she pulls it out and balances it flat on top of the cup.

"How long should it take?"

She hums. "Maybe a couple of minutes? Let me go read the packaging."

Ellie wanders over to the other side of me to grab the bag. I move closer to the test strip and study it as the test area darkens. One line shows up right away, I'm guessing the control line? I look at the area where there would presumably be another, but only see something faint. *Damn.*

"I think it's negative. The second line is really faint. You can hardly see it," I tell Ellie.

It's quiet for a moment. "Second line?"

"Yeah, it's so light compared to the other one." I try to hide my disappointment as I straighten from my position and turn to Ellie. Her face is unusually pale and she's staring where the test still sits over the cup on the counter. "Are you o—"

Ellie pushes past me to grab the little strip and holds it up to her face.

"Holy shit." The words are whispered, barely audible despite the surrounding silence. And unnervingly out of the ordinary for my little non-cusser.

"Ellie?" I venture. "Did we do the test wrong?"

She ignores me and walks over to the toilet, dropping onto the closed seat. She's still staring at the test. I follow her and peer down at it. Everything looks the same as before.

"Baby, is something wrong? We knew it would probably be negative, right?" If one of us was going to react badly to a negative test, I would've put money on it being me. Hence the childish crossed fingers behind my back earlier.

Ellie clears her throat. "This is..." I watch her swallow and then angle the test toward me. "It's, um, positive."

*What?* I squint at the test and see exactly the same lines as when I first looked. One is dark and the other is just barely a line. That can't be positive, right? Maybe the test is faulty? I look at Ellie and then back at the test. Then back to Ellie. She still looks pale. Is she worried because a faint line is a bad sign? My heart rate picks up as if my body is reacting to the news before I can even process it. But I don't think I even want to process it until I figure out Ellie's reaction.

Why does my wife not look happy if the test is positive? I swallow the emotions trying to escape, and kneel in front of her. Gently taking the test from Ellie, I set it on the counter.

"Positive is good, right? You want this?"

She's silent but she nods at me, albeit a little frantically.

"Okay, good. You're happy then?"

"Yeah," Ellie breathes out. "I think so?" She grabs for the test and looks it over again. "Holy shit." The second iteration is no less jarring. "This is crazy. This is crazy, right? Oh my god, babe. How did this happen?"

"I can't tell—"

"We're going to have a baby!" she shouts, standing up and nearly knocking me over.

My entire chest loosens and a flood of *feelings* sweeps in. A *baby*.

She drops to her knees and turns the test around, putting it right in front of my face. "A baby!" she squeals.

I laugh and pull her to me, wrapping my arms around my favorite person in the whole entire world. I get to have a baby with Ellie. A *family*.

I don't know what I did to deserve this—her—but I'm never letting go.

# CONTENT WARNINGS

Endgame contains heavy topics that may be troubling to some readers, including: mentions of a car crash, death of a parent (off page), significant mentions of grief and depression, and miscarriage via ectopic pregnancy.

# ACKNOWLEDGMENTS

I take back ever making fun of celebrities for their long award speeches because WHERE DO I EVEN BEGIN?

Endgame didn't start as a book or even as an *idea* for a book. It was random scenes and snippets of inner monologue I had stuck in my head. Characters I dreamed up and got attached to. I had no plans, no confidence and no formal writing experience (my college English professor *did* recommend creative writing to me after reading my essays, though, so there's that).

I just feel so, so lucky to have found support at every step of my ~~writing~~ journey that made me believe something could actually come of this little dream of mine. I wouldn't be here without countless people involved with this book both directly and indirectly. Writing is inherently something done alone, but I never really felt lonely because of all of you. Thank you.

The list goes well beyond this, but I would like to thank a few specific people:

Thank you to my husband for always making me believe no dream is too small. You make me feel like I can quite literally accomplish anything I want to and you always have. No human, fictional or otherwise, could ever compare to you.

Thank you to my best friend for making me believe in myself as a writer. It was vulnerable and scary sharing those first few scenes, but you made me feel like this story was worth telling. This book wouldn't be what it was without you and the insane number of hours you spent working on it with me.

Thank you to Emily for giving me the confidence to share this book outside of my little bubble. Your feedback and encouragement made me brave and I'm not sure if Endgame would have ever made its way into readers' hands if it wasn't for you.

Thank you to my beta readers for taking a chance on a new author and making my first experience with strangers reading my book so wonderful. Your thoughts and support helped shape the final version of this story and made me believe in a future for this book.

Thank you to Jillian for kindly offering to help make sure I represented hockey accurately. It was important to me that this book felt like a realistic portrayal of the world of professional hockey and I'm grateful for your help with that goal.

Thank you to my editor Julia for being so thorough and thoughtful. Your care for my story was so clear to me from the start and I felt at ease knowing Endgame was in your capable hands. Your feedback and expertise made this story the absolute best version of itself.

Thank you to Dan, my cover artist, for capturing Endgame so perfectly. Your talent blows my mind and I will truly never get over it.

Thank you to my family and friends. Some of you know about Endgame and some of you don't, but you've all helped shape who I am and everything that's led to me getting here now. Feeling loved and supported is the best thing in the world and I don't take it for granted. I'll give a special shout out to A, J and J for being cheerleaders even before I was brave enough to send over the manuscript. Your unwavering encouragement and solidarity is so precious to me.

Lastly, I want to thank anyone who gave Endgame a chance. Being a debut author is scary and exciting and it's just so surreal that anyone would want to read a story I created. Your time and energy is valuable and I'm so honored you spent some of it on this story and me. I hope you felt that time was well spent.

## ABOUT THE AUTHOR

Willa Gray is a romance reader turned writer. She dreams up emotional stories with FMCs you'll root for and MMCs you'll fall in love with. You can find her on a small farm with her husband, three kids, and many cats. A big fan of fizzy drinks, love stories that make her cry, and sad music, Willa is chronically offline but always looking for more #TeamEdward friends.

Follow her at www.willagraybooks.com.

instagram.com/willagray
tiktok.com/@authorwillagray

www.ingramcontent.com/pod-product-compliance
Lightning Source LLC
LaVergne TN
LVHW010308070526
838199LV00065B/5484